THE HAT GIRL'S HEARTBREAK

LINDSEY HUTCHINSON

Boldwood

First published in Great Britain in 2022 by Boldwood Books Ltd.

Cover Design by Head Design Ltd

Cover Photography: Shutterstock

A CIP catalogue record for this book is available from the British Library.

Paperback ISBN: 978-1-80162-671-2

Large Print ISBN: 978-1-80162-672-9

Hardback ISBN: 978-1-80162-670-5

Ebook ISBN: 978-1-80162-673-6

Kindle ISBN: 978-1-80162-674-3

Audio CD ISBN: 978-1-80162-665-1

MP3 CD ISBN: 978-1-80162-666-8

Digital audio download ISBN: 978-1-80162-669-9

Boldwood Books Ltd
23 Bowerdean Street
London SW6 3TN
www.boldwoodbooks.com

For my friend Joyce Pryce, who passed away recently from dementia, and who always supported me in my writing. RIP my little mate.

AUTHOR'S NOTE

My previous book, *The Hat Girl from Silver Street*, was never meant to be a stand-alone book, so I hope those who have read it will enjoy this one. May it answer all of your questions.

1

'You off to the cemetery again?' Flossie Woolley asked as she sipped her tea.

Ella Bancroft nodded, the gold flecks in her hazel eyes shining.

'You'm wasting your life away, gel. It's been five years since your man passed and you should be moving on.'

'I know, Flossie, but I don't seem to be able to,' Ella answered.

'It's maudlin, if you ask me, this visiting that bloody great monstrosity of a family mausoleum. It's become a habit – one you should break, otherwise you'll end up an old maid. Anyway, I need to get home and see how the Sunday dinner is doing. Tarrar a bit.' With that, Flossie went next door to her own house, leaving Ella to think on what she'd said.

Ella's mind replayed the moving pictures of her memories as it had so many times over the last years.

Harper Fortescue, taken in the prime of his life by tuberculosis, shortly before he and Ella were to be married. Again, she saw his chocolate-drop eyes and his black hair; heard his deep resonant voice. She felt the pain stab her chest just as hard as it had the day he died. Tears stung her eyes as she whispered, 'How can I move on when I still love you, Harper?'

Trying to shake off the thought, Ella chose a hat from the latest creations she had finished at home and pinned it in place. Picking up her bag, parasol and the flowers she'd bought the day before in the market and kept in water overnight, she set out.

As she strolled along in the sunshine, she considered her neighbour's words.

After Harper's passing, Ella had thrown herself into her work as a milliner and gone into partnership with her previous employer and rival, Ivy Gladwin. Transforming Ivy's hat shop, now called Ivella, they had built it up into a thriving business.

Ella continued to live in the two up, two down house in Silver Street, Walsall; a town in the middle of England, well known for its leather manufacturing. Saddles, bridles, buckles and chains were all made there and the King, Edward VII, still ordered his saddles from Walsall. Known as the town of one hundred trades, it also boasted limestone quarrying nearby.

The spring sun was warm on Ella's shoulders and she was glad she had decided to wear a cotton blouse and lightweight skirt. She opened her parasol, revelling in the shade it afforded. Crossing the tramway and then the London and North West Railway, she came presently to the large cemetery. Following the gravel footpath, Ella looked at the many gravestones as she passed. *I'll be here one day*, she thought.

Arriving at the mausoleum, she replaced the old flowers with the fresh ones in the little vase. The dead blooms she wrapped in the paper, ready to take to the nearest rubbish container.

Sitting on the grass, her parasol over her head,

she chatted to Harper about the week just gone. Ella was not at all embarrassed at speaking out loud to the love she had lost; many visiting the graveyard did the same thing.

After a while, she rose, and blowing a kiss, she turned and walked away, the dead flowers in her hand.

Once home, Ella had a bite to eat before settling down to work. She'd had ideas about a new range of hats for the shop and hoped that Ivy would agree to them being placed in the window of Ivella.

Gone were the bonnets of the 1850s and also the small Victorian hats. Now it was the Edwardian era, and headgear for ladies had reverted to being large and somewhat fussy. Ivy was delighted, as this style was her forte – the more decoration the better, as far as she was concerned.

Ella held a large circle of straw over the old steam kettle her dad had rigged up for her and felt a stab of nostalgia. Slowly, the stiff straw softened and Ella gently began to bend the brim upwards. Reaching the boat shape she was after, she put it aside to cool and harden, the milk jug on one side and the sugar basin on the other so it would keep its shape. Sorting through her haberdashery, she chose two turquoise feathers which she pinned to one side of the hat, then taking up a piece of rose-coloured silk, she tied it into a large bow. Placing it at the base of the feathers, she sewed it all into place.

Pleased with her efforts, she then picked up a piece of pale blue crin, which she had already steamed into shape, and pinned a small silk rose on the side. Having made her decision, Ella settled to making more roses, which would encircle the wide turned-up brim.

When she was happy with the finished article, Ella stood and stretched out her back. She made herself a cup of tea and turned her thoughts to the next project. It was an order for a feathered hair band. Bending a piece of wire around a wooden block, she then bent the two ends outward slightly to prevent the band digging into the client's head. Wrapping the whole wire in magenta embroidery thread, she secured the ends tightly. After stitching the small black veil in place, she put it aside to concentrate on the feathers. Having already dyed white goose feathers to a delicate pink with cochineal, Ella chose one and added a Lady Amherst pheasant feather, which she tied in place with cotton. Doing the same again with a guinea fowl feather and adding two burnt peacock spines, she slowly built up a bunch. Sewing them all together, she attached them to the headband. Black goose feathers were separated into little clumps which she curled over the steamer. Those were added in strategic places, then she attached goose feathers cut into a long line of diamond shapes.

Finally, her creation was placed onto a poupee, a wooden head-shaped block covered in padded linen. Bunches of feathers curled up and out, down over one end of the veil and along the headband. Ella smiled with satisfaction.

Now it was time to eat and rest. Ella bustled about the square kitchen, placing the kettle on the small range to boil. She crossed to lock the back door before glancing out of the window above the sink, where the stars shone brightly in the inky black sky. From a cupboard on the wall, she took out cheese, bread and pickles for her supper. Placing them on the table in the centre of the room, she then pushed the three chairs into place whilst she made tea. The fourth was missing, as this was where her father's wheelchair had lived.

Once she had eaten and drunk her tea, Ella glanced at the finished articles on one side of the table and nodded. She was pleased with her efforts and tomorrow she would take everything she had made to the shop, where she would be given Ivy's verdict.

Washing her plate and cup, Ella left them to drain and, dousing the light, she walked through the internal door into a small passage, off which lay the front room with a large window that looked out onto the street. The stairs led to two bedrooms. In her room, Ella poured water from the large jug into the bowl on the dresser and bathed her face and hands. She undressed and slipped on her nightgown before brushing her dark hair until it shone in the moonlight coming through the window. With a contented sigh, she climbed into bed and was soon asleep.

The following morning, Ella tied her hat boxes with string, leaving loops for handles before stepping out into the spring sunshine.

Walking the few streets to the shop, Ella returned the greetings of those she passed. Women out washing windows, children playing in the road, careless of the traffic of carts and wagons.

Ella's attention was drawn up high to a circular brush poking out of a chimney before it disappeared again. The rag and bone man's horse and cart made its way slowly along the street, the tatter calling out, 'Any old rags?'

The Caldmore, pronounced Karmer, district had been alive since the early hours with men heading for their work. Others not fortunate enough to have a job carried fishing rods to the Walsall canal where they would spend the day in the hope of a bite. All they ever caught was an old boot or a discarded bicycle wheel, but at least they were away from their nagging wives for a while.

Ella smiled as she saw a young boy run from a ginnel, closely followed by his mother, yelling, 'You cheeky young bugger, I'll tan yer arse!' In an instant, the child was gone. Turning to Ella, the woman said, 'Kids today, what can you do with 'em?' Without waiting for an answer, the woman retreated back down the alleyway.

Moving on, Ella smelled fresh bread emanating from the panniers of the baker's horse. Although she had eaten, Ella's mouth watered at the tantalising aroma. She stopped to buy a cottage loaf, which was still warm from the oven. It would provide a tasty treat mid-morning with a scraping of butter and jam from Ivy's kitchen.

'You're late!' Ivy snapped as Ella entered the shop.

'I stopped to buy bread,' Ella said as she placed the loaf on the counter then piled the boxes next to it. 'I'll put the loaf in the kitchen while you have a look in those.' Ella tilted her head towards the boxes.

'You've been busy again,' Ivy said as she undid the string, lifted the lids and took out the hats.

'I needed something to do,' Ella replied.

'This is nice,' Ivy said as she admired the feathered band, 'the customer will be pleased.' Returning it to its box, she went on, 'I'll make some tea. Let's hope we sell well today.'

Ella nodded and propped the front door open with a doorstop in the shape of a top hat. Gazing through the window, Ella's mind was drawn back over the years to when she was the one to have to make the tea for Ivy.

Ivy Gladwin had been a stern employer, always

quick to pick fault. Then, after Ella had left and set up on her own, Ivy had paid Sally, Ella's sister, to steal Ella's ideas and designs. When her treachery had been discovered, Sally had up and left her husband, and God only knew where she was now, for Ella had received no word of her whereabouts. Eventually Ella and Ivy had joined forces and were glad they had, for the business was doing extremely well.

'Tea up.' Ivy's words broke through Ella's reverie and together they enjoyed their hot drinks while they gazed out of the window.

'I suppose you went to the cemetery again yesterday,' Ivy asked, and Ella nodded. 'You should stop that, it won't bring him back, you know.'

Ella sighed before responding, 'Why did you never marry?' After all these years, Ella still knew next to nothing about her business partner's private life.

Ivy was momentarily taken aback by the question then answered, 'I never had the chance. As a girl, I learned millinery in Birmingham. Then I had to quit to take care of my aged parents. When they passed on, I inherited enough money to buy this place.' Ivy swung her arm out to encompass the room. 'After that, I spent my life working to make it pay so I never found time to socialise and therefore I remain unwed.'

'I'm sorry, I shouldn't have pried.' Ella dropped her eyes to her cup. Ivy's story had been said so matter-of-factly, but Ella's heart nevertheless went out to the woman who had never known love.

'It doesn't matter. It's too late for me now, but it isn't for you. Stop pining for what you can't have and go out and find someone to spend the rest of your life with.'

Although she knew Ivy was right, Ella had no idea how to go about finding love.

2

It was later that evening, as she fussed with frippery for a new hat, that Ella thought about Kitty Fiske, her one-time lodger and assistant. Kitty had fallen in love with a man who, out of an honourable promise and despite his love for Kitty, had wed another woman, Darcie Newland.

Ella shivered as she recalled how her Harper had once been engaged to the same woman. He had broken that engagement to become betrothed to Ella, and it was later that Darcie's father had forged an agreement with Felix for his daughter's hand.

After a disastrous marriage in which Felix Stoddard had been stabbed by his wife, he had sought and been granted a divorce, and he and Kitty had married and moved away. When Felix refused to press charges, Darcie had been whipped away to Scotland by her parents in an effort to escape the gossip. Ella missed Kitty, her friend, and she also missed her support with the business. She and Ivy really did need to employ another assistant and it was something to discuss the following day.

Ella's mind meandered back to Ivy and her advice. Was Ella destined to end up alone with only her work to fill her days? As it stood, she had no social life and no close friends other than her neighbour, Flossie Woolley.

Ella enjoyed interacting with the customers in the shop but at the end of the working day, she returned to an empty house. Even in this modern time of 1906, women didn't go out on their own. Only the ladies of the night could be seen on the street corners, plying their trade. Soirees were only attended by couples and then only by invitation.

With a huge sigh, Ella knew it would be near impossible for her to meet a nice young man, but just the thought brought a shudder of guilt – was she betraying Harper's memory by even thinking such a thing?

Five years ago, when Harper had died, Ella had resigned herself to the idea that she would never marry, and nothing had happened since then to change that notion. Perhaps she might never really be happy again after losing first her father and then her betrothed. She felt stuck, as if waiting for something monumental to happen. Each day was the same routine; breakfast, go to work, come home, eat, then sleep. How to break this pattern eluded her and she had continued to live each day the same as the last.

Ella wondered whether it was time to up sticks and move away, as her sister Sally had done, but where to go? Would she be any better off in another town? She thought not, as at least here in Walsall she had Ivy and her work, as well as her neighbour, Flossie. Somewhere else, she would have nothing and no one.

Was it wrong to want something more out of life? If she met someone, could she love him as much as she had loved Harper? Possibly not, but chance would be a fine thing.

Looking at the bow she had made without thinking, Ella smiled. Memories of her father teaching her this trick warmed her heart.

'Oh, Dad, what would you tell me to do now?' The question was whispered into the quiet kitchen. Placing the bow on the table, Ella picked up the newspaper and as she glanced over a page, something caught her eye. It was an advertisement towards the back of the paper, and it was small. Advertising, she knew, was costly, so it was no wonder folk chose spaces the smaller the better.

As Ella looked up, it was as if a spark had ignited in her hazel eyes, lighting up their gold flecks. Tearing the advert from its place, Ella shoved it into her bag. Tomorrow she would visit the address shown on the scrap of paper, and for the first time in years, Ella felt a touch of excitement.

The following morning, Ella told her colleague that she was going to the rag market in Birmingham to see what new materials were on offer.

Ivy frowned at the thought of being left to mind the shop like an underling and annoyance rose in her which set her piled-up titian hair quivering. 'I could go.'

'Ivy, the last time you went you came back with black, brown and dark red. It's springtime, we need bright colours.'

'I can do bright!' Ivy exclaimed.

'You get side-tracked too easily.'

Ivy harrumphed, reluctantly agreeing. 'You'd best get off then,' she said huffily.

Ella took some money from the small safe in the back room, grabbed her bag and parasol and set off, leaving a none-too-happy Ivy behind.

'Ever since we formed this partnership, you've treated me like a skivvy,' Ivy muttered. 'Oh, I know you came up with all the good designs, but my ideas count as well!'

'It's the first sign of madness, you know – talking to yerself,' a voice said behind her.

Ivy turned to see a customer smiling. With a little cough, Ivy asked, 'Can I help you?'

'I need a hat for a wedding, something big and showy,' the woman replied.

'Certainly,' Ivy said. Moving to the ladder on rollers, she climbed two rungs and pulled out a large box from the shelf. Setting the box on the counter, she removed the lid and lifted out a hat covered in silk roses and large feathers.

The customer shook her head. 'Too fussy.'

Ivy replaced the box and bridled when the woman said, 'I like the pink one in the window.' It was one of Ella's designs, of course. Hiding her disappointment behind a fake smile, Ivy brought out the hat for the woman to try on. Looking into the mirror on the wall, the customer turned this way and that, admiring the fine workmanship.

'It's a bit big.'

'There's a drawstring inside so it can be pulled a little tighter. Here, let me show you.' Ivy took the hat and made the adjustment.

'Oh, now that's much better. I'll take it.'

Ivy put the pink feathered creation in a box which she tied with string from a large ball set on a metal swivel stick attached to the end of the counter.

The delighted woman paid and left, and Ivy threw the money into the till. Another of Ella's designs sold; another of her own dismissed. Even after all these years, and the success of the partnership with Ella, Ivy could not always suppress her jealousy. Still, she refused to believe that Ella's hats were superior to her own. She had tried to be kind to Ella, after all the girl had been through, but at times like this, the green-eyed monster reared its ugly head.

Fetching the besom from the kitchen, Ivy swept the shop floor like a demon, slamming the bristles against cupboards in an effort to dispel her anger.

In the meantime, blissfully unaware of the drama back at the shop, Ella had caught the steam train to Birmingham. Sitting on the wooden board benches in third class, she watched the world race past. The clackety-clack of the iron wheels on the track was, for once, lost to her as she wondered what she was about to get herself into.

3

Gathering her long skirts, ready to jump down from the train, Ella waited for the porter to open the door. An elderly gentleman in a top hat and a three-quarter Chesterfield coat, who was waiting to board, held out a hand to assist her. Ella alighted while giving the man her thanks and a smile. She followed the crowd out of New Street Station in Birmingham and, as she walked, pulled out the scrap of paper from her bag.

Needing to find Smallbrook Street, Ella asked a woman passing by if she knew the way.

'Yes, dearie. Go to the end of the road and turn

left. Follow the tramway past the church and it's the first on the right.'

Ella gave her thanks and moved on, hoping she wouldn't have to make an appointment and could just walk in and be seen. Despite being a couple of streets away, Ella's nose caught the smell emanating from the fish market. The walkways were busy with pedestrians and Ella bobbed and weaved her way through the throng. Carters trundled along the cobblestone roads either side of the tramway, and the noise of their wheels and peoples' tramping feet was loud in her ears.

Turning into Smallbrook Street, Ella found the house she was looking for, but now she was at her destination, she hesitated. Was she doing the right thing? Would the person who lived here be able to help her? Was she wasting her time and money?

Drawing in a huge breath, Ella looked first right then left as indecision took her. Maybe she should forget the whole idea, but having come all this way – what could it hurt?

Ella rapped the knocker and waited, feeling excited but worried. A moment later, the door opened and a brassy blonde-haired woman with a heavily made-up face stood there. Ella wondered if she had the right house and checked the scrap of paper again.

'I... I'm looking for Tilda Hunter,' she stammered.

'That's me.' The woman's red lips parted in a grin.

'Oh... I...' Ella didn't know what to say, she hadn't thought this far ahead. Besides, the woman's appearance had taken her by surprise; she looked like a streetwalker.

'I'm Ella Bancroft and I've come for a... reading?'

Tilda nodded before saying, 'Come in and take the weight off yer feet.'

Ella followed Tilda to her living room, which was dark, the curtains pulled part way across the windows.

'Sit you down,' Tilda said, motioning to a chair. Ella obeyed and eyed the crystal ball in the centre of the table as Tilda sat on the opposite side.

'Now, I take it you've lost someone and you want to see if we can contact them?'

Ella nodded and thought it a good guess on Tilda's part.

Tilda ran her eyes over Ella, making mental notes as she did so. 'It's half a crown, payable up front.'

Ella rifled in her bag and passed over the large silver coin.

Tilda inclined her head as she dropped the money down the front of her blouse. Then, holding out her hands, she nodded for Ella to do the same. Grasping Ella's shaking hands, Tilda closed her eyes. 'Hmm. I see...' Opening her eyes, she looked hard at Ella. 'A man.'

Ella's unintentional smile, known as a 'tell', assured Tilda she was on the right track.

'Yes, he's standing by the side of you.'

Ella began to shiver. Was it excitement or the cold room which had her quivering? 'What does he look like?' Ella asked.

'Tall, handsome and he's smiling,' came the answer.

'Is he happy? Is he well now?'

'He says... yes, he's no longer in pain.'

'Thank God!' Ella breathed.

'He's telling me he's proud of you.'

Ella's eyes welled with tears. Was this Harper or

her father, Thomas? Pulling her hands away, Ella placed one on her chest and sniffed.

Tilda noted the movement before pulling out a pack of cards and asking Ella to tap them three times before shuffling them. Then the clairvoyant spread three cards on the table. Touching the King of Hearts, she said, 'Your visitor passed from... a heart condition.'

Ella gasped – her dad. 'Yes, you must mean my father.'

Tilda saw the look in Ella's eyes change. 'Your father's not the person you want to talk to today, though, is he?'

Ella shook her head guiltily. 'I love my father still, but...'

Laying a finger on the second card, Tilda studied it. The Jack of Diamonds – a lover, maybe? Looking up she said, 'Betrothed.'

'Yes!' Ella could not contain her excitement. 'He passed on before we could wed.'

Tilda screwed up her eyes then muttered, 'John?'

Ella shook her head. 'Harper.'

'Ah, yes, he's here and smiling. What do you want

to say to her, Harper?' Tilda nodded then added, 'He says he loves you.'

Ella was beside herself with joy. 'I wish you were still with me,' she said quietly.

'He wishes he was too.' Then, picking up the third card, the Ace of Spades, Tilda went on, 'He was the love of your life.'

Ella's tears fell like rain as her thoughts were full of her beloved Harper.

'He's fading now – oh, he's gone,' Tilda said in a matter-of-fact manner.

Giving her thanks to Tilda, Ella left the house with mixed emotions. Both her father and Harper had come to speak to her, but was it real? How could she believe this stranger? Half a crown was very expensive for a sitting, but Ella thought it was worth it to commune with the two men she'd loved most in the world.

As she made her way to the market, Ella decided she would pay Tilda another visit soon in the hope of learning more from *the other side*.

Entering the market with its six hundred stalls, Ella wove her way to the one she needed. People pushed and shoved, looking for a bargain, and Ella kept a tight hold on her bag. The market was the ideal place for pickpockets and she had no intention of losing her hard-earned money to a thieving ragamuffin.

Glancing around her, she recalled snippets of history about the city such as that in 1881, the Rubery Hill Asylum opened, and ten years later, the law courts were opened with great ceremony by the Prince of Wales.

In 1889, Birmingham had been endowed with the title of city and was at that time the third largest in Britain. Ella knew that same year had seen a hospital extension to the workhouse built. The arched entrance was known as the Arch of Tears.

As Ella walked on, the noise in the market became deafening, with vendors calling out their prices, and hundreds of people talking at once. Barrow boys shouted for folk to *shift their carcasses* so they could get through to their destinations. The scent of fresh flowers hung heavy in the air before being replaced by the smell of rich soil on newly dug-up potatoes. Crockery clinked and tin pots rattled, laughter sounded and arguments raged.

Coming to the stall loaded down with bolts of

cloth of all colours, Ella sighed with pleasure. She glanced over tweeds, organza, brocades, silks, buckram, satins and nets. Bright cotton in stripes or spots lay alongside boxes of pins, needles, ribbon, feathers and hat pins. Customers were spoilt for choice and Ella was in her element.

Ordering five yards of white silk, Ella stroked some powder-blue felt and pink satin lovingly. Buying some of each, she then sorted through the feathers, making her choice. Adding a selection of hat pins and ribbons, Ella paid before collecting her parcel, which was neatly wrapped and tied with string. The vendor had kindly left a long string handle which Ella looped over her shoulder.

Her errands complete, Ella made her way back to the station and waited on the platform with the other passengers. She was still excited about her sitting with Tilda Hunter and couldn't wait to go again.

Ella stepped back as she heard the huffing of the train as it ground to a halt, wheels screaming when the brakes were applied. Great clouds of steam puffed into the air, smelling of coke, and causing the ladies to cover their noses and mouths with lace handkerchiefs. Porters' whistles blew and doors opened, allowing passengers to spill out onto the platform. Ella was jostled as she moved forward to board but eventually she secured a seat and settled down for her return journey, her parcel on her lap.

As the train trundled along, Ella debated whether to divulge to Ivy the truth of where she had been, or perhaps to Flossie when she called round, as she did every evening. What would they say? Would they consider her a fool for wasting her money? She guessed they would advise her not to see Tilda Hunter again, calling the woman a charlatan. All good reasons to say nothing, but Ella's excitement would most likely burst its banks and she wouldn't be able to resist telling them anyway.

Gazing out of the window, Ella smiled, knowing her dad and Harper were watching over her. The thought was a great comfort in her loneliness.

4

Back at Ivella once more, Ella opened her package and watched as Ivy fingered the material.

'What shall we make with this lot?' Ivy asked.

'I thought you might come up with some of your big fancy designs. This satin would be perfect for that.'

Ivy eyed Ella, unsure if the girl was being sarcastic.

'You're better at big, bold and beautiful than I am,' Ella went on. 'I'm working on a piece of sinamay covered in open weave netting instead. I'll put some wire in the edges to bend it to shape then add a few flowers and cut feathers.'

Ivy nodded and whisked the parcel of fabric up-stairs to the workroom.

Ella guessed she would be up there for quite a while, working on one of her over-the-top creations. Happy to be left alone, Ella's mind again returned to Tilda Hunter and her reading of the cards. Ella was still a little sceptical about what she had been told, but she so desperately wanted to believe that Harper was missing her too, and that her father was proud of her.

Her thoughts were interrupted by the arrival of a customer who was looking for something in the fu-nereal range. Ella took out a few black hats, some with net veils to cover the eyes. She watched as the woman tried them on.

'I like this one,' the woman said, then glanced at the price tag. 'Bloody hell! Expensive, ain't they?'

'We only stock the very best...' Ella began.

'Even so...' the woman turned the hat in her fin-gers. 'I suppose it'll get some use over the years, though.' Trying it on again, she studied her reflec-tion in the mirror on the wall. 'All right, go on, I'll take it.'

Ella boxed the item and took the money. As the

woman left, she thought, *some folks want everything for next to nothing!*

Throughout the day, customers came and went and sales were high. Ivy had been ensconced in the workroom and Ella dreaded to see what she would eventually produce. No doubt it would be very large and heavy with flowers, leaves and giant feathers. It wouldn't surprise Ella to see a bird perched on it somewhere too. Ivy returned to the shop floor at four o'clock, looking full of enthusiasm.

'How's it going?' Ella asked.

'Wonderful!' Ivy gushed. 'The new hat should be ready for display tomorrow.'

'Oh, good.' Ella tried to sound excited at the thought of what she suspected might well be a monstrosity.

At five o'clock, they closed the shop up for the night and Ella left for home, it was still a melancholy time of day, even after all this time. It was hard going back to an empty house. She missed her father's cheery greeting when she walked in through the back door. The winter months were the worst, when the house was dark and cold.

Strolling along, she distracted herself by wondering what to have for her evening meal and decided on ham, cheese and pickles before the meat spoiled and had to be thrown away. Besides, it was quick and easy to prepare. Then she could settle down to work on the sinamay hat she'd told Ivy about.

It was around seven o'clock when Flossie came blustering into Ella's kitchen.

'How do, gel, how was your day?' Flossie sat down at the table and felt the teapot.

'I'll make fresh,' Ella said and got to her feet.

They chatted as the tea was made and poured.

'I swear Birmingham gets busier every time I go.'

'Ar, well, that's cos it's a city now,' Flossie said as if that explained everything.

Ella smiled at her neighbour, who pushed her grey hair back off her face.

'I gave yer winders a quick wash for you today, seeing as you don't have time what with working an' all.'

'Thanks, Flossie.' Ella didn't offer to pay for the good deed, knowing if she did, she would suffer her friend's wrath. Done out of the goodness of her heart, Flossie would not hear of being paid.

'Flossie, do you believe in the afterlife?'

Flossie coughed as she choked on her tea. 'Blimey, where did that come from?'

'Oh, I was just thinking about it earlier today, that's all,' Ella replied.

'No, I can't say as I do. I think once you've gone, that's it,' Flossie answered.

'So you don't think our loved ones watch over us?' Ella pushed on.

'Lord, no! I wouldn't want my mother looking down on me when I take a piddle!'

Ella burst out laughing at the image her mind conjured up. 'The departed would have to be very selective about when to check up on us, I suppose.'

'What's brought this on?' Flossie asked, concern written all over her face.

'I think I'm just missing Dad and Harper today a bit more than usual,' Ella answered evasively.

'I understand. Grief comes in waves, doesn't it? You can be fine for months then suddenly it taps you on the shoulder and you'm fit for nothing.'

'That's about the size of it,' Ella agreed.

'I still say you should get out and about more. Go to the music hall or the theatre – treat yourself.'

'What, go alone? Certainly not. What would people think?' Ella was aghast at the thought.

'Bugger them! Wench, you need summat else in yer life besides working in that shop with battle-axe Ivy.' Ella's laughter rang out. 'Our Josh would go with you to the music hall if'n you asked him,' Flossie finished.

'I couldn't impose on him, Flossie.'

Joshua Woolley was a few years younger than Ella and worked at Junction Saw Mills. Ella considered him like a brother because they'd lived next door to each other for years and had grown up together.

'Josh wouldn't see it as an imposition, and 'sides, he'd enjoy a night out.'

'I'll think on it, thanks, Flossie.'

'Right, I've got snap tins to make up for my lot before my bones see my bed. See you tomorrow, gel.'

'Night night, Flossie.'

Whilst Ella and Flossie were discussing the possibility of there being an afterlife, Ivy had her head bent over the pink satin hat that she had constructed. It was a small dome with a large wide brim and Ivy rifled through the frippery laid out on her work bench, hoping something would catch her eye she could use to bring the hat to life. Silk flowers, huge feathers and bits of jewellery were begging to be used. Ella's edict of 'less is more' came to mind, but Ivy's fingers itched to attach adornments wherever she could fit them.

Pinning a couple of white roses in place on the brim near the dome, she stuck a tigered quill between them. Bunching together a guinea fowl, a peacock and a grouse feather, she stitched them together by stabbing through the end of the quills. Then she attached them behind the roses. The whole thing looked stunning, but Ivy was still not content. She thought the wide brim was screaming out for more decoration.

By the time she had finished, she was tired to the bone. Her eyes were dry and sore from working in the artificial electric light. Although she had baulked at first when Ella had suggested she have electricity fitted, it was at times like these that Ivy was glad of it. Getting to her feet, Ivy stretched out her back and rolled her shoulders, wincing at the pain in her aching muscles. She really felt she was getting too old for this, and despite not wanting to spend the money, she knew it was time to employ more staff. They needed a milliner and a shop girl. A word in Ella's ear tomorrow would have to do; for now, she was heading for her bed.

At the doorway, Ivy glanced once more at her creation and smiled. Turning off the light, she closed the door quietly. The pink hat swamped with decoration was suddenly plunged into darkness.

5

The following morning, Ella smiled at the note wedged in between her back door and its frame.

Glad rags on, you and I are off to the music hall tonight. I'll see you at seven. Josh.

Flossie had evidently told her son about their idle chat and despite her misgivings, Ella found herself quite excited at the prospect of going out in the evening again and her mood lifted.

After breakfast, she locked the house and set off for work. She wondered what Ivy had constructed with the material she had bought. What if it was awful? How would she tell Ivy it might not sell? It was probably better to wait and see. If the hat sat in the shop for a long time, maybe Ivy would get the message without Ella having to say a word.

Ella breezed in through the door to be faced with a tired-looking Ivy. 'Good morning.'

'Hmm,' came the reply.

'I take it you worked late last night,' Ella proffered.

'Hmm.'

'I'll make some tea, shall I, and then you can show me your latest creation.' Ella went to the kitchen as Ivy yawned and plonked herself on the customer chair, her elbow on the counter and her chin on her hand.

Ivy was still yawning when Ella returned with the hot drink.

'I'm going to the music hall tonight,' Ella said by way of conversation.

Ivy sipped her beverage, then asked, 'Who with?'

'Josh, Flossie's son.'

'Oh, well, enjoy yourself. I thought I'd start on another hat,' Ivy said quietly.

Ella's heart sank. When would her partner realise her designs sat gathering dust for months on end, only to be reworked into something more saleable later on?

With her tea finished, Ivy went to the workroom, returning with the pink hat which she laid reverently on the counter.

'Oh, my!' Ella exclaimed.

'Lovely, isn't it?' Ivy said, admiring her handiwork.

'You should put it in the window straight away,' Ella said, then thought, *out of my sight!* There was no way on God's green earth that hat would sell, and Ella could see no possibility for it to be renovated down the line.

Ivy fussed around with the window display, putting the large pink hat in pride of place in the centre.

'Ivy, I've been thinking, we really need to employ extra staff,' Ella ventured, expecting an argument as there had been with everything else.

'I had the same idea last night,' Ivy replied, her bottom now back on the chair. 'We should put up a sign in the window.'

'Good thinking. A milliner and a sales assistant.'

'We don't need a milliner, we do all right together,' she said, despite having had the same thought herself, the words were said now and she couldn't take them back. 'But a shop girl would be useful,' Ivy said huffily.

Here we go!

'Look at yourself, Ivy, you're tired out. I enjoy putting hats together, but I'd prefer to design them and have someone else bring them to life.' Ella was not about to back down on this.

'I like to design as well!' Ivy spat.

'Exactly. So if we join forces and produce some really good ideas, we can leave the rest to the staff. In fact, we should have two milliners while we are at it, because once we get going, there will be too much work for one woman. Besides, it will save money advertising for someone else if your new designs really take off.'

'That will cost and I'm not sure we can afford it!' Ivy felt her control slipping away and as if Ella was taking over yet again.

'If you check the books, I think you'll find we can.'

Ivy's sigh was loud, and Ella knew she had won, but she didn't gloat on the victory.

'All right, let's try it then. Write out a sign and we'll see if anyone applies.'

Ella grabbed paper and a pen from behind the counter and began.

Two experienced milliners wanted. Also a sales assistant. Please apply within.

Propping the sign in the window, Ella was followed back to the counter by a customer.

'Can I help you?' Ivy asked tiredly.

'Ar, you can tell me where you got that pink blancmange from, 'cos wherever it was, you need to send it back!' The woman laughed at her own quip, oblivious to the look of hurt on Ivy's face.

Ella winced. At least she knows now how awful it is, she thought.

'What can I do for you today?' Ivy asked, fighting to keep her temper under control. What was that old saying? The customer is always right. Not in this case, however, Ivy determined.

'I need summat ickle,' the woman said. 'I don't

want my good looks hidden by a bloody great big hat!'

Ivy grimaced as the woman smiled, showing her decaying teeth.

'Might I suggest a teardrop?' Ella asked, raising her eyebrows. 'Did you have a colour in mind?'

'Nah, not really. I ain't bothered as long as it's cheap.'

Ivy passed down three boxes from the rack of shelves and Ella took out the hats.

'How much?' the woman asked.

'The white silk is seven shillings and sixpence. The red sinamay two pounds one shilling, and the green one is one pound five shillings and sixpence.'

'Christ above! You two must be raking it in!' the woman gasped.

'Had you a price in mind when you came in?' Ivy asked.

'Ar, about two bob!'

'Two shillings wouldn't even pay for the feather!' Ivy lambasted.

'Fair enough, I'll get my arse to the market and see what they've got.' With that, the woman marched out.

As the hats and boxes were placed back on the shelves, Ella gave a shudder, saying, 'Ivy, we have to aim for a better class of clientele.'

'Ain't that the truth?' Ivy concurred.

As it was, the day turned out to be busy and both Ivy and Ella were tired by the end of it. Walking home, Ella thought about her evening out with Josh. She would much rather have put her feet up by the fire with a good strong brew. *Don't be such an ingrate!* she berated herself, and by the time she got home, Ella found herself actually looking forward to an evening out socialising.

6

Whilst Ella was readying herself for a trip to the music hall, Ivy snatched a quick meal of reheated broth with fresh bread before settling herself in the workroom. *Pink blancmange, indeed!* she thought as the woman's words sounded again in her mind. Grabbing the powder-blue fabric, she stared at it. What design to use it for? Large or small? Less or more decoration? Feathers or flowers – or both?

Cutting a length of white silk, she ruffled it until it looked like ripples in the sand left by the outgoing tide. Pinning it so it kept its shape, she then cut the blue felt and began stretching it over a dome-shaped block and secured it with blocking pins. She had half an eye on a huge ostrich feather which she planned would adorn the side of the hat. Once the felt was steamed, she put it aside to cool.

With a huge yawn, Ivy decided she was too tired to continue. What she needed was hot tea and to sit in her armchair by the fire.

* * *

Josh and Ella had arrived at the theatre at the end of Wolverhampton Street. They were near the front of the queue for tickets as they waited for the doors to open. Being among the first in would ensure they could find seats close to the stage. The sound of excited chatter grew louder as more people joined the line and a busker played to his audience in the hope of a coin or two coming his way.

Eventually, the doors were flung open and cheering broke out. Slowly, Ella and Josh moved forward and at the booth they each paid for their own ticket. Hurrying inside the theatre itself, they scrambled for seats right at the front and centre stage.

The noise of the auditorium filling up was tumultuous and over it all, Ella heard a man shout, 'Hey, missus, tek yer hat off, I can't see a thing!'

'I'll have you know this hat is an Ella. I paid a lot of money for it, so I'm wearing it!' came the reply.

Ella beamed with pleasure at hearing the hat was one of hers.

'Well, you was robbed!'

'You shut yer cake 'ole!'

Ella giggled at the riposte. Looking around, she noted the wealthier patrons settling themselves in the boxes high up on the walls. The old gas lamps had been replaced by electric lighting which revealed that the red and gold décor was starting to look a little shabby.

The musicians filtered into the large orchestra pit and began to tune their instruments and the excitement of the audience grew.

As the house lights went down, the applause rang out. The curtains parted and a man strolled onto the stage. Catcalls and whistles greeted him.

'All right, you rowdy lot,' he yelled, 'you all know me, I'm the comedian.' More whistling sounded before the man shouted, 'I'm not as stupid as I look, you know!'

'You couldn't be!' a female audience member retorted to the amusement of all around her.

'My family are in the iron and steel business –
my mother irons and my father steals!'

Laughter rang out – the evening had begun.

The next couple of hours were filled with jug-
glers and a magician who was booed offstage. A
mime artist was pelted with food and a ventriloquist
was ridiculed as he couldn't keep his lips still. A lion
comique entered dressed as a toff and sang a song
about drinking champagne and going to the races.
Then came a female singer who encouraged the audience to join in with the chorus.

All in all, Ella had a thoroughly enjoyable
evening and thanked Josh profusely as they strolled
home.

Josh saw her indoors safely before he went next
door to his own house.

Making tea, Ella sat to reflect on the evening's
entertainment. She smiled as she recalled some of
the bawdy jokes. She realised how much she had
been missing over the years. 'Thank you, Josh,' she
whispered into the empty kitchen.

The following morning, Ella regaled Ivy with

what she'd seen the previous night, but soon realised Ivy wasn't listening.

'I'm going to the workroom, I have a hat to finish,' Ivy said before disappearing through the door.

'Oh, Lord!' Ella said quietly.

It was about mid-morning when a young woman came in, asking about the job of sales assistant. Ella yelled for Ivy to join them to interview the girl together rather than do it herself and be accused of taking over again.

'What's your name?' Ivy asked, annoyed at having been disturbed when she was in full creative mode.

'Katy Woodbine.'

'Like the cigarettes,' Ivy said with a sniff.

'Like I ain't heard that before!' the girl answered sarcastically.

'Do you have any experience of sales?' Ella asked quickly, after introducing herself and Ivy.

'No, but it can't be that hard now, can it?'

Ivy harrumphed. 'We really need someone who has worked in a shop before.'

'Then you should put that on your sign!' Katy snapped. 'Wasting my time and what for? Nothing!'

'That's no attitude to take if you're looking for work!' Ivy said harshly.

'Look, I've tramped the town for days *looking for work*, and there's nothing doing anywhere. So if you don't want me here, just say so and I'll bugger off!'

Ella sighed. This was going to be hard work. 'Ladies, please. Everyone needs to start somewhere, Ivy, but Katy, you would have to be a little more polite.'

'I'm sorry, it's just that I'm desperate for work. Sometimes I speak before I think, but I promise I can rein it in. Please give me a go, I won't let you down.' Turning to Ivy, Katy went on, 'I apologise for being rude, it won't happen again.'

'Then I say we give Katy a try out and see how she gets on,' Ella said. 'What do you say, Ivy?'

'Please yourself,' Ivy said with a shrug before returning to the workroom.

'Bloody hell, she's a rum 'un and no mistake!' Katy said, making Ella smile.

'You have no idea. Now, tell me a bit about yourself, Katy.'

The dark-haired, brown-eyed girl launched into a precis of her life. 'My folks are drunkards –

Mother, who is pregnant *again*, loves her gin more than her kids. Father spends his life in the pub and only comes home to eat and tup me mother.'

Ella did her best to hide the smile coming to her lips at Katy's description of her home life.

'I've got two brothers and two sisters, all younger than me,' Katy went on.

'Pardon me for asking, but how does your family manage for money?' Ella asked.

'Me mother sells her favours for a couple of bob, which she won't be doin' for much longer now she's up the duff.'

'How old are you, Katy?'

'Fifteen, sixteen next month. I need to find a job quickly before my father decides I can earn more than Mother by doing the same thing.'

Ella was shocked at the idea of this young girl being made to work the streets and by her own father no less, as well as the forthright way Katy had spoken.

'Well, we treat all our clients as special. The customer is always right, even when they're wrong. Be polite and hold on to your temper because some people can test you to the limit. So let's see how you manage with the next customer before I make my decision, but I'll be on hand if you need me.'

The girl nodded and wandered around, having a good look at everything as Ella explained where everything was kept. Katy was shown how to work the till by pressing the required numbers together then turning the large handle on the side which released the coin drawer.

Ella liked Katy, she reminded Ella of her old friend, Kitty. She hoped Katy would be able to join the staff, even though Katy and Ivy's relationship could turn out to be volatile.

Just then, a woman walked in and Ella nodded to Katy.

'Good morning, how may I help you?'

So far, so good. Ella stood back and watched.

'I've gorra funeral to go to, so I need summat as is cheap.'

Ella pulled out a few boxes and laid them on the counter before stepping back again.

'Right then, let's have a look at what we have,' Katy said, taking off the lids and lifting out the hats.

'Nice,' the woman said and plonked one on her head, 'but two quid is out of my price range.'

Katy passed her another to try, then she helped arrange the net veil to only cover the eyes.

'Seven and six, a steal at that price.'

'Ain't you got anything a bit cheaper?' the woman asked, checking her look in the mirror.

Ella gave an imperceptible shake of her head.

'Ivella only produces the very best and at these prices you can't go wrong,' Katy said.

'I don't know. Can I try the other one?' Katy passed her the third at the same price. 'What do you think?'

Katy walked around the woman, studying her intently. 'This one ain't for you.'

'Why not? I like it.'

Ella held her breath for a few seconds.

'It's a little big on you and it's hiding all your lovely hair,' Katy answered simply.

Ella breathed again as the woman smiled.

'The other one it is, then.'

The happy customer left the shop and Katy, after passing the money to Ella, replaced the boxes on the shelf, having noted where Ella had got them from.

'Well done! That was excellent, Katy!'

'You gonna give me the job, then?'

'I am happy to give you a trial period. Let's discuss wages and I'll tell you a bit more about myself and Ivy. Welcome to Ivella!'

Katy emitted a whoop of joy, and upstairs Ivy sighed, knowing they now had a new assistant.

7

The following morning, Katy arrived right on time and was immediately ushered by Ivy to the kitchen to make tea.

'I thought I was a shop girl, not a servant!' Katy complained indignantly.

'We take it in turns,' Ella explained.

Katy nodded and went on to complete the task.

Returning to the shop, Ivy said to Ella, 'That one will cause trouble, you mark my words. I finished my hat – I'll fetch it down.'

A moment later, Ella was staring at the blue hat with a wide brim supporting a white ostrich feather.

The silk ruffle was attached to the dome, giving the whole thing an untidy appearance.

'Blimey!' Katy exclaimed as she brought in the tray of tea.

'Do you like it? It took me forever to make it,' Ivy said as she turned the hat on her bunched fist.

'If you want an honest answer – no.'

Ivy bridled. 'Why not?'

'It don't need that top-knot thing. The feather does all the talking. It says *class*.'

Ella clamped her teeth together to prevent a laugh escaping.

'No, I think you're quite wrong. I'll put it in the window and we'll see!' Ivy retorted.

'I should take the pink one out, if I were you, it looks a right mess.'

Ivy kept her back to the others as she closed her eyes tight and breathed through flared nostrils. Then she swapped the pink for the blue.

'Forgive me for saying, but I'd remodel that one if it were me,' Katy said with a nod.

'Mind your mouth, young lady, or you could find yourself looking for another job!' Ivy rasped before taking the *blancmange* upstairs.

'I was only telling the truth,' Katy mumbled.

'I did warn you, but don't worry, I'm on your side regarding those creations. However, it might be prudent to choose your words more carefully in future,' Ella whispered.

'Well, I'll try, but I can't change the way I'm made, Ella. I say it like I see it, and if Ivy don't like it – that's tough!'

Ella couldn't help the grin that crossed her face. Katy was so like Kitty.

The morning was filled with customers coming and going, and at ten o'clock, Ella made tea.

'Hello,' a cheery voice said when she came back through to the shop. 'I believe you're looking for an experienced milliner.'

'Indeed we are, come in, please.' Ella led the woman through to the back room where Ivy sat brooding.

'I'm Thora Skelton,' the woman said, nodding in Ivy's direction.

Ella made her introductions and asked Thora to take a seat.

'Tell us a little about yourself, Thora,' Ella said.

'I worked in Birmingham for a good many years, but when my old man died, I came home to Walsall.'

Ella nodded; Ivy showed no interest.

'You're knowledgeable about the construction of hats, I take it?' Ella asked.

'Oh yes, been making 'em all my life. Toppers, bowlers, pork pies, stove pipes, and for the ladies – boaters, riding hats, walking out, winter, summer...'

'Clever dick!' Ivy muttered under her breath.

'Beg pardon?' Thora asked.

'I would like to see some of your work, if at all possible,' Ella said.

'Oh, right. Here, I made this myself.' Thora took off her hat and handed it over to Ella to inspect.

'This is really very good. I'll tell you what, we can give you a month's trial and see how you fare,' Ella put in quickly.

'Sounds good to me. When would you like me to start?' Thora asked, her blue eyes twinkling.

'Can you begin immediately?'

'Yes! Show me to my work bench and tell me what you want doing.'

Ella led their new employee to the work room where she explained about the wages on offer.

Thora accepted readily and sat down on a well-worn stool.

'This is what I've been working on,' Ella said, passing over a sketch.

Thora nodded, her grey hair wobbling free of its pins. 'I can do this, what colour did you have in mind?'

'Oh, erm...'

'I reckon white satin with these feathers...' Thora pointed at the paper, 'dyed to a royal blue.'

'Ooh, now that I can see,' Ella enthused.

'Right, leave me to it.'

'You'll find everything you need, just have a good poke around. I'll bring you a cup of tea.'

'Thanks. That's a new one on me, the boss making tea for the workers,' Thora said with a grin.

'We're a team here, we all pull together.' With that, Ella went to fetch the promised tea.

While she'd been interviewing Thora, Ella was delighted to learn that Katy had sold two more hats. Having provided Thora with a brew, Ella then went to speak to Ivy.

'We need to do an inventory,' she said.

'Whatever,' Ivy responded sluggishly.

'What's the matter with you? You're like you lost a pound and found a penny.'

Ivy glared. 'I'll tell you, shall I? You're here again taking over. Hiring folk left, right and centre!'

'We need the staff, Ivy, and you left me to it! You didn't seem very interested.'

'I guessed I would be to blame.'

'Oh, for God's sake, pull yourself together, woman!' Ella's temper flared. She would not stand by and allow Ivy's jealousy to get in the way again. Staring at Ivy, Ella went on, 'It's not just that, though, is it?'

'I don't know what you mean,' Ivy said.

'Yes, you do. It's because of those hats you made, isn't it? The pink and the blue.'

Ivy shrugged.

Ella sighed loudly and dropped onto the other armchair.

'I can't do it any more. I've lost my creativity,' Ivy whispered.

'No, you haven't. You just get carried away with frippery, that's all,' Ella answered quietly.

'That style is all I know, I can't remember ever doing anything else.'

Ella became concerned. Why was Ivy behaving like this? It was as though she had given up and lost all interest. 'Rubbish. You know all there is to know about making hats, you simply need to redirect your ideas. That's why if you and I work together, we could make this place great.'

Ivy looked up at the girl she'd been envious of for so long.

'Honestly, I really do think we could be *great*,' Ella emphasised, 'but I need you with me.'

Ivy gave a single nod and Ella breathed easier. 'Thora is working upstairs and Katy is minding the shop, so why don't you and I get to designing some new headgear for the summer range?'

'What did you have in mind?' Ivy asked, her interest piqued and her mood lifted.

'Large – but not too fussy!'

'Right, where's that bloody paper and pencil?' Ivy said as she jumped up.

'I'll give you some peace and quiet while you work, then we can compare our sketches and tweak them where necessary,' Ella said and left Ivy to it, returning to the shop floor. Looking out of the window, she saw the weather had turned.

The rain came short and sharp and an elderly gentleman dashed in through the door. 'Great galloping gods! That came on quickly!' he said, shaking the droplets from his hands.

'I'll fetch a mop then, shall I?' Katy said.

'I'm so sorry to make a mess!' the man apologised.

'It ain't no bother. You stand there and drip while I nip to the kitchen.'

The man's laughter boomed out before he said, 'Oh dear, I fear I have upset your salesgirl.'

Ella shook her head with a smile. 'That's just Katy's way, please don't worry about it.'

'You're most kind.' Removing his top hat, he went on, 'I'm in need of a new topper, this one is on its last legs, don't you know!'

'Would you like one in black?' Ella asked as she slid the ladder along on its rollers.

'Rather!'

Ella grinned, already warming to her customer.

'Oh, I say!' the man said as he ran a finger over the crown of the hat Ella passed to him. Trying it on, he looked around for a mirror and, spotting the one on the wall, he made his way over to it.

Katy quietly mopped up the raindrops before returning the mop and bucket to its place.

'This is splendid! I'll take it.'

'Don't you want to know the price first?' Katy asked, causing Ella to wince.

'It's of no consequence, m'dear,' he answered.

'Of course not, silly me,' Katy mumbled.

Again, the man laughed loudly.

Ella boxed the hat, making a mental note to have words with Katy about her manner with customers.

Paying his money, the man said, 'Thank you so much, ladies, for the hat – and the entertainment. Be assured I will be recommending my friends call in to your delightful shop. Cheerio!' Then he was gone.

Ella and Katy looked at each other, then they burst out laughing, all thoughts of reprimand lost in the joviality of the moment.

It was as if their joy had sparked another change in the weather when the sun appeared and, within half an hour, the streets were dry again.

Ivy made lunch of cheese and onion wrapped in pastry and baked to a golden brown. Chutney and crusty bread accompanied the pasties with hot tea for all. They closed the shop for an hour so they could get to know each other a little better.

When Ella opened up again, a woman was waiting to come in. 'I've come about the job – the position of milliner,' she said, clearly hoping the post was still available.

Inviting her into the back room of the shop, Ella went through the interview process once more with Ivy listening in.

'Freda Harlow's the name and I'm a milliner by trade.' The woman's dark hair was unkempt and her clothes had seen better days. Obviously she was down on her luck and Ella noted the sadness in her grey eyes. 'I lost my husband last month and I'm desperate for work so I can pay my rent.'

Ella passed over a large square of felt and asked, 'What would you do with this?'

Freda thought for a moment then, laying it over her kneecap, she began to pull and shape the material. 'It would need doing properly, block pinned onto a pupae and steamed, then when it's cool, I'd stitch a band around the base of the dome. I think it might look nice with a wavy brim and maybe one small silk rose on the side. I ensure the stitches are small so can hardly be seen, I can show you if you like.'

Ella nodded, liking what she heard, so she led Freda upstairs to the workroom where she asked the woman to show off her handiwork. Pleased with the results, Ella offered the same terms and wages as she had given Thora.

'Thank you! Thanks very much!' Tears welled in Freda's eyes, so grateful was she to be given the opportunity of working at last, and not only that, but working for Ella Bancroft.

Once she had shown Freda upstairs and introduced her to Thora, Ella set them each a project to be getting on with then left them to their tasks. She wanted to see how they worked without supervision. Just as she was about to close the workroom door, she heard Freda say, 'Fancy me working for the great Ella Bancroft! She's famous all over the place!'

'I know, I heard of her when I was in Birmingham,' Thora answered. 'I was made up to be given this chance.'

'Me an' all. Now let's have a look at this that Ella has asked for.' Freda stretched the material over the wooden head block and began to press the blocking pins in place.

Ella went downstairs, her heart beating fast. *Me, famous?* She could hardly believe what she'd overheard. How had that come about? Deciding to keep what she'd overheard to herself for fear of upsetting Ivy, Ella smiled inwardly. It was a nice feeling to think of herself being famous, but it wouldn't do to allow this to turn her head.

Taking the card out of the window, Ella was pleased they had new staff and hoped they would become like a family now Katy, Thora and Freda had joined them. The idea that they could all be close had Ella thinking about her father. She still missed him dreadfully and knew he would be proud of her. This in turn made her think about her trip to the medium in Birmingham, and although she was trying to resist going again, the pull of it was getting stronger. She couldn't help wanting to know more.

With a curt nod of her head, Ella gave in to temptation, deciding it was time for another visit to Tilda Hunter.

8

Up bright and early the next day and on the pretext of going in search of more textiles, Ella boarded the train to Birmingham. Her excitement rose as the engine chugged along. Would Tilda Hunter be able to see her? She hoped so, but would her sitting be fruitful? Ella tapped her foot in time with the iron wheels rattling along on the rails, but she stopped when she caught a woman scowling at her in annoyance. She was eager to be there so, rather than tap, she wriggled her toes inside her shoes.

First on her feet as the train squealed to a halt, Ella jumped down onto the platform and pushed her way through the crowd. Hurrying along the streets, she didn't notice the smells or noises, and instead she raced onwards until at last she was rapping the knocker on Tilda's door.

'Oh, back again, are we?' Tilda said as she opened the door. 'Come in, I have a vacancy so you're in luck.'

Sitting as she had previously, Ella waited and watched as Tilda closed her eyes. 'Harper, are you there?'

Ella was impressed the woman had remembered Harper's name.

'Is there anybody there?' Tilda called out.

Ella had a sinking feeling. Maybe she shouldn't be doing this. Perhaps it was all a sham.

'Ah, there you are, dear,' Tilda said and Ella looked around. Seeing no one, she felt a little silly that she'd even looked. Tilda was obviously conversing with someone on the other side.

'Ella's here, what do you want to tell her?'

A shudder took Ella as she wondered who Tilda was talking to.

'All right, lovey. Harper says to keep your hat business going.'

Ella gasped. How could this woman know she was in millinery?

'What was that, dear? I see, yes, I'll tell her. Ella, he says he loves you and will forever.'

Tears sprang to Ella's eyes as she listened.

'Can you ask him – tell him – I need to...' Ella faltered, unable in her heart to let him go.

'He knows what you want, bab, he's aware you need to move on with your life.'

'Oh, Harper!' Ella's tears ran down her cheeks.

'He wants to be able to talk to you through me as much as he can, though,' Tilda said with a little cough.

'I'll come every week!' The words were out of her mouth before she realised what she was saying.

'He's pleased, he's smiling.'

Ella sobbed, wishing he could come back to her.

'I've got a Thomas here now.'

'My dad.'

'Ah, yes. He wants you to know he's happy now. No more pain.'

'Are his legs mended?' Ella asked.

'Oh, yes, lovey, they are.'

'Thank goodness!'

'He's fading. Is there anybody else who has a message for Ella?' Opening her eyes, Tilda gave a tight smile. 'They've gone.'

'Thank you, Tilda, I appreciate it. I feel so much better now.' Ella handed over her half a crown.

'Come back anytime,' Tilda said as she saw Ella out.

'I'll come next week.'

Tilda wriggled her fingers in a little wave before closing the door. It was worth all the questions she'd asked around the market because now Ella Bancroft was hooked. That extra two shillings and sixpence would come in very handy.

Ella sniffed and wiped her nose as she walked towards the market. Harper and her dad were watching over her still and she was glad of it. She couldn't wait to come again and chat with them some more. The week would drag past and she considered whether she could afford to visit again sooner. It was so expensive for the short time she was there, but Ella felt she *had* to go. She couldn't live without Harper's messages now. They were the brightest part of her week.

Deciding against shopping in the market, Ella

headed instead for a huge textile shop. Now there were two milliners working in the business alongside Ivy and Ella, Ivella would need plenty of stock. She chose bolts of lemon and silver brocade, peppermint green silk, cream chiffon, pink organza, along with large and small feathers from all types of birds. Requesting the merchant deliver to the shop, she was given an invoice to be paid at the end of the month.

Delighted with her purchases, which were promised for the next day, Ella thought she deserved a treat. A cup of coffee and a sticky bun were called for.

Sitting at a window table in the coffee shop, Ella watched the people passing by. Men stepping around women, children laughing or crying, carters and horse riders, it was incredibly busy.

Sipping her hot drink, Ella thought about her reading with Tilda again, and her heartbeat increased. Harper still loved her even from wherever he was.

The little shop bell tinkled, and Ella looked over as she saw someone enter. She was hardly able to believe her eyes as the fair-haired woman snapped,

'No! Over there!' The woman strode over to a table in the corner, the man accompanying her trailing behind.

Ella quickly turned away so as not to be seen.

Darcie Stoddard, née Newland was a woman she'd hoped never to see again.

Ella quickly finished her refreshment and left her money on the table, slipping quickly out of the coffee shop and hurrying to the train station. What were the odds of seeing Darcie in Birmingham after all this time? Ella was sure her parents had whisked her off to Scotland some years earlier.

As she sat on the train, Ella realised she was shaken to the core at seeing the spiteful Miss Newland once more and she hoped their paths would not cross in the future. Ella felt sorry for the man, whoever he was, who had followed behind Darcie like a kicked dog.

That evening, Ella told Flossie about her shock in the coffee shop.

'Oh, bugger!' Flossie exclaimed.

'My thoughts exactly,' Ella said simply.

* * *

Ivy sat by her fire, mulling over the day's events. The shop girl, Katy, had turned out to be really rather good with the customers, as the day's sales could testify. She was outspoken, it was true, but folk appeared to respect that. The girl had no qualms about telling a customer that a certain style or colour did not suit them, but for all that, she didn't lose a sale.

As for Thora and Freda, the two new milliners, time would tell. Making hats took a lot longer than selling them. The women seemed nice enough and it *did* leave Ivy free to do her designing. The problem there, however, was she had no ideas to get down on paper. It perplexed her to admit it, but Ella was the best she'd ever known when it came to thinking up new creations. So where did that leave her? With Ella's notions, Thora and Freda to bring them to life and Katy to move the finished article on – what was left for Ivy Gladwin?

Feeling redundant in her own shop, Ivy had spent the day roaming from room to room and watching Katy doing a roaring trade.

Ivy had been all fired up after Ella's little speech about making the place great, but that feeling was soon reduced to ash when all her sketches looked the same. Where had her millinery talent gone? She must have been good once upon a time, for hadn't she started the business and kept it going these long years?

Then Ella Bancroft had come along and Ivy's world had been turned upside down. It was sad the girl had suffered the loss of her father and then her betrothed, something Ivy would not wish on anyone, but Ella had then thrown herself into her work. This in turn had slowly pushed Ivy into the background. Already, after five years, people knew Ivella as Ella's shop. It galled Ivy but what could she do other than sit back and watch it grow without her? Yes, she would benefit financially, but what good was that, having nothing to spend it on? She had no one to leave her money to, either; all she'd had to stop her dying of loneliness was making her hats. Now it seemed she couldn't even do that. Perhaps a good night's sleep would help. Maybe she would wake refreshed, her imagination stirred, and raring to go.

With a sigh, Ivy thought, and one day pigs might fly!

9

The following day, Ivy had not woken up inspired and she was moping about in the shop when Ella arrived. Katy was dusting and humming to herself as she did so, but Ivy was ignoring her.

'I thought I'd visit Harper's parents today,' Ella said brightly.

'Out yet again!' Ivy snapped.

'Do you need me here for anything?'

'Oh, no, you go right ahead and socialise. I'm sure we can manage without you for an hour or two.' Ivy's remarks were scathing and had Katy watching with interest.

Not wishing to get into a contretemps on such a

lovely day, Ella merely nodded. Going upstairs, Ella ensured that Flora and Freda had enough work to keep them busy for the day. Satisfied, she returned to the shop and, clutching her bag and parasol, she left the shop and began her walk to The Cedars to see Eléna and Rafe Fortescue.

Strolling down Wednesbury Road alongside the tram line, Ella passed New Mills Pool, where out of work men sat holding fishing rods. It wasn't as though they thought they would be dining out on what they caught; families couldn't be fed on old bicycle wheels, but it had become a daily ritual. Seeing Ella, they tipped their caps and she waved in return.

As she walked, she thought about Ivy and how sharply she spoke to people lately. Ivy had always been awkward, it was true, but recently she was sarcastic, bordering on rude, which had become far worse since they had gone into business together.

Crossing over the railway line, she sauntered past Oxford Street, the noise from its two public houses loud even this early in the day. The Methodist chapel was all closed up and Ella continued on to pass by The Hollies. She gave a little shiver as memories flooded back to her.

Stafford Darnell, who had lived there, was once one of Harper's friends. He had overstepped the mark one day and tried to force his attentions on her, but thankfully Harper had come just in time and given Darnell a sound thrashing. She heard Darnell had left for America shortly afterwards but passing that house always reminded her of her ordeal and her heart rate increased rapidly.

Two streets later, she had arrived at The Cedars. Instantly a sadness covered her like a shroud as she looked at the building where her beloved Harper had lived for so long.

Given entry by the maid, Ella was shown to the sitting room, where Eléna sat reading a book.

'Ella! How lovely to see you. Come in, take a seat.' Eléna nodded at the maid who bobbed a knee and disappeared.

'Hello, Eléna, how are you?'

'Fine, dear, and Rafe is too. He's off somewhere doing something or other.' Eléna flapped a hand and smiled when Ella laughed at her lack of interest in her husband's business.

'It's good to see you looking so well,' Ella said as

the maid trundled in with a tray of coffee and biscuits.

'Thank you.' Eléna spoke to the maid who again left quietly. Then to Ella, 'What news do you have to tell me, my dear?' She poked a finger at the tray, indicating Ella should pour their drinks.

'Well, I had a surprise the other day that has prompted this visit. I was in a coffee shop in Birmingham and who should walk in? None other than Darcie Stoddard!'

'Good grief! What's that madam doing back here?'

'I have no idea, but it's a bit of a worry,' Ella replied.

'Was she alone?'

'No, she was accompanied by a man who appeared to be besotted with her.'

'Oh, dear, another lamb to the slaughter!'

Ella contained the grin threatening to erupt.

For a while they discussed the whys and wherefores of Darcie's return.

'Did you know the man accompanying her?' Eléna asked.

'I'm afraid not, but the poor man was being ordered about and he complied without a complaint.'

Eléna nodded, then, seeing Ella's expression change, she said, 'I feel there's something you wish to ask me. Come on, let's have it.'

Ella took a deep breath and plunged in. 'Do you believe in the afterlife?'

Eléna was surprised by the question, but being an astute woman, she guessed there was more to it. 'I believe in God and heaven but anything more than that – no, dear, I don't.'

'So you don't think that those who have passed over can contact us?' Ella asked tentatively.

'No, I don't. It's my belief that when you die, you go to heaven, although exactly what that would be like I have no idea. As for speaking to the dead, it gives me the chills just thinking about it. Why do you ask?'

'I... was just wondering.' Ella knew her faltering was a dead giveaway but had been unable to prevent it.

'Why don't you start at the beginning and tell me everything?' Eléna asked as she plumped the cushion behind her and settled back to listen to what was on Ella's mind.

* * *

Ivy had gone upstairs to see how the new milliners' work was progressing. The windows were open and the door was ajar to circulate the warm air. She stopped on the landing to listen in to the conversation between Thora and Freda.

'I ain't sure about the background of them but Ella is the driving force, I think,' Thora said.

'Definitely,' Freda concurred, 'but it was Ivy's business to begin with, so I heard. I don't know what happened to bring them together as partners, but I *do* know they were rivals at one time.'

'I thought there must have been summat because you can feel the tension, can't you?' Thora said.

'I'll tell you something else, you can see at a glance which are Ivy's hats and which are Ella's,' Freda added.

Ivy bristled, but continued to eavesdrop.

'Ella's good reputation is spreading far and wide, it wouldn't surprise me if she moved to London. That's where the money is.'

'Bloody hell, I hope not! I couldn't afford to go with her, much as I'd like to,' Thora answered.

'It's such a shame, though, ain't it?' Freda asked.

'What is?'

'That Ella has to try and sell those horrendous creations that are ruining the window display.'

'I can't argue with that,' Thora said with a little chuckle.

Ivy turned and walked away. She was close to tears with the hurt, frustration and anger fusing together in a dangerous mix. Stomping down the stairs, she marched into the shop area where Katy was serving a customer.

Once the customer had gone, Ivy said, 'Go and fetch some empty boxes from the spare room.'

'What for?' Katy asked.

'I don't have to explain myself to you! Just do as you're told!'

Katy stepped away, wondering what had got Ivy in such a flap. She came back with a pile of boxes, which she set down on the floor.

Ivy scrambled into the window and began removing all of her hats. 'Put these in those boxes, they need to go to the workroom,' she called out.

Katy obliged, and before long, the display was littered with gaps that needed to be filled. Ivy crawled out, her long skirt hampering her efforts, then she studied the shelves. She knew without checking what was stored there, she just had to decide which to use.

'What are you going to do in the window now?' Katy asked.

'I'm not sure yet,' Ivy mumbled behind a hand held to her mouth, her other hand resting on her hip.

'What about a theme of some sort?'

'I was thinking the same,' Ivy responded, but in all truth, she hadn't a clue. She tried to think back to years ago and what displays she had used then, but those memories appeared to be lost to her.

'Springtime, summer maybe?' Katy proffered.

'Old hat, if you'll pardon the pun.'

Katy roared with laughter and even Ivy smiled.

'When you take those upstairs, ask the others to pop down and see me, please.'

Following Katy back down the stairs, Thora and Freda stood before Ivy, feeling afraid. Were they about to lose the jobs they had so recently acquired? Had Ivy somehow overheard their conversation earlier?

'We need a new display and I'd like to hear any ideas you might have,' Ivy said. *If you can't beat 'em, join 'em!* The old adage came to mind as she looked from one face to another.

'What about weddings?' Thora suggested.

'Or funerals,' Katy put in, then, seeing the looks directed at her, added, 'maybe not.'

'It is the season for weddings,' Freda added.

'Hmm. We could go with that and see how it looks. Thank you, ladies, you may return to your work.'

Exchanging a relieved look, Thora and Freda made their way back up to the workroom.

'You get in there and I'll pass you the décor, before we place the hats,' Ivy said.

Katy lifted her skirts and deftly climbed into the space. 'Shall we shift everything out first?'

Ivy rubbed a finger beneath her nose as she pondered. 'Yes, good idea, then we can start afresh.'

Hat after hat was removed and placed on the long counter, then Ivy pulled out white ribbons to be draped in loops at the top of the window and down the sides. Top hats, gloves and a walking cane came next, being passed to Katy to arrange.

A white silk creation with a piece of net veiling was strategically placed, followed by four brides-maids' hats, each of a different design but roughly the same colour. One of the hats for the bride's attendants was a pale cream sinamay dome with a single feather on the side. Another was oyster-coloured teardrop, the feathers situated at the back. The third was white satin with a wide brim which held a cream rose, and the last was a small cartwheel in a pale fawn with white flowers attached to the side. A white lace parasol was opened and propped over the bride's hat. A packet of confetti, tiny white pieces of paper, was scattered liberally over the whole ensemble.

Katy carefully manoeuvred herself out of the window and joined Ivy outside to admire her handiwork.

'That'll do nicely,' Ivy said. 'Now to tidy up.'

Would it have hurt you to say, 'Nice work, Katy'? Katy thought as she followed Ivy back indoors.

The rest of the day was spent cleaning in between the serving of customers. Katy swept the shelves with a duster while Ivy dealt with a lady who needed a hat for a wedding.

'I like the one in the window with feathers at the back,' the woman said, tilting her head as she spoke.

'The teardrop, but that's a bridesmaid's hat,' Ivy informed her.

'So? That don't mean I can't wear it, does it?' the woman persisted, clearly intent on buying the headwear.

'Of course not, if that's what you want,' Ivy relented. At least it would be a sale and they could replace it with another from the stock.

Lifting the piece from the window, Ivy passed it to the customer, who tried it on.

'Oh, ar, that's bostin'! I'll tek it.'

Ivy boxed the hat and took the money before watching the happy woman leave the shop.

In the space in the window, Ivy set an off-white boater adorned with a silk band.

Ivy wrung her hands as she watched Katy cleaning the window outside. She was feeling nervous about what Ella would say about the new window display.

10

'Oh, Ella, surely you don't believe what this woman tells you!' Eléna said when Ella finished explaining about Tilda Hunter.

'I do! How can I not?' Ella instantly felt defensive. 'She knew about my hat business...'

'Of course she did! Your excellent reputation precedes you!' Eléna was trying to make Ella see sense without upsetting her too much.

'Harper said he wanted to talk to me through Tilda!'

'No, darling, Tilda said that. It's her way of making sure you keep going back and spending your money there. How much does she charge, by the way?'

When Ella told her, Eléna gasped. 'Good grief, Ella! You cannot continue to keep spending your hard-earned money like that!'

'Eléna, I *have* to, it's the only way I can have more time with Harper.'

'But you are not having more time with him, my dear! Look, I loved my son as much as you did, but Ella – he's gone. You have to accept it now. You've been in mourning long enough.'

'Tilda knew about my dad too, she called him by name.'

'Sweetheart, she would have asked around. She would have found that out from people who know you. Don't you see how easy it is for her? She knows how desperately you are holding onto hope. That's what these people do, Ella, they prey on the heart-broken, the vulnerable.'

Ella's tears came in a flood. Part of her knew Harper's mother was right, but another part was unwilling to let go of the possibility of Tilda being a true medium.

Eléna looked on sadly as Ella cried herself out,

then when the tears had subsided, she said, 'Ella, promise me you won't go back to this charlatan.'

'I can't, I'm sorry. I have to know if it's real.'

Eléna nodded resignedly. She understood. Ella had to find out for herself that this Tilda was a fake. Only then would she be able to move on with her life.

After Ella had left to go back to the shop, Eléna's thoughts remained on their conversation. It was hard enough for Eléna, after losing her son, but Ella was wasting her life pursuing something that would break her heart all over again.

People like this Tilda Hunter should be stopped from stealing folks' money under what she saw as false pretences. The trouble was they were breaking no laws as far as Eléna knew. As long as the bereaved sought comfort, these confidence tricksters would prevail. It was all very sad but there was nothing to be done about it.

Ella left The Cedars, making her way back to Ivella and as she walked down the street, she noticed a group of three women busy gossiping. Their scowls were directed at a woman across the road who was washing her windows. Clearly better off, the neighbour was dressed well despite doing her household chores. The group stood with arms folded beneath their bosoms and every so often they glanced towards the window washer. It was obvious to Ella that they were verbally ripping the woman to bits.

Ella sighed. Life was too short for this animosity. Striding past the huddle, she was surprised when they nodded at her with a smile. She returned the greeting and moved on.

As Ella walked along the streets back towards the shop, she chided herself for revealing to Eléna what she'd been up to in Birmingham. She should have kept her mouth shut, but she really thought Eléna, of all people, would understand.

Mixed emotions flowed through Ella as she trudged along. She felt a fool for confiding in Eléna, embarrassed that she was wasting her money according to Harper's mother. She was sad that Eléna didn't believe, for she was hoping Eléna might want to join her on the next trip. She was also afraid that this might all turn out to be a sham and she'd be hurt again.

Eventually, arriving back at Ivella, she stared at

the window display. In the time she had been away, it had all changed. Thinking hard, she was sure Ivy had not mentioned anything about swapping the hats before she left for her visit to The Cedars. Ella was a little perplexed at why Ivy should suddenly decide to make these changes.

The wedding scene portrayed was lovely, but Ella thought they needed something completely different. It was then she realised all the hats in the window were hers, which added to the mystery of it all.

Going indoors, she said, 'The window looks nice.'

'Ivy and I did it between us,' Katy replied.

Just at that moment Ivy came through. 'Oh, you're back then.'

'Yes. I was just telling Katy that I like the new display.'

'I told you before you went out it was time for a change,' Ivy said.

'I don't remember that, I'm sure we didn't talk about it, Ivy.'

'We most certainly did, so I got down to it!' Ivy responded.

Ella was shocked at Ivy insisting that they had discussed the window change when she knew perfectly well that had not happened. Had Ivy imagined it?

'With my help!' Katy put in. She was not about to let Ivy take all the credit.

'Hmm,' Ivy allowed, annoyed at the girl trying to steal the praise she felt belonged to her.

'Ivy asked Thora, Freda and me for our ideas,' Katy added.

Ella was surprised at the revelation and smiled inwardly, seeing Ivy scowling. She could see the relationship between these two women was fragile but neither would back down. Ivy would take every opportunity to remind Katy that she was the shop girl and she, Ivy, was the boss.

'*I* thought we needed something different,' Ivy said.

'We did, but...' Ella began.

'What?' Ivy snapped.

There she goes again with the nastiness, Ella thought but instead said, 'Well – is it different enough? I mean, the wedding scene is lovely and all...' Ella let the sentence hang in the stuffy air of the shop.

'I suppose we have done it before,' Ivy conceded. 'So what would you suggest?'

Ella frowned and sighed loudly. 'Let's leave it as it is for a while and see how it goes. Then maybe we could we do something around – a carnival, maybe?'

Katy clapped her hands, a broad grin on her face. 'What a cracking idea!'

'Perhaps,' Ivy said, cupping her chin with her thumb and forefinger. 'Then again, everyone needs a hat for a wedding, but who would want a carnival hat?'

'Wasn't there something in the newspaper the other day about a masked ball being held some-where? I didn't take that much notice, but I re-member thinking it would be nice to attend something like that,' Ella replied.

'We could have masks on the heads!' Katy said.

'Pupae,' Ivy corrected, then added, 'it could be worth a try. I like the idea of a masked ball and we could decorate the window with ribbons and flowers and such.' Despite herself, she was warming to the idea and the excitement was contagious.

'We could decorate our own masks with paints and feathers, and have the Melpomene and Thalia in a prominent position.'

'The what?' Katy asked.

Ivy closed her eyes and sighed at the girl's ignorance.

'Melpomene represents the tragedy mask and Thalia represents the Muse of Comedy. They are associated with the theatre,' Ella explained.

'Well, I never. You learn summat new every day, don't ya?' Katy said, elbowing Ivy in the ribs.

Ivy scowled again and Katy just grinned.

'Of course we would need a new range of hats, but not too many, in case they don't sell,' Ivy said as she turned back to Ella.

'Indeed, so I think you and I should get our heads together and come up with some fancy designs.'

Ivy gave a single nod and pushed back her shoulders in a self-important manner.

Retiring to the back room to begin their work, they left Katy to mind the shop.

'Fancy you not remembering we were going to

change the window,' Ivy said as they scratched out designs on old butcher's paper.

'I was certain we hadn't discussed it,' Ella responded.

'Right, what do you think of this?' Ivy passed over her paper and waited for Ella's reaction.

Ella sighed. 'Well, it's nice, but a cartwheel doesn't really scream carnival, does it?'

Ivy frowned as she took back the paper. Staring down at the drawing, she shook her head. 'When did I sketch this? It must have been years ago.'

It was then that Ella really began to worry about her colleague. Ivy was forgetting things more and more often and her temper at having this pointed out could well become a problem.

'Add an eye mask to it and it might look totally different,' Ella suggested. Then, with a stretch, she said, 'I've had enough for one day, I'm going home.'

That evening, as Ella was preparing her meal of boiled potatoes to go with a meat and onion pie, the back door opened and in bustled Flossie.

'Hello, chick.'

'I thought you'd got lost. I haven't seen you for a

few days. The tea is fresh, help yourself,' Ella said with a smile.

'I've been spring cleaning. I hear you had a nice time at the music hall.'

'I did, but you shouldn't have made Josh take me.'

'I d'aint! I was just telling him I thought you needed some fun in your life and he came up with the idea,' Flossie said indignantly.

'Oh, I'm sorry, I didn't realise.' Ella gave an apologetic look as she spoke.

'It's all right. He enjoyed it and said he wouldn't mind going again.' Flossie's eyes were on her cup as she poured the tea.

Ella glanced over, wondering if Flossie was trying to match-make. Was she trying to set Ella up with her son?

Ella said she wouldn't have time to go out now for a while as they had decided to bring out a new range of hats; she noted the look of disappointment on her neighbour's face.

'Ar, well, all work and no play...' Flossie commented.

'Flossie, it wouldn't work,' Ella said quietly.

'What wouldn't?' Flossie asked, as she forced an innocent look to her face.

'Your Josh and me. I can see that's what you're up to, even as I know you'll deny it.'

Looking shamefaced, Flossie said, 'Ah well, it was worth a try.'

'I love Josh like a brother, Flossie, and one day I'll be making you a hat for his wedding. He just won't be marrying me.'

Flossie's head nodded slowly in acknowledgement. Ella was right, of course, they had always been like siblings.

'Right, I'm away. I need to black lead my range before bedtime. I'll see yer tomorrer.'

Whilst eating, Ella thought about the wedding hats in Ivella's window, and how Ivy had sworn they had discussed the change. Now Flossie was thinking Ella and Josh would make a fine couple if they began to court each other. This then led her to wonder if she would ever be a bride herself. It was no use even considering the prospect until she was sure in her own mind of the truth about Tilda Hunter and her chosen profession.

11

Whilst Ella and Ivy were working hard on the new carnival collection, Tilda Hunter had been out and about asking questions once more.

She knew Ella would be true to her word and come every week after what Tilda had told her about her lost love wanting to continue communications. Now she had to gather as much information as she could in order to drip-feed titbits to Ella on each visit. That way, Tilda would be half a crown better off every week. It was money for old rope and, as she trawled the market, she smiled.

She came to one stall that sold all kinds of every-thing to do with millinery, such as pins, needles, ribbons, thread, and feathers, as well as materials of all textures.

Picking up a feather, she twirled it between her fingers.

'What can I help you with, duck?' the vendor asked.

Now she could begin asking her questions. 'I wish I could sew. I need a new hat but... who would you recommend as the best person to see to have a hat made for a special occasion?'

'Oh, Ella Bancroft, to be sure,' the market trader told her.

'And where would I find her?' Tilda asked, replacing the feather in its box on the stall.

'She lives in Silver Street in Walsall, but trades from Ivella in Junction Street.'

'Is she good, do you know?'

'The best, and of course she buys all her fabric from me,' the vendor said proudly.

'Is that the same woman who lost her fiancé just before the wedding?'

'Yeah, bloody shame if you ask me. She's a lovely girl.' The vendor leaned forward and went on in hushed tones to explain how she'd heard that

Harper Fortescue had dumped someone called Darcie Newland to wed Ella. Warming to her theme, she carried on to share the story of how Ella and Ivy had been rivals at one time but were now a team – which many in the trade had found very mysterious.

Tilda thanked the woman and moved on. She had a lot to formulate in her mind before Ella's next call. She also needed to find out what she could about this Darcie Newland. Despite there being no mention of Darcie being bereaved, Tilda was intrigued and wanted to know what kind of woman she was and whether she would be a good client.

It was the Fortescue family she needed to research, though. It could be that with a name like that they might be monied, and if she could snag one of them, maybe Harper Fortescue's mother, as a client too, she'd be raking it in.

Making her way to New Street station, Tilda decided a little train journey was in order. She was going to Walsall to see what more she could learn about the life of Ella Bancroft.

Knowing the best gossip to be had would be in the market, Tilda decided to start there.

Tilda ignored the strange looks from other passengers, knowing what they thought of her, and instead she looked out of the train window. After the engine pulled into the station, Tilda alighted and asked the way to the market. A harassed woman with six children yanking on her skirts pointed before bending to slap whoever was within reach as she yelled at them to 'get on home, *now*!'

Tilda walked on and entered the market, which was laid out in the street leading to a large church on the hill.

Again, she asked her questions, and the answers provided her with the knowledge she sought, and on the train homeward bound, she considered what she'd learned.

Ella's intended in-laws, the Fortescues, came from old money. They were high on the social ranking and Rafe Fortescue, Harper's father, owned the Alma Tube Works. After losing their son, they had retired from the social part of life, but Rafe still managed his works.

As for Ella, new information had come to light. It appeared her sister, Sally Denton, had been selling Ella's new designs to Ivy Gladwin. When her treachery had been found out, Sally had left the area; no one knew where she had gone.

Tilda mentally rubbed her hands together as she left the station and trudged home to Smallbrook Street. She had enough juicy snippets to keep Ella coming back for months.

Once indoors, Tilda made tea, sat down and began to work out a plan in readiness for when Ella Bancroft graced her doorstep again.

* * *

Whilst Tilda had been trudging the streets, Ella was chatting with Katy in the shop. Ivy was working up-stairs with Thora and Freda, helping to bring their new designs to life.

'That landlord of mine – I swear if he slips an arm around my waist one more time, I'll kick him in the trossocks!' Freda exclaimed.

'Touchy-feely sort, is he?' Thora asked.

Freda nodded. 'And some. He thinks he's God's gift to women, but he's just a dirty old sod!'

Ivy listened to the conversation, her eyes on the work in her hands.

'Tell him, then,' Thora replied.

'What, and find myself out on the street?'

'Hmm, I suppose that does pose a problem.'

'I really have to find somewhere else to live,' Freda said as she pushed her needle through the white satin.

'I've got a spare room, why not come to mine?' Thora suggested. 'We'd be company for each other and we could share the bills. You'd be most welcome.'

'That would be bostin'! Thanks ever so,' Freda gushed.

'Right, then. You can move in right away and you can tell that old lecher to stick his rent up his arse!'

Ivy sighed loudly but the women ignored her and continued to chat. They decided that Freda would move in that very evening and Thora would help carry her friend's belongings.

Downstairs, the bell tinkled and as Ella turned, she thought her heart had stopped. There in front of her stood a very handsome young man. Tall with dark hair and twinkling brown eyes, he smiled, showing pure white, even teeth. But the most striking thing about him was his skin, which was a dark coffee colour.

'Ella Bancroft?'

Ella stepped forward and whispered, 'That's me.'

'Ah, how very nice to meet you. My name is Paul Sampson and I'm in need of a new bowler hat. I was told you could help me.'

'Of course, Mr Sampson. Please take a seat.' Ella directed him to the padded Queen Anne chair she had purchased some time ago to replace the old kitchen seat.

Turning to Katy, who stood with open mouth, she said, 'Katy! Black bowler, please.'

Katy's jaw snapped shut as she swung the ladder along its rails before climbing the rungs. She pulled down a box and passed it to Ella, then went back to staring at their most unusual customer.

Paul Sampson stood and laid down his walking cane on the counter, before taking the hat held out to him by Ella. He stroked a long finger around the crown, enjoying the feel of the material.

Ella pointed to the mirror on the wall and watched as he tried it on. Her heart was beating like a drum as she studied him. Well-built but slim, he had powerful shoulders. His voice was like honey as he praised the workmanship. She had never before seen anyone with skin so dark and she was fascinated.

'Very nice. It's a little small, though, do you have a bigger one?'

Katy obliged by pulling down another box and handing the hat over.

'Thank you, this fits much better, I'll take it,' he said turning to face Ella.

Ella nodded, unable to speak; her tongue seemed glued to the roof of her mouth, and her eyes roamed over the smooth darkness of his face.

'You were recommended as being the best in the business and I can see why,' he said.

Blushing scarlet, Ella muttered, 'Thank you, Mr Sampson.' Her tongue released now, she went on, 'May I ask who was kind enough to suggest you visit me?'

Katy, who was boxing the hat and tying it with string, could hardly keep her eyes off the man in the shop.

'Mrs Eléna Fortescue,' he answered.

'Ah, yes, she's a fine lady.'

'Indeed. I have known the family for a number of years, as I am their accountant.' Paul's eyes crinkled at the corners in a smile.

'I see,' Ella said, wondering why she'd not heard of him before. But why should she have? He had a business relationship with the family, not a social one.

'It was a sorry thing, them losing their boy the way they did.' Paul drew out his wallet and paid for his hat. 'Just before his wedding too – very sad.' Then he stared at Ella and she could have sworn he paled. 'Ella Bancroft – oh, my dear, I'm so sorry, the penny has just dropped. You and he...'

'Yes, we were betrothed,' Ella said as her eyes dropped to the box in her hands passed over by Katy.

'Forgive me for being so thoughtless. It was not my intention to upset you. I feel wretched.'

'Please, Mr Sampson, it's all right. It's been five years since Harper left us.'

Paul Sampson gave a nod, but his eyes never left hers, the gold flecks nestled in their hazel nest glinting in the light. She was a beauty and no mistake. Her dark hair shone in its intricate coiffeur, and her smile was enchanting. Tearing his eyes away from her, he glanced around. 'You have some beautiful designs here, Miss Bancroft, are they all yours?'

'Some of them are. The others belong to my business partner, Ivy Gladwin.'

Katy had melted into the background and watched the interaction between the two. She was also very interested in the unusual man.

'I wonder, may I see a topper whilst I'm here?'

Ella gave him a winning smile and turned to see Katy swinging the ladder again.

Laying a new box on the counter, Ella picked out the hat and passed it to the man who intrigued her so much.

His fingers touched hers as he took the hat and Ella could have sworn they lingered there a little longer than was necessary. Or was that her imagination?

Ella's heart lurched; she had not touched another man since holding Harper's hand and kissing him. Was this feeling telling her she was at last beginning to heal?

Paul Sampson stroked the brim of the topper, but his eyes stayed on Ella's. 'Lovely,' he muttered.

Ella's cheeks flamed, her mouth tilted up at the corners and she allowed herself to be drawn into the depths of his chocolate-drop eyes.

It was Katy's cough that broke the spell.

Paul looked at the hat. 'Yes, this will do nicely, but it's not my size.'

'I can take your measurements and have one made up for you,' Ella replied. 'Katy, help, please.'

Katy wrote down the figures as Ella called them out. She was measuring his head with a tape measure and was nervous about being so close to the seated man.

For his part, Paul Sampson drank in her scent, savouring it. He could feel the warmth of her body and his senses came alive at being so near to this stunning young woman, but he stamped them down.

'That should do it, it will take a couple of weeks as we are working on a new range for the shop. I hope that will be all right.'

'Of course,' Paul said. Reaching into his pocket, he pulled out a little white card. 'My card, in case you should need to contact me.'

'Thank you,' Ella said as she held out her hand to be shaken in farewell.

Paul Sampson took her hand, gave it a firm shake and said, 'Until then.'

Ella's heart exploded with an exquisite pain, a joy she hadn't known in a long, long time.

With a grin and a wave, Paul Sampson left the shop.

'Bloody hellfire and damnation!' Katy gushed.

'I was thinking much the same myself,' Ella muttered as she stared at the open shop door.

12

Katy was happy to run upstairs with the new order for Paul Sampson's top hat, and to tell everyone of their strange customer. She'd never seen anyone like him before and was bursting to share the news.

'He was brown, I tell you!' she said excitedly.

'What, from being in the sun too long, you mean?' Thora asked.

'No! Like a African you see in the books!'

'An African,' Ivy corrected.

'Whatever, but I tell you he was handsome as the day is long!' Katy replied dreamily.

'There are brown people in Birmingham, Katy.

Next time he comes in, I wish to be informed,' Ivy said icily.

'So you can have a good gawp?' Katy asked unashamedly.

'Don't be impertinent! Get yourself back to work.'

Thora and Freda exchanged a look and wiggled their eyebrows, knowing Katy had been right in her summation.

Katy harrumphed but did as she was told, mumbling that *she* had never seen anyone like the brown man in her life and was very surprised to have seen him.

Down in the shop, Ella was daydreaming about the very good-looking Paul Sampson. She couldn't believe he had affected her the way he did. She was trying to convince herself she hadn't been struck by Cupid's arrow, but to no avail. The man had taken her breath away; he had stirred feelings she thought long since dead and left her wanting to see him again.

Ella went to the kitchen to make tea for everyone, where she could think in peace. She couldn't allow herself to be drawn to this man, it would be betraying Harper's memory. If he was looking down on her, he would know and he would be hurt.

Making the tea, she took a cup to Katy before carrying a tray upstairs for the others.

'Katy told us about our new customer,' Ivy said nodding her thanks for the beverage.

'It's nice to be gaining new clients, he bought a bowler too,' Ella said, feeling a blush come to her cheeks.

'Katy thinks he may be from Africa,' Ivy pursued.

'I'm sure I have no idea,' Ella replied before glancing at the work being undertaken. 'Is that the same as the sketch?' she asked Thora.

'Not quite, Ivy said to...'

'Ivy, for goodness' sake! We designed these together and now you're changing things!'

'I thought it needed a little something.'

'Well, that *little something* is in the form of a bloody big feather!'

Ivy was shocked – she'd never heard Ella swear before.

'Remove it please, Thora, and in future, ladies, please follow the sketches to the letter. Ivy, a word, if you don't mind.' Ella turned and went downstairs to the back room with Ivy in tow.

Thora sighed as she began to unpick the tiny stitches holding the feather in place.

'Blimey! Ivy's done it now. Ella weren't best pleased, was she?' Freda asked.

'I'm not surprised. Look at it.' Thora wobbled the hat, setting the huge feather swaying. 'It's awful, but Ivy's the boss, so what can you do?'

'I can see there being a parting of the ways before too long,' Freda said.

'Ar, me an' all. The question then would be, where would Ella go? This is Ivy's house as well as her shop,' Thora returned.

'We could find ourselves out of work again as well.' Freda gave a huge sigh.

'Not me, I'd follow where Ella led,' Thora said.

'She wouldn't be able to afford us if she went out on her own again, though.'

Placing the hat on her worktable, Thora picked up her cup and gave thought to Freda's remark. 'In that case, let's hope they sort things out and quickly.'

Down in the back room, Ella rounded on Ivy.

'Why do you do it? Why change a perfectly good design and turn it into an abomination?'

'That's a bit strong!' Ivy spat.

'No, it's not. I'm sick of constantly having to watch you ruin good hats, Ivy!'

'Well, if you ain't happy, you can always go back to your little house in Silver Street and try and sell from there again!' Ivy was as angry as Ella now.

'I thought we had an agreement, but clearly I was wrong! You simply cannot accept the fact that I'm the more modern designer!' Ella's voice rose in pitch as her fury mounted.

'That's the thing, I don't think you are!' Ivy yelled.

'Look, either you leave the hats to be made according to the sketches, or you can tear up the contract and go it alone once more!'

'And what will you do?' Ivy asked sarcastically. 'Where will you sell your hats?' she went on, feeling she had won this round of the verbal battle.

'I have more than enough in the bank now to rent a small shop, where I *know* my millinery will sell. Can you say the same if you were left trying to shift yours?'

Ivy dropped into a chair. Round two to Ella. Of course Ella was right, Ivy's business would fail if they broke up the partnership.

Ella quietly took a seat as she watched a dejected Ivy. She felt bad for the woman, but Ella's livelihood depended on keeping the business going. She could not back down and let Ivy ruin things, she had to stay strong and stick to her guns.

'I just wanted to help. I feel redundant in my own shop.' Ivy's words were hardly more than a whisper.

'I'm sorry you feel that way, Ivy, but we *must* stand by our agreement. If we waver, we're lost.' Ella kept her voice low too for fear of triggering Ivy's temper again, something which was happening more and more often.

'What's left for me to do? You design, Katy has the sales in hand, and Thora and Freda make the hats. All I do is supply the premises for you all to work from.'

Ella was shocked to see tears rolling down Ivy's cheeks. She'd never seen the woman cry before. Passing her handkerchief over, she whispered, 'Don't get upset. We can work together, we simply have to try a bit harder. You've made the window look lovely, and once the new range is complete, goodness knows how fabulous it will look.'

Ivy sniffed and eyed the girl she envied with her heart and soul.

'You're just trying to make me feel better.'

'No, I'm not – I mean, yes, I am, but...'

Suddenly both women burst out laughing at Ella's poor attempt at lightening the mood and all the tension was gone.

'I was thinking,' Ivy ventured, 'when the collection is finished and our carnival window is done with, maybe we could have a fashion day, like all the clothes designers do.'

'Ivy, that's brilliant!' Ella gushed. 'What a spectacular idea!'

Caught up in Ella's enthusiasm, Ivy went on, 'We could send out invites to the nobs – something along the lines of a champagne party.'

'Fantastic, although I'm not sure we could afford to run to champagne. We could manage wine, though,' Ella said brightly. 'You know all the elite, so...'

'I'll send out the invitations, but you have to word them. I'll get them printed up. Oh, we'll need to decide on a date and do something with the shop and window – again!'

'That's your department as well. I'll help the girls with getting the hats finished,' Ella said.

'Right, let's get to it!' Ivy beamed with pleasure at being useful once more.

Ella watched as Ivy found pencil and paper and began to draw a new layout for the shop. Then she went to inform the others about Ivy's idea.

Katy sighed when she heard the news. 'She'll have me run ragged shifting things about. *Empty the window! Move that cabinet!* It will be a bloody nightmare!'

'We might be able to persuade her to give you girls a bonus for all your hard work,' Ella suggested.

'Oh, well, that could make it worthwhile,' Katy said with a grin.

Both laughed as the shop door tinkled and Ella's heart leapt in the hope it might be their special client. She berated herself for being so foolish, of course it wouldn't be Paul Sampson back so soon, but it didn't stop her thinking about inviting him back to the shop. All she needed was a reason to do so.

13

Despite Ella's longing, the customer was not the one she had hoped to see. It was a young woman wanting a hat for a christening.

Ella decided that as all was running smoothly in the shop, she would again visit Tilda Hunter. She had a lot of questions and hoped they would be answered by the so-called medium. Ella was torn between wanting to believe the things Tilda told her and wondering whether the woman was indeed a charlatan.

She wanted to remain true to Harper's memory; however, she could not deny she was drawn to Paul Sampson. Her heart was not dead after all, and even if it turned out Paul was already married or not interested in her, she knew now she could possibly love again.

Looking smart in her high-necked white blouse and blue and white striped skirt, Ella grabbed her white boater with its blue ribbon tied about the dome. Taking up her bag, she left the shop on the pretext of shopping. Ella walked briskly towards the railway station, pleased to see the train waiting at the platform. Buying her ticket, she entered the third-class carriage at the end of the train.

Boarding, Ella found a place and smiled inwardly; one day, she would travel first class and sit in the plush blue velvet seats. She would be served coffee and pastries to enjoy on her journey. For now, she was content at not having to walk to Birmingham.

A young boy further down the carriage began to cry, which soon turned into a wail, then on into a full-blown tantrum. Ella watched as he stomped around, yelling at the top of his voice, eliciting stares from other passengers. Suddenly the sound of a slap rang out and the child's noise stopped in an instant.

'I warned you, you little bleeder! Now shut yer

row before I tan yer arse good and proper!' The child's mother sat the child next to her and acknowledged the congratulatory nods and smiles from those around her. The boy sniffed but remained quiet otherwise. Ella wondered how she would have dealt with the child had he belonged to her; she hoped she would have raised him so that he would behave in public in the first place. However, she silently praised the mother for having settled him at last.

Arriving at the station, Ella alighted and walked out onto the busy streets. Was she doing the right thing coming back here again? Should she just accept that Harper had gone and would never come back? She knew she would not forget him but was it time, as everyone kept telling her, to move on with her life? Somehow, something was drawing her back here time after time and she knew that was becoming a problem. Until she could discover the truth of whether everything Tilda was telling her was real or not, Ella knew she would continue to return.

Walking along the streets, Ella took note of the hats she saw as women passed her by. She found herself mentally redesigning them and committing these ideas to her memory. She also looked hard at the fabrics of the long skirts and dresses, and it was then she saw a lady in a bright red tartan outfit. That, she thought, would look grand as a hat!

Arriving at Tilda's house, she knocked soundly. She was greeted with a warm smile by the heavily made-up Tilda and led through to the sitting room.

Paying her money, Ella waited and watched quietly while Tilda closed her eyes and called upon the spirits to join them.

'Harper, are you there?' After a moment, Tilda smiled. 'Ooh, that was quick! He's here, Ella. What did you want to ask him?'

Ella sighed. How could she put it? She wanted his blessing to live her life again and be able to not hanker after something she couldn't have. 'Does he need to say anything to me?'

'All right, dear, I'll tell her. He says he misses you. He says you must forgive Sally. Your sister has learned her lesson.'

Ella gasped. How could Tilda know about Sally? She felt the colour drain from her face and her stomach roiled.

'What was that, dear? Right. Ella, are you keeping an eye on Eléna?'

Again, Ella's sharp intake of breath was audible in the quiet room and Tilda knew the girl was now well and truly hooked.

'Yes, Harper, I am.' Then, after a moment, Ella whispered, 'Harper, I have to let you go.'

Suddenly Tilda banged a hand on the table, making Ella jump. 'No! He's saying you can't leave him.'

'I must, Harper, I can't go on like this!' Ella's whisper became more urgent.

Tilda thought hard, she felt Ella was slipping away from her. She wanted to keep this client; she desperately needed the money. 'Harper is upset, Ella. He's saying this is the only way he can speak with you.'

'I understand that, but it's making me ill!' Ella's tears welled in her eyes. 'I can't see him, or touch him. I only have the words you are telling me and it's not enough!'

'He's saying he can't be with you any more, Ella, but he can't let you go.' Tilda pushed, hoping the girl would believe what she was being told.

'No, if I can't have him back here with me, then I must hold him in my memory and move on with my life!'

'Oh, dear!' Tilda opened her eyes and went on, 'He's gone! I don't think he was very happy.'

Ella was distraught at having upset Harper's spirit, but she knew she had made the right decision. Getting to her feet, she ran from the house in tears, Tilda's words ringing in her ears. 'Come back soon, dear.'

Dashing back to the station, it was all Ella could do not to break down and cry. The train journey seemed to take forever and she held back her emotions with monumental effort.

Finally arriving at Ivella, Ella pushed her shoulders back and tried to pull herself together. She heard Katy's voice ring out as she walked into the shop. 'I ain't moving it again! Make your bloody mind up and stick to it!'

'Problems?' Ella asked with a forced smile.

'No, I'm just trying a new layout, but *madam* here is being obstinate!' Ivy snapped.

'I am not! You've had me shift that cabinet three times and it's heavy!' Katy retorted.

'I like it where it is, Ivy, it would be useful to put the trays of drinks and canapes on,' Ella said tactfully.

'Hmm. All right, leave it there.' Turning to Ella, Ivy asked, 'Weren't you going shopping? You'd best get a move on if you want to bag a bargain.'

Ella frowned and she and Katy exchanged a puzzled look.

'Now, how are we going to display our millinery?' Ivy asked, returning once more to the task in hand.

'What about those pupils?' Katy asked.

'Pupae,' Ivy corrected.

'What about live models?' Ella suggested.

'We can't afford to hire models!' Ivy was aghast.

'No, but we could do it ourselves. I'm sure for a financial incentive the girls would be happy to oblige.'

'Ooh, I'd love to!' Katy responded quickly.

'Well, you'd have to wear something plain,' Ivy said looking down her nose.

'Why?'

'Because the whole idea would be to show off the hats, not your best frock!' Ivy explained exasperatedly.

'Oh, right.' Katy was clearly a little disappointed at that.

'We should ask Thora and Freda if they would be willing to model the creations they've worked so hard to make,' Ella put in.

'I'll do it.' Ivy cast a frustrated look at Katy before disappearing upstairs.

'Blimey, that woman is a slave driver!' Katy said as she dropped onto the customer chair. 'She's had me at it all day, I'm worn to a frazzle!'

'I'll make some tea; that will revive you.' Ella smiled as she walked to the kitchen. She gave her mind over to her sitting with Tilda as she prepared a tray. How could she make reparation with Harper now? Why had he stormed off the way he did? Suddenly it dawned on her that she was thinking about him as if he was still alive and she shuddered. Was she going mad? These visits were not conducive to good mental health and Ella considered yet again whether she should refrain from going to see Tilda again as she had decided on her last visit. She had discussed it with Eléna, who had said it was all a sham; a way of relieving Ella of her hard-earned money. Who else could she talk to about it? Flossie

Woolley popped into her head. Her neighbour would tell her the truth and not what Ella needed to hear, which was that Harper was really communing with her.

With the decision made to broach the subject with Flossie, Ella carried the tray through to the thirsty workers. Just how she would actually ask Flossie's advice, however, was something else entirely.

14

That evening, as Ella worked on the wording for the invitation to the fashion show, her mind whirled from one thing to another. Harper's quick disappearance during her sitting at Tilda's, her meeting Paul Sampson, the new range of hats and whether they would be ready in time, and how to tell Flossie about Tilda Hunter.

Throwing down her pencil in exasperation, Ella dragged her hands down her face. Why was life so complicated? Ivy wasn't helping matters either with her changing designs and upsetting the staff; she was harsher in her comments, too.

The business was doing well, but there was still

so much potential untapped. They needed to branch out to the wealthier people of the town, the higher echelons of society.

Ella had heard that her reputation for being an excellent milliner had preceded her to Birmingham, but what about other towns? Wolverhampton, Bilston, Darlaston, West Bromwich, surrounding areas still to be reached. Should they try an advertising campaign in those local newspapers? It would be expensive, but it might prove fruitful. Would they see any returns for their outlay? Ella felt they would, but of course it would take time. Could she be wasting her time, energy and money? If she didn't try, she'd never know.

What would you do, Dad? Ella's thoughts always turned to her father when she was weighing up a problem. Somehow Thomas Bancroft could provide answers, no matter how difficult the questions.

The back door flew open, breaking her thoughts, and in bustled Flossie. 'Is the kettle boiled? I'm parched!'

Ella smiled and pushed the kettle onto the hotplate of the range. Once the cups had been made ready, she spooned loose tea into a warm pot and poured the hot water over it, dropping the lid into place. With the teapot on the table, she slipped the knitted cosy over it.

'Whatcha doing here?' Flossie asked, eyeing the pencil and paper.

Ella explained about the invites.

'Ooh, can anybody come?'

'Sorry, invite only, I'm afraid, for this time anyway. We're asking the wealthier clients in the hope of making some serious money. Maybe we could have an open day some time later on and I'll make sure you'll be the first to know.'

'I'll come to that one then,' Flossie said as she removed the cosy, stirred the tea and, satisfied it had mashed long enough, poured.

Ella brought out some cake and cut them a slice.

'Mm, lovely,' Flossie said through a mouthful of crumbs.

'Flossie, can I ask your opinion on something?'

'Course you can, gel.'

Ella sighed, not knowing where to begin. Then, in a rush, she said, 'I've been seeing a medium.'

Flossie coughed, her sharp intake of breath carrying cake crumbs to the back of her throat. She sipped her tea to dislodge them before she spoke.

'Oh, Ella love, why?'

'I needed to know if Harper was – well, happy.'

'It's all a load of rubbish, sweet 'eart, surely you know that?'

'I... oh, Flossie, I'm so miserable!' Before she realised what she was doing, Ella had poured her heart out and told the older woman everything.

'Right,' Flossie said at last, 'the business is taking care of itself. As for Ivy – don't take no shit from her!'

Ella couldn't help but laugh.

'Stick to your guns because it's your name on people's lips – not Ivy's.'

Ella nodded. Flossie had confirmed what she had already heard.

'This Paul Sampson, you have to wait and see whether anything comes of it.'

'Flossie, I don't think it will.'

'Why not?'

'Because I think he's from Africa.'

Flossie's mouth dropped open.

'Ella, I wish you happiness, God knows I do, but an African fella? He won't be accepted here, and you probably wouldn't be accepted in his community. It could cause untold misery for you both in years to come.'

'I've only met him once, he could be married for all I know. So let's not get carried away. He's given me no cause to think he would be interested in me, but I have to admit he set my heart aflutter and no mistake.'

'Well, time will tell. Now then, this medium. Tell me who, when, where, how and why,' Flossie said as she refreshed their cups.

When Ella had explained all, Flossie said, 'I think the only way you will have peace of mind is if you get proof that this woman is a lying cheat!'

'How, though? How can I do that?'

'Look, why don't I come along with you the next time you go?'

'Would you? That would be better for me because I get all flummoxed and don't know what to ask.'

'Ask? Oh, blimey, Ella! You shouldn't be asking anything! Any medium worth their salt would be telling you without prompting. That settles it, we'll go and see this woman tomorrow, because I'm convinced she's a fraud!'

'Thank you, Flossie.'

With a nod, Flossie stood to leave. 'I'll see you at nine o'clock in the morning.'

Ella felt better knowing her friend would winkle the truth out of Tilda Hunter one way or another. Then that would be one thing Ella had no more need to worry about.

Going back to the invites, she began again.

You are cordially invited to the unveiling of Ivella's new millinery collection on 3rd April at 7 p.m. R.S.V.P. Ivella, Junction Street, Walsall.

Short and sweet. Now to decide how many invites to have printed and sent out. Ivy could deal with that, Ella thought, as she considered how well the carnival window was coming along. Once that was out of the way, they could concentrate solely on their big day. With a yawn, Ella decided enough was enough for one day and retired to her bed.

* * *

Whilst Ella was putting together an invite, over at Thora Skelton's house, she and Freda were enjoying a hot beverage by the fire.

'So you ain't been a widow long, then?' Thora asked.

'No, a couple of months,' Freda answered sadly. 'My Stan died of the asbestosis in his lungs. He had a nasty coughing fit one night and by the morning he was gone.'

'Bloody hell! Laid right next to you? That must have been a shock.'

'It was, I never expected to find him dead in our bed. Luckily his funeral plan was enough to see him laid to rest,' Freda said with a sniff.

'D'aint you have any kids?' Thora probed.

'No, I lost three in a row, so we decided not to try again.'

'Blimey, wench, you've had a rough trot an' no mistake,' Thora said, her heart going out to her new friend.

'What about you, Thora? How long have you been widowed?'

'Going on ten years now. My old man was a drunken waster. He was handy with his fists as well.'

'I'm sorry, I didn't mean to...' Freda began.

'It's all right, I'll tell yer, but you have to keep my secret,' Thora said in earnest.

'I will, I swear.'

Thora nodded, feeling sure Freda would stay true to her word. 'One evening, Jim comes in drunk as a lord. Had his arse in his hand cos there was no tea ready. I couldn't cook cos there was nowt in the larder and he'd drunk all the housekeeping money up the wall. Any road up, he gives me a good hiding and buggers off out to the boozer. After years of this, I decided I'd had enough, so I waited outside the pub for him. I hid so he d'aint see me and I followed him – all the way to the cemetery. He got maudlin when in his cups, so I guessed he would go to his mother's grave. It was the early hours of the morning, pitch black and silent. I watched him lie down by the gravestone and before long, I heard the snores. I picked up the biggest rock I could find and I stove his head in.'

'Oh, my God!' Freda gasped. 'You killed him?'

'Yeah, I did, and damn good riddance! He'd battered me since the day we were wed, and I couldn't take any more.'

'What about the police?' Freda asked, hardly able to believe what she was hearing.

'They came to tell me they'd found him, thought he'd been robbed. He had an' all, 'cos I took what little money he had left.'

'Didn't they suspect anything?'

'No, and they never found the murder weapon either because it's sitting in the middle of my rockery,' Thora said with a grin.

'Good grief! Remind me never to aggravate you,' Freda said.

Silence descended as the two women stared at each other, then suddenly they both began to laugh at Freda's comment, despite Thora's grisly confession.

After a while, Thora groaned as she stood up. 'I'm ready for my bed,' she said.

'Me too, although I'll be locking my door tonight,' Freda said with a laugh.

Thora laughed as she placed the guard around the fire. Then the friends retired for the night.

* * *

The following morning, Ella was ready when Flossie arrived.

'Won't they be expecting you at the shop?' Flossie asked.

'I'll make an excuse later,' Ella replied as they set off for the station.

Finding seats on the train, Ella whispered, 'I'm not sure this is such a good idea.'

'Of course it is, she'll think she's got another customer.'

Ella nodded, but she wasn't convinced.

'I love being on the train,' Flossie said as she watched the steam whizzing past the window.

'Hmm,' Ella replied.

'Cheer up, gel. This visit will be very enlightening – one way or another,' Flossie said with a grin.

15

Flossie was surprised when Tilda Hunter opened the door. She wasn't sure what she had expected to see, but it certainly wasn't a woman who looked like a streetwalker.

'Oh, you've brought a friend. Come in, come in, you know the routine,' Tilda said cheerfully.

Sitting in the living room, Flossie frowned when Ella handed over her money. The woman purporting to be a medium must be raking it in if she was charging that much with each client. Gazing around, Flossie noted the none-too-clean curtains. There was an odour she couldn't quite identify and suspected it was coming from the carpet. The décor was shabby from what she could make out in the dim light. Flossie waited quietly as Tilda closed her eyes.

'I see a woman, someone to be wary of,' Tilda began.

Flossie rolled her eyes.

'I'm being told you will come into money.'

Flossie sighed. I bet she says this to everyone, she thought.

'Thomas is here.'

Ella looked at Flossie, who shook her head and raised a finger to her lips. They had agreed on the train that Ella would say as little as possible. That way, Tilda could not use the tells to feed nonsense to Ella.

'He knows you're unhappy and it's breaking his heart.'

Ella's face fell but when Flossie gripped her hand, she nodded. She had to be strong.

Tilda was decidedly uncomfortable at Ella staying tight-lipped, as she was hoping for more information to draw on. Was it because Ella had brought along a friend and was afraid to speak up? Whatever it was, Tilda was struggling. She searched her mind, trying to recall what she'd learned about Ella in the market.

'He says he's proud of you.'

Flossie shook her head. Tilda would have to do better than this to convince her.

'Has your sister passed over?'

Flossie squeezed Ella's hand, warning her to give nothing away.

'No, not your sister – this is your mother.'

Flossie nodded to Ella.

'Yes,' Ella replied.

'I thought so.' Tilda was relieved to have received an answer.

'I have an aunt here as well,' Tilda said.

Ella and Flossie exchanged a look. Ella didn't have an aunt.

'I'm thinking that's where the money comes in. She's left you a lot in her will.'

Flossie raised one side of her top lip in a sneer, and it was all Ella could do not to laugh.

'Hello, lovey. Harper's here, Ella.'

Flossie opened her eyes wide in warning, and Ella gave a little nod.

'Do you need to ask him a question?'

'No,' Ella replied.

Tilda shifted on her seat. 'Are you sure, dear?'

'Yes.'

Flossie smiled at Ella, reassuring her she was doing well.

'Righto, then. He says to tell you he loves you.'

Ella bit her bottom lip, her heart racing.

Tilda snapped her eyes open and blew her cheeks out. Then, turning to Flossie, she asked, 'Do you want a sitting as well?'

Flossie nodded and handed over the money Ella had given her.

Tilda palmed the coin and again closed her eyes.

Flossie rubbed her hands together. This should be interesting.

The staff back at the shop didn't know that Ella was in Birmingham and Katy, Thora and Freda were chatting excitedly about modelling the new range when Ivy's voice yelled up the stairs. 'Katy, we have a customer!'

Katy hitched up her long skirt and tripped

lightly downstairs. 'Sorry, Ivy,' she said with a cheeky grin. Then, turning to the woman waiting to be served, she asked how she could help.

Ivy left Katy to it and went to join the others in the workroom. She watched as they stitched feathers into place, desperately wanting to tell them to add some flowers. She refrained, however – she didn't want Ella raging at her again.

'What exactly will you be wanting us to do at this here fashion show?' Freda asked as she snipped the cotton.

'Just walk around, showing off a hat,' Ivy responded.

'That ain't very exciting for the customers!' Thora exclaimed.

'What would you suggest then?' Ivy asked, feeling a little put out.

'I don't know, but it will need more than merely ambling about in a titfer,' Thora replied.

'Hmm, I'll have a word with Ella when she deigns to grace us with her presence.'

'Ain't she in yet then?' Thora asked.

'Wouldn't I have said if she was?' Ivy snapped.

'I wonder where she is,' Thora replied, ignoring Ivy's harsh tone.

'I'm sure we'll find out, but for now let's keep busy, shall we?' Ivy said before she turned on her heel and left the women to it, with Thora's, 'Ooh, she's got her drawers in a tangle this morning,' ringing in her ears as she went.

Having stamped downstairs, Ivy went to the back room and, having nothing to do in there either, she strolled into the shop area. 'How did you get on with that customer?'

'Good, the woman bought that cream affair with the pink feathers,' Katy answered.

Ivy nodded. Yet another of Ella's designs sold.

'Cream affair – really, Katy!'

'Well, what else can I say? These hats should have names!'

Ivy looked like she'd been struck by lightning. 'What a marvellous idea!' Hurrying back to the back room, she began to list the hats she could recall they had in stock. Beside each, she wrote names as they came to her. It took a long time to put the list together as she thought carefully about whether each name would match the millinery.

Ella would be surprised when she learned of Ivy's notion of naming the hats, for that's what she would be told. Ivy fully intended to take the credit for the ideas she now had down on paper.

* * *

Over in Birmingham, the reading was not going well. 'Who is Harold?' Tilda asked.

'No idea,' Flossie returned with a raise of her eyebrows in Ella's direction.

'Herbert?'

'No.'

Tilda sighed heavily. This sitting was a nightmare, and she felt she might have met her match.

'No, it's Horace.'

Flossie shook her head.

Tilda's eyes remained closed as her brain scrabbled around for something to tell her client.

'He's telling me you are an unbeliever.'

That's the first thing you've got right, Flossie thought, but she said nothing.

'I have May here – your mother's sister.'

'No.'

'Margaret?'

'No.' Flossie grinned. Her mother didn't have a sister; she only had brothers.

'There are so many wanting to speak to you it's hard to distinguish...' Tilda said, by way of a get-out. 'Who was it who drowned?'

'Look, missus, you should be telling, not asking. Now, if you can't tell me anything I can associate with, then I'll have my money back!'

In a panic now, Tilda said, 'It's potluck whether anyone comes through which, you understand, is no fault of mine.'

'I think you're a fraud and I want my money, otherwise I'll have the bobbies on your doorstep!' said Flossie.

Tilda's eyes snapped open and she said, 'You've broken the connection.'

'There was no bloody connection in the first place! Money – now!' Flossie held out her hand and nodded when Tilda placed a coin in it.

'Come on, Ella, I've heard enough rot to last me a lifetime!' Flossie said, grabbing Ella's arm.

'Why, Tilda?' Ella asked, full of disappointment. 'Why are you duping people into believing what you say? I am, like many others, grieving lost ones. You gave me hope and now I have none.' Close to tears, Ella saw Tilda lower her head.

'I have to eat and pay my bills,' Tilda said quietly.

'Well, you won't be dining out on our money,' Flossie said, 'so I think you should return Ella's as well.'

Tilda did as she was asked, feeling thoroughly miserable at being found out.

'Take my advice and find other work because you might have a client who won't be as nice as we've been.' Flossie turned and walked out, dragging Ella behind her.

Tilda saw them pass her window and muttered, 'Bugger! That was a nice little earner an' all!'

On the train home, Ella and Flossie quietly discussed Tilda and her lies.

'I know you wanted so desperately to believe it, sweet 'eart, but now you've seen for yourself that she's a charlatan. And you won't be wasting your money lining her pockets – or should I say bodice?'

Ella grinned, thinking how Tilda shoved the coins into a pouch sewn into the top of her dress.

'I was a fool,' Ella replied. 'Thank you, Flossie, for showing me the truth of it.'

'You were grieving and she took advantage of you. But now it's time for you to move on and concentrate on your business.'

Ella nodded. Suddenly she felt free of the shackles of grief and knew Flossie was right. Ella would always have Harper in her heart, but her mourning time was over. She would no longer cry for what she couldn't have. A whole new chapter of her life was opening up and Ella determined she would meet it head on.

Alighting from the train and walking out of the station, Ella was brought up sharply as she spied Paul Sampson with a very beautiful dark-skinned woman.

16

'Miss Bancroft! How very nice to see you again!'

'You too, Mr Sampson,' Ella said, trying to compose herself.

'May I present my wife, Imelda. This is Ella Bancroft, the lady I told you about.'

Imelda's hazel eyes twinkled and her smile showed even, pure white teeth. 'I'm pleased to meet you. Paul has told me all about you and your business, and I have to say, his bowler hat is one of the best I've ever seen.'

'Thank you, Mrs Sampson,' Ella returned. She noted the long fingers encased in an open weave lacy glove as they shook hands. 'This is Mrs Woolley, my good friend.'

After exchanging pleasantries, they parted company and, as they walked home, Ella's emotions threatened to overwhelm her. Firstly, she and Flossie had revealed Tilda to be a fraud, and now she had discovered Paul Sampson was married. What else would life throw at her?

'I'd best get back to the shop, otherwise Ivy will be in a foul mood,' Ella said.

'Here's your money,' Flossie said, taking the half-crown from her bag.

'Keep it, Flossie, it's worth it to have unveiled Tilda's lies.'

With a hug, the women went their separate ways.

Arriving at Ivella, Ella braced herself for Ivy's tirade, which she felt certain would hit her no sooner she stepped in through the door. She was surprised when it didn't come. Instead, Ivy led her straight to the back room, leaving Katy in charge of the shop, humming quietly to herself.

'I've had an idea,' Ivy said, shoving a piece of paper into Ella's hand.

'What's this?' Ella asked, glancing at the writing.

'I've named all the hats! When we have our fashion show, we can introduce each one by name!'

Ella looked down the list. 'This is smashing, Ivy!'

Ivy's chest puffed up at the compliment. 'Flower names for hats with flowers – naturally, and women's names for others.'

Ella nodded. 'Sunrise and Sunset?'

'For yellow and red!' Ivy explained.

'Smashing, and what about for blue and green?' Ella asked.

'We'll think of something,' Ivy answered, feeling a little narked at Ella's question. She should have thought of that herself.

'What about Azure Sky and Emerald Jewel?'

'Lovely!' Ivy beamed with pleasure.

'I need a cup of tea,' Ella said as she dropped into an armchair.

'I'll make it,' Ivy said. 'Oh, and Thora said she thinks it might be a bit boring with the models just walking about.' With that, Ivy disappeared into the kitchen, having completely forgotten about asking where Ella had been.

Ella thought Thora could well be right, but what

could they do about that? The shop wasn't particularly big, and they had moved furniture to make space like a catwalk. The guests would stand either side to be afforded a good view of the millinery on show.

Ivy brought in tea and the two women began to mull over plans. 'I think we should have wine for our potential customers,' Ivy said. 'I know it will cost, but you have to speculate to accumulate.'

'That's another good idea, Ivy,' Ella said as she took the tea offered. A small frown creased her brow as she recalled they had mentioned this before. Dismissing the thought, she went on, 'So how can we liven up the fashion show?'

Ivy shook her head. 'I honestly don't know.'

It was then they heard Katy singing rather than humming, and Ella and Ivy exchanged a questioning look as they listened to the beautiful voice filtering through from the shop floor.

Simultaneously, over in Birmingham, Tilda Hunter was angry at being caught out by Ella and her friend.

It was true she was not a medium, but so far her lies had brought in a handsome reward. Her fear was that if she continued to work and advertise, Ella could well report her to the police. She might find herself hauled off to jail for taking money under false pretences. It was actually Ella's friend who was the unbeliever, and Tilda thought she had persuaded Ella to change her mind about the afterlife. *Bloody woman!*

Tilda sipped her hot tea and thought hard about what to do. It was certain Ella would not be back for further readings now, but Tilda had other clients. Not many, if truth be told, but a few who depended on what she would tell them. Besides, Ella was in another town, so it was unlikely she would visit this part of Birmingham again.

With a nod, Tilda felt she was safe enough to continue her work. A knock on the door had her on her feet.

'Hello, my name is Darcie Newland and I've come for a sitting.'

Taking in at a glance the woman's fine clothes, Tilda smiled. 'Please come in, I'm between appointments right now.'

Darcie looked down her nose at the poor sur-roundings and dusted off the seat offered with her gloves before sitting down.

'May I ask how you found me?' Tilda asked as she took the chair opposite.

'Oh, you are quite well known! I heard your name mentioned while attending afternoon tea with acquaintances. I also saw your advertisement in the newspaper.'

'I see. Well, that's lovely. Tell me, do you have someone on the other side you wish to speak with?'

'Not particularly, but I was interested to see if there might be a message for me,' Darcie said.

Tilda felt this reading could be difficult unless she worked hard at it. 'There is always someone who may want to pass on greetings. Now, let's get to it, shall we?'

Darcie nodded, feeling a little excited at what could be revealed.

* * *

Approximately seven miles away at Ivella, Ivy and Ella went into the shop and Katy instantly ceased her singing.

'You have a lovely voice, I didn't know you could sing so beautifully,' Ella said.

'Thanks, and I'm sorry. I won't do it in the shop,' Katy replied.

Ivy nudged Ella, who stepped forward. 'Katy, we have a proposition for you.'

'What would that be?' Katy asked, her fear of being sacked for singing in the shop disappearing.

'At our fashion show – well, we need to liven it up a bit,' Ivy put in.

'We wondered if, when our models come through, you would sing a song to complement the hat on show,' Ella explained.

'Oh, don't I get to be a model, then?' Katy's disappointment was evident by the look on her face.

Neither Ella nor Ivy had considered this, but Ella was quick to come up with a solution.

'Of course you can. Whilst you are modelling, I can describe the hat you're wearing, then you can sing for the others.'

'I suppose I could,' Katy said tentatively as she considered the proposal.

'We could make it worth your while. We can manage a little bonus for you and the other models,' Ivy said quickly, hoping to help Katy make up her mind.

'All right, then,' Katy said. 'What songs am I to sing?'

'Come through to the back and we'll discuss it,' Ella said. Then to Ivy, 'Would you mind the shop while I chat to Katy about your great idea?'

Ivy's smile was broad as she nodded. She was delighted Ella had credited her with coming up with the suggestion.

Ella showed Katy the list of hat names and waited whilst the girl read them. Shaking the paper, Katy said forcefully, 'These are great, but naming the hats was my suggestion!'

'Oh, I thought...' Ella began.

'No, it was me, not Ivy! I'm gonna have it out with her!' Katy said, getting to her feet.

'Katy, wait! Listen to me a minute, please.'

Katy retook her seat but she was still fuming at Ivy taking the glory for what had been her idea.

Ella explained quietly how Ivy had done the same to her when she was an apprentice.

'A lady came in for a riding hat as I recall but didn't like all the frippery, so she didn't buy it. Afterwards, Ivy asked my opinion and I suggested a simple tie of net around the brim saying that was all it needed. Later, another customer was shown the same hat and Ivy claimed the idea as her own, even using the same words I had spoken!'

'How did you feel about that?' Katy asked.

'I was furious, so I understand your anger.' Ella then told how her father had encouraged her to break away and start her own business because of it, and that she'd never looked back.

'But she'll keep doing it if we don't take her to task, Ella!'

'I'll have a word with her, Katy. I'll tell her I know it was your idea in the first place. Can I say, in confidence, that I'm rather worried about Ivy, she keeps forgetting things.' Ella was trying her best to prevent Katy confronting Ivy, who might well sack the girl out of spite.

'I noticed that an' all, but it doesn't excuse what she's done.'

'Leave it with me and I'll sort it all out,' Ella encouraged.

'All right, but in future, any other notions I'll bring straight to you.'

'Very well. Now, let's get back to the list.'

By the end of the day, Ella was exhausted and walked home wearily. She had been indoors but a moment when Flossie bustled in.

'I haven't even got the kettle on yet!' Ella said with a grin.

'I'll set it on the range, you put your feet up,' Flossie said.

Ella nodded. What was this all about?

'I just came to apologise again about this morning,' Flossie said.

Ella smiled. So that was it. 'No need, you did me a favour. Anyway, Flossie, I have a favour to ask.'

'Spit it out then, my wench,' Flossie said affectionately.

'Our fashion show is short of a model, so I wondered...'

'I'll do it!' Flossie answered before Ella could finish her sentence.

'Oh, thank you!' Ella gushed. She had been

feeling bad about Flossie not receiving an invitation, knowing her friend really wanted to come to the show. 'There will be a small remuneration for all the models too.'

'Even better!' Flossie said as she prepared cups. 'So how's the organisation going?'

Over hot tea, Ella explained how Ivy had stolen Katy's suggestion and the girl was livid about it.

'She don't get any better, does she, that Ivy?'

Ella shook her head. 'But Katy has agreed to sing whilst you models parade up and down our shop.'

'Ooh, nice touch,' Flossie said. 'Oh, blimey, I'll have to get me hair done!'

'No, just pin it up in a nice French pleat,' Ella suggested.

'Very chic,' Flossie said as she patted the back of her hair.

Ella laughed at her friend's antics.

'Right, I'm away. I have to put the kids' snap tins up. See ya tomorrer.' With that, Flossie left Ella to her thoughts, of which there were many after such a busy day.

As she considered again the models and Katy's voice accompanying them, suddenly Ella realised that the following day they would need to change the window display yet again to show off their carnival creations. With a tired sigh, Ella opened the doors of the range and propped her feet up on a chair, enjoying the heat warming her. Tomorrow would take care of itself; for now, she would simply rest and relax a while.

17

Whilst Ella had been thinking about the day's events and those of tomorrow, over in Birmingham, Tilda Hunter was doing the same. She had gained a new client and a wealthy one, judging by the woman's apparel. Tomorrow, she needed to visit the market – in Walsall. Darcie Newland had said that was where she had once lived, so Tilda needed to find out what she could in readiness for Darcie's next visit. Tilda wasn't about to be caught out again. She had to research this woman thoroughly so she could ensure Miss Newland kept coming back.

The sitting had gone well, considering it was a

new client, but Tilda had picked up on the little things as they spoke. Such as that Darcie was a divorcée, rather than a widow. She now lived in Birmingham but was raised in Walsall. Tilda wondered if Darcie knew Ella Bancroft. Possibly, but not for certain. Maybe questioning the stall holders in the market would provide further information on that.

Rubbing her hands together, Tilda was delighted to have a rich young client. It could prove very lucrative for her, especially if Darcie Newland encouraged her wealthy friends to have a sitting also.

Tilda studied the images in her mind of Miss Newland. A little hard-faced, there was no kindness in her blue eyes. Her blonde curls had been pinned up expertly beneath a flowered hat. Her outfit was cut from the finest cloth, and her matching leather bag, gloves and shoes must have cost a packet. Tilda got the impression that Darcie didn't smile much and, from the way she spoke, Tilda thought her a spoilt brat. No matter, Tilda would continue to take the woman's money.

Taking up her coat, she slipped it on. It was a fine night for a walk and Tilda decided to visit the

friends she had made when standing on street corners, looking for business. She was not afraid to
wander the streets in the darkness, she had done it
for many years, and as she meandered between the
pools of light shed by the streetlamps, she wondered
who would be at their chosen spot.

Her boots clicked on the cobblestones as she approached the corner where the girls stood and one
yelled, 'Well, I never! Look here, Jinny, it's our very
own Tilda!'

Tilda's face split into a grin as she approached
the women standing by the lamp post. 'Hello, girls,
how are you all?'

'All the better for seeing you,' Jinny replied. Seen
as the leader of the little coterie, Jinny did most of
the talking while the others listened intently. 'So
what you been up to?'

'Not a lot, I'm still doing my readings, but it's not
going so well. With luck, it will pick up, though,'
Tilda replied.

'Stick with it, girl, no offence but we don't want
you back here now you've managed to get out of this
work,' Jinny said with a warm smile.

Tilda watched as, one by one, the girls left with a punter after a brief consultation about prices, and before long, they returned, rattling their coins in their pockets. Eventually, she said her goodbyes and left the women to their gossip, promising to visit again soon.

The following morning, Tilda caught the steam train to Walsall. Walking towards the market, she ignored the disdainful looks from people passing by. They took her for a prostitute, she knew, but she didn't care.

The first stall she came to sold fruit and vegetables and, buying two apples, she peppered the vendor with questions. Did anyone know a Darcie Newland? When asked why she wanted to know, Tilda said she had found a drawstring bag with the name embroidered inside and she wanted to return it to its owner. Before long, Tilda was inundated with information about the lady and warned to be on her guard. Darcie was said to have a dreadful temper and had stabbed her husband in the leg before they were divorced. Taken back to her parents, who were full of shame, they had whisked her off to Scotland. The stallholders were surprised that Miss Newland had returned to England and possibly to live in Birmingham.

Loaded down with shopping, having bought something at a few stalls, Tilda made her way back to the station. When she got home, she needed to write down what she had been told lest she forget.

Ignoring the disdainful looks from other women, Tilda walked towards the railway station. She knew what they thought of her. They considered her to be a streetwalker by dint of her make-up and clothing. Her blouse was low cut and showed a small amount of cleavage, but it was all she had. She could, she supposed, not use so much rouge on her cheeks, but why should she? This was Tilda Hunter – take it or leave it! Beneath her bravado, Tilda still felt the sting of hurt and thought people would always see her as a prostitute, no matter what she did.

The train was waiting at the platform, puffing out clouds of steam, and Tilda hurried to board.

Finding a seat in the third-class carriage, Tilda bit into one of her apples and, as she chewed, she went over in her mind all that she had learned about Darcie, like the fact she had reverted to her maiden name of Newland.

Seeing a child staring at her, Darcie smiled. The child snuggled closer to his mother, who looked down at him.

'Is that lady a clown?' the boy asked innocently.

'No, now don't be so rude. Sit quietly or else.' The woman gave Tilda an apologetic look.

Tilda diverted her eyes rather than let the woman see the tears welling there.

* * *

As Tilda alighted from the train in Birmingham, over at Ivella, Katy was rehearsing the songs she would sing at the fashion show, and Ivy couldn't help but join in. 'I'm Shy Mary Ellen' was followed by 'Sunbonnet Sue'. Upstairs in the workroom, Thora and Freda gave a rendition of 'Bye Bye Dolly Gray'.

The window now sported the carnival theme put together early that morning by Katy and Ivy, and customers poured in to see what was on offer.

Ella sat in the back room, writing out the name and description given to each hat, which she would read out before Katy began to sing. She smiled as she listened to the refrains filtering from the shop.

Considering the guest list, she thought back to her meeting with Paul Sampson and his beautiful wife, Imelda, who had been invited, and her smile dropped away. She should have realised he would be married, and in all honesty, he had given her no encouragement to think otherwise. Ella wondered if she was so desperate to be wed herself that she was clutching at straws. There and then, she determined that she would concentrate only on her work, refusing to allow herself to moon over every gentleman who came into the shop; all it would bring her was heartache.

With a mental shake, Ella returned to her work as the singing ceased. There must be a customer in the shop.

The day passed with intermittent bouts of singing and at last closing time arrived. The new window display had been a great success, as evidenced by the money in the till.

Ella wound her way home wearily. She was tired but happy with what she had accomplished. Now to find something to eat before she could rest in the heat from the open doors of the range.

Flossie made her usual visit around seven o'clock and over tea, she and Ella discussed the grand showing of Ivella's spring collection of millinery.

'You gonna have blokes attending?' Flossie asked.

'Yes, why?'

'They'll need to see what's on offer for them an' all, won't they?'

'Oh, Flossie! I never thought of that!' Ella gasped. 'How can we show off our range of toppers, bowlers and boaters to their best?'

'You'll need a male model,' Flossie replied, as though it was obvious. She raised her eyebrows as she helped herself to more tea.

'Who? How? Where will I find a man willing to do it?'

'What about our Josh?'

'I can't see Josh wanting to parade round the shop in our hats, Flossie, he's a real man's man.'

'You won't know unless you ask him.'

Ella began to wonder if her friend's son would actually be interested, especially if she offered a small payment as a sweetener, as with the female models.

'There's summat else as well,' Flossie went on. 'You'll need waiting staff to offer glasses of wine and regular top-ups.'

'I wish we'd never started all this!' Ella said, feeling exasperated. No sooner had she thought everything was in readiness, something else popped up to be organised.

'Do you want me to ask our Phoebe and Margaret to help out with that?'

'It would be marvellous if they would!' Ella enthused.

'I tell you what, I'll go and fetch all three around now and we can thrash out the details,' Flossie said, and in a moment she was gone.

Ella brewed a fresh pot and before long, her kitchen was full of excited chatter.

'Can we wear a hat an' all?' Phoebe asked. At eighteen years old, she was a beauty with dark hair and eyes, as was her younger sister, Margaret. Both girls worked in shops in the town so were used to dealing with customers.

'How would it be if you both chose a hat to wear

which will be yours to keep after the show? I'm sure we can arrange a small wage for you too.'

'That'll do for me,' Margaret said and smiled when Phoebe agreed.

Turning to Josh, Ella said, 'We need a male model as well.'

The girls gave out little whistles as Josh placed the tea cosy on his head and strutted around the kitchen, one hand resting on his hip.

Ella and Flossie laughed until tears ran down their cheeks.

'Do I get the same deal as the girls?' Josh asked at last.

Ella nodded as she dried her eyes.

'Then count me in!' Josh said as he replaced the cosy over the teapot.

Turning to Flossie, Ella said, 'I think you should come with me to the shop tomorrow so we can share the news with the others. Then we can iron out the last few details, which you can pass on to Josh and the girls.'

'Good thinking. I'll be round first thing,' Flossie said as she ushered her excited brood through the back door.

Alone again, Ella felt the silence close in around her. Would she ever get used to living on her own? Deciding to have an early night, Ella locked up and, dousing the lights, she climbed the stairs. She needed to sleep before the loneliness threatened to drag her down into a pit of despair.

18

The following morning, when Ella and Flossie arrived at the shop, Ella asked if they could have a meeting in the back room before the day's work began, when she explained about Phoebe, Margaret and Josh agreeing to help them out.

'I had the invitations delivered and already we've had some replies. Mr and Mrs Fortescue and Mr and Mrs Sampson will be attending, Ella.'

Ella nodded, pleased that Harper's parents were still supporting her.

'The mayor and his wife are coming, as well as the wealthy industrialists; the owners of Cyclops Iron Works, Walsall Tube Works, James Foundry and the Staffordshire Galvanising Works will be in attendance, along with their wives, so we should have a packed room,' Ivy added.

'Our models will be in the back room, where we will have all our hats and accessories in the correct order so there's no mix-up with Katy's songs.' Ella was making notes as the discussion proceeded.

'Are we having canapes?' Ivy asked.

'I hadn't thought about that. What does everyone think?'

'It's classy,' Flossie said, 'and we could all make some and bring 'em down during the daytime.'

And so it was agreed.

'I'm not sure there will be enough room in the shop area when everyone arrives,' Ella said thoughtfully.

'Well, let's shift the cabinets out, that will give us more room,' Ivy suggested.

'Here we go,' Katy mumbled, 'shifting furniture yet again.'

'This time we're all here to help,' Ella said with a grin.

Before long, the cabinets had been dragged to

the back room and stacked in the corner. The shop looked totally different now it was empty.

'It's so big!' Ivy gasped as she looked around. 'I'd forgotten.'

'We only have a few days left, ladies, so I suggest we get on and give the place a good clean. Then we can move what we'll need into the back room,' Ella said.

'It'll be cramped now with those cabinets in there,' Ivy said.

'We'll have to do the best we can.'

'What about the window?' Katy asked.

'Oh, yes, we'll need to add to it. Sorry, but it's the first thing our guests will see. Any ideas, ladies?'

Ivy was not happy at having all her hard work being disturbed, but she could see the need.

'I'll make us all some coffee while you throw out some suggestions. Katy, make notes will you, please?' Ella asked.

Each sitting with their drink now, Ella cast a glance over Katy's handwriting. 'We really need something special,' she said as she mentally dismissed the ideas written down.

'Oh, by the way, Judge Landor and his wife from Birmingham are unable to come, but their son, Mason, and his fiancée will attend in their stead,' Ivy said.

Ella nodded and returned the conversation to the window display. She had noticed the sudden change in Ivy's concentration but said nothing.

'In the spare room upstairs there are two dress dummies, could we use those?' Ivy asked.

'Great idea! Let's go and have a look,' Ella gushed.

Ivy led them to the spare room and they brought down the forms of a man and woman.

'These are just the job, Ivy, well done for remembering you still had them!' Ella said as she dusted them off. 'Flossie, would you help Katy to make space in the window, please?'

As the two women set about their task, Ivy disappeared, coming back with a ballgown and a man's black suit. 'These could be useful, don't you think?'

'Excellent!' Ella enthused.

'We can dress the dummies,' Thora put in as she took the clothes from Ivy, passing some to Freda.

'Thank you. All we'll need to do then is fit them

in and maybe move the other things around a bit. We need to make a real show of this window.'

All day, the women worked well together in between serving customers and having lunch, which Ivy prepared. By closing time, Ivella's window resembled a masked ball, the dummies posed as if they were dancing.

'I think we should leave the lights on in the window tonight so people will stop and look in as they pass by. Hopefully they'll like it enough to tell their friends, which could mean more custom,' Ella remarked as she and the others stood outside admiring their hard work.

Everyone agreed before leaving for home.

Ella and Flossie chatted excitedly as they walked, both tired after their exertions but happy with the results.

'I do hope it all goes well,' Ella said as they reached home.

'It will, I have no doubts about it,' Flossie replied.

'Thanks for all your help today, I really do appreciate it.'

'I know you do, pet. I'll see yer tomorrer,' Flossie said as they parted company.

Ella let herself in through the back door. The kitchen was dark and cold and she shivered. She quickly fed the range and poked it into life. She lit the gas lamps and the room was bathed in a warm yellow glow.

Looking at the space by the table where her father's wheelchair used to be, she mumbled, 'I miss you so much, Dad.'

* * *

The next few days fled past in a flurry of activity as Ivy, Ella and their staff worked hard to get everything ready for their showcase evening. On Saturday afternoon Josh, Phoebe, Margaret and Flossie arrived, the ladies in smart long skirts and white blouses and Josh booted and suited in black.

In the back room, Katy was warming up her vocal cords and Thora, Freda and Ivy were arranging canapes on trays covered with doilies. On tiny pastries were smoked salmon, devilled eggs, radish and parsley, crabmeat fondue, oysters in a creamy sauce, dill cheese, chicken and mushrooms, and salmon mousse. The wine and cordial had arrived, along with glasses hired for the occasion.

Ella and Ivy had agreed to close the shop for the day so all could be prepared in readiness for their guests arriving at 7 p.m.

Chatter and nervous laughter filled the air as the women stepped around each other in the confined space.

'I'm going out the back for a smoke, Ella, I can't cope with all these clucking hens!' Josh said with a little laugh.

Ella grinned as she glanced around her. This was it, their very first fashion show!

The window display had been a great success and had brought in many new customers over the previous days, much to the delight of everyone.

As the time approached when the door would be opened, Ella called for quiet. 'Now, whilst a model is in the shop showing off our hats, we need to have silence in here. Sound carries at night, remember.'

'I'm nervous,' Flossie said.

'Don't be, just walk around slowly so everybody can have a good look at your hat, and don't forget to smile,' Ella encouraged.

'I hope all this is worth the expense,' Ivy muttered.

'It will be, Ivy, you'll see. Right, ladies and gentleman, are we ready?' Ella asked. At the nods, she went on, 'Ivy, would you open the door, please?'

With a smirk at being asked to open her own shop door, Ivy was secretly delighted at being given the honour.

Phoebe carried through a tray of glasses filled with wine and cordial and Margaret's tray held an array of tantalising canapes.

Ella stood at one end of the counter with notes in hand and Katy was at the other end. She would begin to sing quietly without musical accompaniment as the guests arrived and the girls would replenish their trays as and when needed. All were wearing hats from the new collection, and Ivy waited by the door to welcome the guests. Lines of carriages arrived and, after the occupants had alighted, they moved off, making way for others queueing up.

Ivy greeted people she knew, as well as those she didn't, and Katy's gentle refrain sounded in the background.

Phoebe and Margaret were kept busy offering

wine and nibbles until at last the room was full and no more carriages arrived.

Ella tapped her glass with her pen, calling for attention. 'Good evening, everyone, welcome to Ivella. Thank you for taking time out of your busy lives to attend the launch of our new collection of millinery. If you see something you like – which I'm sure you will – please let one of the staff know and we will put it aside for you. Now, without further ado, we will introduce our first model. Thora is showing a hat in blush rose sinamay decorated with cream roses and a white ostrich feather.' Katy began to sing 'Ma Blushin' Rosie' as Thora came through, a big smile on her face. She walked around, mingling with the guests before returning to the back room as Katy's song finished.

'Thank you, Thora. Next, we have Flossie in a cartwheel hat of cream feathers with a single peach rose. Perfect for any occasion.'

Katy sang 'Peaches 'n' Cream' as Flossie made a grand entrance, enjoying herself immensely.

'We haven't forgotten the gentlemen, you'll be pleased to hear. Josh is sporting a black silk top hat.'

Katy's 'Don't You Think It's Time to Marry?'

sounded and Josh strode out, silver-topped cane in hand. He stepped along, tipping the cane as he acknowledged the gentlemen guests. Then, with a bow to the ladies, he swept off his topper, allowing them to see the fine workmanship inside. His grin was infectious and rapturous applause sounded as empty glasses were placed on passing trays.

'Our next model, Freda, is wearing Emerald Jewel, a green ladies' riding hat with a silk band and adorned with black curled goose feathers.' Katy's refrain of 'Pretty Polly Perkins of Paddington Green' rang out.

As the evening moved on, the applause got louder with each showing until Josh appeared in a white boater. He moved to an older lady and held out his hand. As she took it, Katy sang 'I'm Shy Mary Ellen', and the audience erupted as he danced the lady around in the tiny space afforded to them. Taking her back to her place, Josh kissed the back of her hand and shook her husband's.

Ivy and Ella were over the moon with how things were going. Next came Freda and Thora in blue hats of different shades and designs. They kicked up their heels as Katy sang 'Two Little Girls in Blue'.

Eventually the show came to an end, and more wine was served as sales were made. The whole evening was a roaring success and Ella couldn't have been happier.

It was then that she heard a voice that chilled her to the bone.

19

'You've certainly done well for yourself.'

Ella turned round to come face to face with Darcie Newland.

'Hello, Darcie,' Ella said, feeling as though all the life had suddenly been sucked out of her.

'This is my fiancé, Mason Landor, he's the son of Judge Landor,' Darcie said haughtily as she indicated the man standing next to her.

'I'm pleased to meet you, and congratulations on your engagement,' Ella said as they shook hands. She realised it was the same man who had been with Darcie that day in the coffee shop in Birmingham.

'What a wonderful evening! Thutch a thucceth!' Mason said with a pronounced lisp.

'Thank you,' Ella said.

'I'm not sure there was anything good enough to grace my wardrobe, though,' Darcie put in spitefully.

'Oh, I wath thinking about a new boater for the thummer.'

'Not from here, Mason. We'll go to London and get you one. Come now, we really must speak to the mayor and his good lady.' Darcie stuck her nose in the air and wandered away.

As Mason followed meekly behind, Ella thought, *he really is like a dog who has been kicked!*

'Ella! What a fantastic evening,' Eléna Fortescue gushed as she kissed Ella on both cheeks.

'Indeed,' Rafe commented as he did the same.

'Thank you both for coming, I'm so glad to see you.'

'Was that who I think it was?' Eléna asked as she tilted her head at the disappearing Darcie.

'Yes, she's engaged to Mason Landor, apparently.'

'Ah, well, third time lucky,' Eléna muttered.

'She gave me quite a start. She was the last person I expected to see,' Ella confessed.

'I'm so glad Harper didn't marry her. It was a shame Felix Stoddard didn't have the same insight because look how that ended up – stabbed in the leg before he divorced her.'

Ella nodded. 'I know, it was so sad. Eléna, it's lovely to see you, but if you'll excuse me, I need to save Ivy. I think she's drowning in boxes!'

Making her way over to Ivy, she was greeted with, 'Thank God you're here, I'm so busy I don't know which way to turn!'

The rest of the evening was spent boxing hats, taking orders as well as money, and chatting with guests before seeing them safely into their waiting carriages.

When the shop was finally locked and in darkness, Ella made tea for everyone as they sat in Ivy's back room, having kicked off their shoes.

'Well done, all of you, for making the night such a success,' Ella said. 'Josh, you're a natural! Ladies, you were fabulous. Ivy – congratulations.'

Ivy beamed at the applause given her. 'We'll have to do it again.'

'Next time, make it for regular folks, though,' Flossie suggested.

'I agree,' Thora added.

'I think so too. You can't forget your bread and butter customers,' Katy said.

'That's true, but we'll give it a little while – maybe in the summer,' Ella agreed.

'On Monday, we'll have to strip the window again,' Ivy said and wiggled her eyebrows as Katy groaned.

Thora and Freda left for home as did Ella and Flossie, Phoebe and Margaret. Josh insisted on walking Katy to her door, saying it was dangerous for a young woman to be out alone so late at night.

'I think Josh has set his cap at Katy,' Ella said as she and Flossie strolled along, Phoebe and Margaret having hurried home in front of them.

'I like her, and he could do a lot worse,' Flossie said.

'I do too. It's nice to see romance in the air,' Ella said on a sigh. She stopped and looked up into the sky. 'Look at that moon,' she said as she stared at the great white orb.

'Nice, ain't it?'

'Beautiful,' Ella whispered before they resumed their journey.

Neither realised that they were being watched.

* * *

Darcie Newland sneered as she walked away, having seen Ella and her friend leave Ivella. Darcie had sent her fiancé home early from the show, saying she would get a cab home. Mason had not been happy but when Darcie threatened to make a scene, he had complied with her demands.

Following Ella and the other woman to Silver Street, she saw them enter their respective homes, helping Darcie to deduce that Ella still lived alone. The house was in darkness, telling her there was no one else at that address, otherwise the windows would be lit up. Seeing the lights finally spark into life, Darcie's grin was one of pure evil. If she wanted to scare the life out of Ella, this would be the place to do it.

Turning on her heel, she strode away. Seeing a cab waiting for a fare, she stood beneath a street lamp and waved to attract the cabby's attention. Giving her destination, Darcie climbed aboard and settled herself for her journey back to Birmingham.

As the cab rolled along, Darcie's thoughts slipped back in time. Having once been betrothed to Harper Fortescue, she had been heartbroken when he had called off the engagement. It didn't take her long to find out why. He had met someone else, and that woman was Ella Bancroft. Then Darcie's father had arranged for her to wed Felix Stoddard, a handsome and prominent businessman. She had been happy for a while but had known all along that Felix didn't love her. For him, it had been a marriage of convenience and all too soon, she had realised he was in love with another. This other woman was none other than Ella's friend and lodger, Kitty Fiske.

Recalling how, in a rage one evening, she had stabbed her husband in the leg, Darcie winced. He had deserved it, as far as she was concerned, and fully expecting him to obey her demands for him to give up this Kitty, Darcie had been sorely disappointed. Having sought medical attention, Felix had then bundled Darcie and her belongings into a cab and taken her straight back to her parents. It was clear from the reception she was given that they didn't want her either, and they had then whisked her off to Scotland to escape the gossip and, a while later, she learned Felix had divorced her. He had gone on to marry Kitty and they had moved away from the area. Now Darcie was engaged again, to a milksop called Mason Landor.

Sitting in the darkness of the cab, Darcie thought about her new beau. Mason was short in stature and prone to being overweight, his love of all things sweet ensuring he would never be slim. His ginger hair was thinning, and his skin was fish-belly white. His blue eyes appeared to hold no life in them, and his pronounced lisp grated on her nerves. Mason had no backbone and was a complete and utter yes-man. He obeyed her instructions to the letter; he never argued or disagreed with her, which only served to make her angrier. Although she insisted Mason should do as he was told, there were times when she wished he would fight back. At least that would make their relationship a little more interesting. The saving grace was that Mason had money. Lots of it – and he was very generous. He bought her anything she wanted and had set her up in his large house in Birmingham. She had a cook and a maid and plenty of cash to spend. She had Mason's love and devotion; what she didn't have was happiness.

Darcie Newland was lonely and miserable, but she would never let the outside world know that. To them she appeared carefree and gay, a young woman planning her wedding to a wealthy man.

Darcie scowled as she again thought of Ella Bancroft and how the woman had stolen her man and her life. Now all that kept Darcie going was the thought of taking her revenge. One day, she would see Ella ruined; her business, her life and her happiness. Ella Bancroft would rue the day she had met Darcie Newland.

The cabbie shivered as he heard the loud cackle coming from his cab. The sound carried in the quiet of the night and cold fingers of fear ran up his spine. Slapping the reins against the horse's rump, the carriage picked up speed. The sooner this woman was dropped off, the happier the cabbie would be.

20

Over the next few days, the talk in the shop was all about the fashion show and how successful it had been.

'We should definitely do another one,' Ivy gushed.

'I agree, but I would suggest having it as a special open day,' Ella replied.

'How do you mean?' Ivy asked with a frown.

'We could organise it during the afternoon and open it up to the public.'

'We are open to the public anyway,' Katy said, pulling a face.

'Yes, but normally we are just a shop. With this,

we will turn it into a proper fashion show.'

'That's all well and good, but what about our models? Josh and his sisters will be working,' Ivy pointed out.

'True, but we're all here. Flossie would love to join us, I'm sure, and even you and I could take a turn at showing off our products.' Ella waited for Ivy's refusal, she thought her business partner would consider it outrageous to strut about the shop in a hat, being the boss and all. However, Ella was most surprised when Ivy beamed.

'I rather like the idea of being a model.'

'Good. All we have to decide now is when to hold it,' Ella said.

'The sooner the better because we don't want our customers feeling left out,' Ivy stated.

'I thought we'd agreed on the summer when the weather would be better?' Ella reminded Ivy.

'We did, but why let the grass grow under our feet? Let's get it done now while it is still fresh in people's minds,' Ivy suggested.

'You have a point, but do we have enough stock?' Ella asked, knowing how much had already been sold and fearing there would be a lack of designs to show.

'Plenty. There's all those hats in the workroom and those in the back room,' Ivy answered.

Ella's heart sank a little. The hats Ivy was referring to were ones that had been stored for an age. Almost all of Ivy's creations. Ella wasn't at all sure they would sell now unless...

'Ivy, how about if we used those as an enticement – a sale? We could reduce the prices a little to be sure of selling them on and that would leave us with valuable space for new stock.'

'What? Put all my beautiful hats out like a – rummage sale?' Ivy was mortified to think of her lovely hats being reduced to such a lowly status.

'You know how women love a bargain, Ivy, and just think, all your hats will be paraded around the town with pride.' Ella had to think on her feet where Ivy was concerned, but seeing the smile cross Ivy's face, Ella knew she had won that round.

'What about more expensive items?' Ivy asked.

'We should have time to make some and display them, but I'm betting the cheaper ones will be of more interest. I think they'll fly out of the shop.'

'We could use the same designs as before but not have them quite so elaborate, that way we can keep the prices down,' Ivy suggested.

'An excellent idea!' Ella praised her partner again before planting another seed of an idea in Ivy's brain. 'How will we draw in customers, though?' Ella waited for the seed to grow and, before long, it sprouted.

'Well, we would have to advertise in the local paper! Also have a notice in the window.'

'Of course, yes!' Ella grinned, knowing that Ivy would come up with the answer and she, Ella, would not have to persuade her of the need to spend money on an advertisement.

Ivy pulled out the order ledger and scanned its pages. Then, stabbing a finger on the book, she announced, 'Then. That's when we'll hold the open day because all the orders will be finished by then and any new ones will take us to – here.' Ivy flipped the pages, showing Ella.

'I agree. Right, we'd best tell the girls about our Grand Sale,' Ella said.

'Before we do, may I suggest we find a trustworthy accountant?' Ivy said, taking Ella by surprise.

'That's another marvellous idea, Ivy, and I think I know just the man,' Ella replied. 'Now, let's go and tell the ladies about our plans.'

In the back room that afternoon, Ella donned her hat and grabbed her bag and parasol, ready to go out. She also had a hat box tied with string.

'Where you off to now?' Ivy asked sharply.

'I'm going to see an accountant.'

'You're never in the shop these days,' Ivy remonstrated.

'If we had a telephone installed, I wouldn't need to keep popping out,' Ella replied as she eyed the other woman.

'It would be expensive.'

'It would but then we'd save on cab and train fares and I could spend more time here helping out.'

Ivy studied the young woman, who was checking in her bag that she had everything she might need. Weighing up the costs against the usefulness of a telephone, Ivy had to agree it would be worth it and made perfect sense.

'While you are out, you'd best visit the telephone company as well then,' she relented.

Ella smiled kindly. 'I'll try not to be too long.'

With that, she left the shop and put up her parasol before striding away.

Ivy couldn't help but feel a little excited at having a telephone in the shop. It was a step up, and when they advertised their Grand Sale, she could add the number.

Striding into the shop area, Ivy looked around.

'You lost something?' Katy asked.

'No, I'm wondering about the best place to put a telephone.'

'Ooh, a telephone!' Katy enthused.

'Yes, but it will be for business purposes only,' Ivy snapped.

'Who do you think I would know who has one?' Katy asked sarcastically.

Ivy bristled, then decided next to the till would be the ideal place. With her nose in the air, she went upstairs to tell Thora and Freda the exciting news.

* * *

Striding to the railway station, Ella boarded the train to Birmingham and searched for a seat. The third-class carriage was crowded and all the wooden benches were full.

'Get yer arse up and give the lady yer seat,' a woman said to her young son. Doing as he was told, the boy smiled as Ella gave her thanks.

Women were gossiping loudly over the clickety-clack of the wheels on the rails, and Ella's ears pricked up at mention of her name further along the carriage.

'I bought a bostin' hat, it was really classy. I'm keeping it for best, though. I'm going back to get another of Ella's designs,' one woman said.

'I don't blame you; they are the best,' another said.

Ella smiled and looked out of the window. The landscape appeared to race past, and the chugging of the steam being released through the chimney beat a steady rhythm.

Pulling into the station, the train ground to a halt. Whistles sounded and doors opened, allowing people to pour out onto the platform.

Ella fought her way out of the station and waved to a cabbie. Giving the address, she settled in for the ride.

Ella arrived at her destination and walked into the small office, after paying the cabbie.

'Can I help you?' the secretary asked.

'I wonder if I may have a moment with Mr Sampson.'

'May I take your name, please?'

'Ella Bancroft.'

The secretary disappeared through a door and, a moment later, called Ella to follow her.

'Miss Bancroft, how very nice to see you, please take a seat,' said Paul Sampson.

Ella did as she was bid and smiled at the handsome man.

'How may I help you?' he asked with a smile of his own, which lit up his whole face.

'Firstly, I have brought the hat you ordered,' she said, passing over the box.

'Many thanks.' Paul relieved her of the box and set it on top of a cabinet.

'Secondly, I find myself – or rather Ivella – in need of an accountant and I was hoping you would be able to take us on.'

'Of course, dear lady. I'm happy to come to you to save you a journey.'

'Thank you, I'm sure my partner Ivy Gladwin will want to keep an eye on everything,' Ella said with a little laugh.

'I understand, and rightly so, if I may say. Have you had your books audited before?'

Ella shook her head. 'No, Ivy has dealt with all that, but we both feel that a professional should now take over the task. That then would leave us to do what we do best; designing and making hats.'

'Very wise. Let me see when I'm next free.' Checking his schedule, Paul Sampson went on, 'I can visit tomorrow morning at ten o'clock, if that suits?'

'It does indeed. Thank you.' Ella stood to leave.

Paul Sampson hurried from behind his desk to open the door for her.

Ella nodded her thanks to the secretary as Paul saw her out of the office after shaking hands.

Waving to a cabbie, Ella asked to be taken to the telephone company. Climbing aboard, she settled onto the padded seat, happy that the first of her errands had gone well.

After securing a time for the telephone installation, Ella's cabbie returned her to the railway station for her journey home. He tipped his hat at the tip given and Ella walked onto the platform.

Once back at Ivella and in the back room, she told Ivy, 'Mr Sampson is coming at ten in the morning to go over the books and the telephone company will be here in the afternoon.'

'We'll need new cards printed with the number on,' Ivy said grudgingly. It meant more money going out of the account, but as Ella explained, they would reap the rewards in no time.

The rest of the day was spent discussing the Grand Sale and the best way of advertising it, as well as how to plan for it.

'If we use the same designs but not so fancy, it would help to keep the prices down,' Ivy suggested, completely unaware that she had suggested this earlier.

Ella frowned, which she forced into a smile as Ivy asked, 'What do you think?'

'It's a marvellous idea, Ivy,' Ella replied, but she was distracted from their discussion now and more focused on why Ivy really couldn't remember having said this before.

21

The following morning, Ivy couldn't stop staring at the man who had his head over their books. She wanted to reach out and touch his tightly curled dark hair to see if it felt as wiry as it looked. She had never before seen a man with such dark skin and she was fascinated by his look and his accent.

'Ladies, this is Mr Paul Sampson, who has graciously agreed to become our accountant. Mr Sampson, this is Katy Woodbine, our marvellous modiste. Freda Harlow and Thora Skelton, our top-class milliners, and my partner, the famous Ivy Gladwin.' She smiled inwardly as Ivy puffed up her chest.

'I'm very pleased to meet you all.'

'Same here. Oh, if I were twenty years younger, I'd give your wife a run for her money!' Thora said with a grin.

Ella's mouth dropped open as Katy muffled a giggle with her hand.

Paul Sampson's deep voice boomed out in a great belly laugh and Ella visibly relaxed again.

'Thank you, ladies, time to get back to work,' Ella said.

Seeing her about to speak again, Paul waved a hand. 'Please don't apologise, which I suspect you were about to do. Anything that makes you laugh has to be a good thing, am I right?'

Ella nodded.

Paul then turned his attention to Ivy. 'Miss Gladwin, you have done an excellent job in keeping your ledgers up to date,' he said, giving Ivy a beaming smile.

'Thank you, please call me Ivy,' she responded with a warm smile of her own, delighted at the compliment.

'I'd be pleased if you'd call me Ella too.'

Paul nodded. 'Ella and Ivy, it is then, and I'm Paul. Now, I will audit these,' he said with a finger tap on the books, 'at the end of each month, thereby releasing you, Ivy, of the task. I can also sort out any taxes to be paid.'

'I can't say I'm unhappy about that. I always found it a bit of a bind,' Ivy confessed.

Paul went on, 'However, if you have any questions or queries, just let me know.' He handed over a small card.

'We're having our telephone installed later today, so I will use it to let you know our number,' Ivy said with an air of grandeur.

Paul nodded as he stood to leave. Shaking hands with both women, he saw himself out at his own insistence.

'What a thoroughly nice man,' Ivy said once they were alone.

'I think so too. Now, I suggest we see how Thora and Freda are getting on with the orders, then we can decide on a layout for the shop in readiness for our Grand Sale,' Ella said.

* * *

At the same time as Ella and Ivy were making their plans, over in Birmingham, Darcie Newland was sitting in Tilda Hunter's dim room.

'Oh, my dear, you've known heartbreak,' Tilda said quietly.

'Oh, I have!' Darcie snapped.

'You were let down badly by a man.' Tilda was fishing for confirmation.

'Harper Fortescue!'

Tilda smiled inwardly, this was going better than expected. 'He's here and he's apologising...'

'Too late now!' Darcie cut across sharply.

'There is a new man in your life now, though. I'm seeing the letter M.'

'Mason, yes.' Darcie's lip curled in distaste.

The movement was not lost on Tilda. 'He adores you.'

'Hmm.'

Tilda blinked rapidly. 'I'm being told you will marry Mason and the wedding will be a grand affair.'

'And rightly so. He has money enough for the wedding of the century!'

Tilda ploughed on. 'You bear a grudge – a woman has wronged you.'

'Yes!' Darcie was amazed that Tilda hit the nail on the head every time. How could the woman know all these things? Was there really someone on the other side telling her? Or was it simply good guesswork?

Seeing doubt flit over her client's face, Tilda upped her game. 'I'm seeing the name Felix – is that your cat?'

'No, it was my husband, we're divorced now. He remarried – a woman named Kitty.'

Suddenly the funny side of the question and answer hit Tilda and she burst out laughing. 'Your cat – Kitty!' she muttered. Then, composing herself once more, Tilda went on. 'You seek vengeance on the one who...'

'Yes, I do!' Darcie butted in.

'It shall be yours.'

'Good, because I can't wait!'

'I have nothing more for you today, I'm afraid.'

'Thank you, I'll come back next week,' Darcie said as she handed over a tip, having paid her money up front for her reading. She grimaced as she watched the shilling disappear down the front of Tilda's grubby dress. Leaving the house, Darcie stepped into the waiting cab and determined, the moment she got home, she would call for her bath to be drawn.

Tilda gave a little wave and closed her front door with a grin. Another satisfied customer. Grabbing her hat and coat, Tilda then set off for the nearest public house which sported a 'snug' – a room kept aside just for women. Tilda Hunter felt she'd earned a gin or two.

* * *

As Tilda made her way to the nearest public house, back at Ivella, Ivy was overseeing the telephone being installed and taking note of the instructions being given for its use.

Katy was excited and was dying to have a go with the new contraption.

After the workmen had left, both women stared at the new addition to the shop, willing it to ring. Of course, it didn't, for no one had their number yet.

Ella wandered in, waving a piece of paper. 'Our

new advert to go into the newspaper,' she said. 'Will you telephone it through, Ivy?'

Snatching the paper from Ella, Ivy grinned.

Picking up the receiver, she heard a voice say, 'What number do you require?'

'The newspaper office, please,' she answered.

After dictating their advert, Ivy replaced the receiver on its cradle, feeling extremely pleased with herself. 'This will make life so much easier,' she said before retiring to the back room to make tea, pride bubbling in her chest.

'That was a wise move on your part,' Katy said. At Ella's frown, she whispered, 'Getting Ivy to use it first.'

Ella grinned. 'Now I can let Paul Sampson know our number,' which she promptly did.

The rest of the day passed in a flurry of activity, with customers coming and going. Orders were taken and appointments for adjustments made. Locking up at the close of business, Ella walked home, feeling tired to the bone. That evening, Flossie popped in as usual and chatted excitedly about being a model again at the Grand Sale.

'Will it be like last time?' she asked, accepting the beverage offered.

'More or less. We'll have a sale of some of the older hats too in an effort to shift them, which will give us space for new stock.'

'Good idea.'

Ella went on to tell her neighbour about Paul Sampson and the new telephone in the shop.

'Ivella's really taking off now and it's all thanks to you,' Flossie said.

'The girls say my name and reputation is widely known,' Ella said timidly.

'I ain't surprised. Your dad would be so proud of you.'

Ella nodded sadly as she glanced at the space yet again where her father's wheelchair used to be.

'Oh, guess what I found,' Flossie said as she delved into her apron pocket. Pulling out a gold wedding band, she passed it to Ella.

'Mum's ring! I'd forgotten about it.'

'I was having a tidy up and I remembered it. It was a while ago now when you asked me to keep it safe for you so your sister d'aint sell it,' Flossie reminded her.

Ella looked at the ring and gave a half-smile. 'Yes, indeed. Our Sally was set on it being sold and having the money for her baby. I wonder where she is now and whether I have a niece or nephew.'

'She might turn up again one day, you never know,' Flossie said, hoping in her heart it would not come to pass. Sally had hurt Ella deeply by stealing and selling her hat designs to Ivy. It was the worst betrayal as far as Flossie was concerned.

22

It was Grand Sale day at last, and everyone was buzzing with excitement.

'Now, do you all know what you have to do?' Ella asked and at the nods, she went on, 'Good. Let's get the door opened, then.'

Walking into the shop to unlock the door, Ella was amazed to see a queue of women waiting to be given entry. Propping the door open, she welcomed the customers as they poured in and found a place to stand.

Spying a particular woman, Ella's heart sank. Darcie Newland marched in like she owned the place.

'Ella.'

'Darcie,' Ella responded.

The fashion show began with Ivy showing off a huge brimmed hat sporting a peacock feather. One after another, the articles of millinery were paraded in front of potential buyers.

Eventually, it was time for customers to inspect the hats they had their eye on.

'Ooh, I love this one!'

Ella smiled at the comment as she squeezed her way through the throng. She was delighted as she heard the rattle of the till as time after time, items were paid for.

'I'm having this,' an older woman said as she held onto the peacock-feathered creation.

'I wouldn't if I were you.' The voice of Darcie Newland grated on Ella as she watched. 'This isn't very secure.' Ella saw Darcie bend the feather until its spine cracked, leaving it hanging at an awkward angle.

'You did that on purpose!' the woman yelled.

'I most certainly did not! It's shoddy workmanship!' Darcie retorted.

Ella closed her eyes for a second. She had

prayed that there wouldn't be an upset, but with Darcie in attendance, she knew it was a forlorn hope.

'Is there a problem, ladies?' Ella asked.

'Ar there is. She's just bosted this feather and deliberately an' all!'

'I can assure you...' Darcie began as all eyes turned to the contretemps.

'No matter. If you are interested in the hat, we can have a new feather attached very quickly for you.' Ella's attention was on her prospective client.

'Go on, then, but might I suggest you keep *her* away from your goods!'

'How dare you be so rude? I'm about to marry a judge's son and you could find yourself up in court very easily should I tell my fiancé!'

'Well, you ain't wed yet, so you can stick it up yer arse!' The woman gave as good as she got.

'Ladies! Enough, please. Ivy, will you take this customer and her hat to the back room and ask Thora to do the necessary repair, please?' Ella asked and watched as the woman strode away with a last defiant look at Darcie.

Cupping Darcie's elbow, Ella led her towards the

door and out onto the street. 'Why are you doing this to me?'

'You mean you don't know? My, but you have a short memory!'

Ella sighed. She did know, of course, but had been hoping she was wrong. Surely Miss Newland wasn't still bearing a grudge after all these years?

'You stole Harper away from me! The man I was engaged to, who I was to marry!'

'That was his decision, not mine,' Ella said quietly.

'He jilted me – for you!' Darcie's voice was like a rasp on metal.

'I think it's time you left. I also think you should not return, otherwise I may have to inform the police of your harassment.' Ella kept her voice low, as she could feel eyes watching her from inside the shop.

'You won't get away with this because I know you killed Harper!' Darcie yelled.

The silence in the shop was deafening now as tears formed in Ella's eyes. 'Harper was taken by tuberculosis and well you know it! How then could I have killed him?' Ella raised her voice for all to hear. 'I'm sorry to have to say this, Darcie, but he never loved you. Harper was forced into the engagement by his father. Now, if you don't get away from here, I *will* call the police and have you removed!'

Darcie stamped her foot before marching away.

Ella watched her go before letting her shoulders slump. Turning to go back into the shop, she was greeted with rapturous applause. With a half-smile, she re-entered and began to mingle once more, but Darcie's outburst had taken the shine off Ella's day.

For hours, people came and went, and hats of all descriptions were sold; men's as well as women's. By five in the afternoon, and with the door finally bolted, everyone had gone home except Ella. She sat with Ivy in the back room, sipping a much-needed hot drink.

'We did incredibly well today,' Ivy said. 'I think it might be a good idea to have a Grand Sale at least once a year.'

'Hmm,' Ella mumbled.

'The ones on the sale all went as well,' Ivy went on. Then, seeing Ella was barely listening, she asked, 'You still thinking about that Newland woman?'

Ella nodded. 'I can't believe she still holds me responsible.'

'She's bitter, Ella. She needs someone to blame for what she thinks is her misfortune. People like that never own their mistakes, they always lay them at others' feet.'

'I know, but...'

'Ella, you dealt with it extremely well – the customers thought so too. Let it go now and enjoy our successful day.'

'You're right as usual, thanks, Ivy.' Ella smiled over the rim of her cup, but inside, she couldn't help feeling Darcie hadn't finished with her yet.

* * *

Ella could not know that over in Birmingham, Darcie Newland was spitting fire, she was so angry.

'Darling, you really mutht calm down,' Mason Landor said.

'Don't tell me what to do!' Darcie snapped back.

'But thweetheart, you'll make yourthelf ill.'

Darcie glared at the man she had promised to marry. Mason's cheeks were rosy and he was sweating again. His short stature meant he had to look up at her, adding to the sense of his subservience. His stomach bulged, stretching his waistcoat tight, and his fat hands mopped his brow with a handkerchief as his piggy eyes surveyed her. How had she come to be betrothed to this awful man? She gave an involuntary shudder as a fleeting thought of the wedding night crossed her mind. Whatever else, that was one thing she could not do – she refused to share a bed with Mason Landor.

'I want that woman arrested, Mason, and thrown into jail!'

'My petal, there ith nothing to arretht her for,' Mason said gently and stepped back out of reach lest Darcie decide to land him a slap.

'She said she would have me in police custody! She was rude and virtually threw me out of the shop!' Darcie was fuming at being treated in that manner and was now directing her anger towards this unofficious little man. Would he ever grow a backbone and stand up for her?

'I'm thorry, my thweet pea, but you can't arretht thomeone for being rude. Father would tell you the thame thing.'

'Oh, thut – shut your mouth! And can't you sort that bloody lisp out, for God's sake!'

Mason sighed and lowered his head. He idolised this woman, who was treating him like something she'd scraped off her shoe, but this was the first time she'd mentioned his affliction. He couldn't help it, he simply could not pronounce certain words properly, and all the so-called professional help given him growing up hadn't helped.

'Don't sulk, Mason, it really doesn't become you.'

Would it have hurt you to apologise? Mason thought, as he lifted his head to look at the woman he adored. Besides being beautiful, Darcie had chosen him and had accepted his proposal of marriage. He had never thought he would marry, as women really didn't seem to take to him. Darcie, however, was different. She had welcomed his attentions and was happy to be seen out with him. He loved having her on his arm and showing her off.

'Look, go home and change and then we'll go out for dinner and take a trip to the theatre,' Darcie said as she walked to open the sitting room door.

'All right, my love.' Mason stood at the door,

waiting for a kiss, but seeing he was out of luck, he left.

Closing the door behind him, Darcie gave a little shiver. Then, crossing to the fireplace, she pulled the bell rope to summon the maid. She needed a cup of tea whilst she hatched a plan to seek her revenge on Ella Bancroft.

The Pet Shop Dilemma

23

'Ella, did you put the takings in the safe?' Ivy asked the following day.

'No, you did. Don't you remember? You said one of us could take it to the bank the next time we went to town.'

'Oh, I must have forgotten,' Ivy said.

'We were so busy and both very tired by the end of the day,' Ella reminded her.

'Very true.' Ivy wandered away to the shop area, leaving Ella in the back room. Ella's brows drew together as she considered the short conversation. This wasn't the first time Ivy had been unable to recall something. It was little things like where she'd put certain objects, or asking the same question time after time. Ella had put it down to the fact that the shop was the busiest it had ever been, and she and Ivy were helping out. Selling a hat and putting the money in the till was an automatic action; one doesn't stop to consider every step, Ella thought. So why couldn't Ivy remember? Ella made a mental note to keep a keener eye on Ivy. Something wasn't right. It might be mental exhaustion, or it could be something more sinister. If it persisted or got any worse, Ella would have to suggest Ivy see a doctor.

In the shop, Ivy was thinking much the same thing. She could recall incidents from her childhood, and yet putting away the money yesterday was a blank to her.

Was she losing her mind slowly and bit by bit? Or was she, as Ella stated, just tired out? Maybe she should take more rest or more notice of what she was doing. One thing for sure was – worrying about it wouldn't help. On that thought, Ivy went upstairs to see how Thora and Freda were getting on with the orders.

* * *

While Ivy fretted about her forgetfulness, in Birmingham, Darcie Newland hailed a cab to take her to Smallbrook Street. Although she had told Tilda Hunter she would visit the following week, Darcie couldn't wait that long. She was seeking answers and hoped Tilda would provide them. She wanted to know what the future held for her. Was it likely she would heap her revenge on Ella for stealing her man and making her a laughing-stock? If so, would she get away with it?

Snapping out the address, Darcie waited on the street. She heard the cabbie sigh before he jumped down and opened the door for her. Darcie gave him a curt nod and climbed aboard. The cabbie slammed the door shut and retook his seat.

Darcie smiled as the cab rolled away. Glancing out of the window, she watched people ambling about. The streets were busy with folk side-stepping around others; women with hordes of unruly children shouting the odds. Men were hanging about on street corners smoking rough tobacco, or playing dice on the pathway.

The closer they got to her destination, Darcie noticed, the dirtier the buildings became. Soot-blackened brickwork and smoking chimneys gave this part of town a grimy look. The pall of smoke hanging in the air filtered the sun's rays, which tried desperately to penetrate the thick dark layers.

Feeling the cab draw to a halt, Darcie again waited and a moment later, the door opened. Stepping down, she said, 'Wait for me, I shouldn't be too long.'

'Sorry, missus, I can't. I've an appointment to collect the mayor,' the cabbie replied, tipping his cap.

With an explosive sigh, Darcie paid the man but gave him no tip. Then she hammered on Tilda's door.

The cab set off and the cabbie chuckled. He had no such appointment but would not be at this woman's beck and call. It was his job to drive the cab, not open bloody doors for women with ideas above their station. Had she not been so condescending, he might have waited, but now she would have to walk to find a cab home. With another chuckle, the cabbie was glad it wouldn't be his.

'Ah, Miss Newland, do come through. I wasn't expecting you today,' Tilda fawned.

'Well, I'm here now.' It had never occurred to

Darcie that Tilda could already have a client with her.

'My last lady has just left, so you're in luck. I have half an hour before my next arrives,' Tilda lied. She had no one booked in for the rest of the day.

'Right, let's get on with it then!' Darcie said sharply as she brushed the seat with her glove before sitting down.

The movement was not lost on Tilda, and she seethed inside. It was true she was not house-proud, but even so... Forcing a smile to her lips, she asked, 'Is there anyone in particular you wish to speak to today?'

'No. I want to know what my future holds for me.'

'I... that's not how I usually work. I only pass on messages from the dead to the living.' This had taken Tilda by surprise, and she wondered what Darcie was up to.

'Then ask someone, surely they could help!'

With a sigh Tilda nodded and laid her hands flat on the table.

Noting the woman's dirty fingernails, Darcie shuddered.

'Is there anybody there?' Tilda called out, all the while thinking rapidly about what she could tell her wealthy client. 'I have an older man here, a grandfather, maybe?'

'Ask him if I'm destined to become a wife again!'

'He's nodding.'

Darcie sighed loudly. She was hoping that would not be the case. The thought of being tied to Mason for the rest of her life made her stomach turn.

'I have the initials E. B.'

'That would be Ella Bancroft.'

'She's a thorn in your side,' Tilda went on. 'She's done you a great wrong in the past.' She could sense she was on the right path with this thread, and besides, she was drawing on what she'd been told by the market traders. 'I'm seeing hats – a lot of them.'

'Yes! She makes them!' Darcie could not contain herself.

'Fear not, you will have your revenge,' Tilda said, looking directly into Darcie's eyes, and what she saw there made her shiver inwardly. Those eyes held a hate so raw it made Tilda afraid. She wondered in fact if she was doing the right thing in feeding this woman's need for vengeance.

Having heard enough, Darcie rummaged in her bag and slapped her coin on the table. Getting to her feet as the dirty hands scooped it up, she turned and walked out without so much as a thank you.

When Darcie had gone, Tilda turned the coin over in her fingers and stared at it. If something terrible befell Ella Bancroft at the hands of Darcie Newland, could she, Tilda, be held responsible? Would the police find her accountable for encouraging Darcie to commit a crime? It was possible.

Tilda felt the cold fingers of fear caress her spine as she imagined herself standing in the dock beside Darcie. Right then and there, she made up her mind – she would not be seeing that particular client again. Despite it being good money, it wasn't worth the worry.

Striding out to find a cab, Darcie had a big smile on her face. Now she was certain, she would see Ella Bancroft ruined – or dead.

24

Ella watched Ivy closely and was very worried to see her business partner's memory failing more often. The little things began to add up, like Ivy losing her pencil, and repeating her questions. Ivy started to get frustrated and angry and Ella chided herself for not having noticed it before now. How long had Ivy been like this? Was it getting worse, or did it seem that way because Ella was more observant now?

'Did we order new stock?' Ivy asked as they helped Katy re-dress the window.

'Yes, I told you yesterday,' Ella replied, exchanging a glance with Katy.

'Oh, all right.' Ivy continued to pass items to Katy.

'I think we should have a cuppa,' Katy said.

'I'll do it,' Ivy volunteered.

As soon as Ivy left the room, Katy whispered, 'What's going on with her?'

'I think her memory is going,' Ella whispered back.

'I thought the same, should we get the doctor out to see her?'

'Not yet. Let's see how she goes and if it doesn't improve, we will.' Ella's reply was quiet.

'Tea up,' Ivy called as she carried in a tray. 'Oh, Ella, I meant to ask, did we order new stock?'

Ella stole another quick glance at Katy as she answered, 'Yes.'

'Oh, good. I'll take this up to... erm, the girls.'

'Ella! She couldn't remember Thora and Freda's names!' Katy said.

'I know. Whatever it is, it's come on very quickly,' Ella replied. Now she was really worried. 'I'm going to see the doctor and ask him about it.'

'Good idea, at least we might have an idea what the problem is.'

Ella sipped her tea, a worried expression on her face. If it was a disease of some sort, how fast would it progress? Was it contagious? 'I'm going now,' Ella said suddenly.

'What shall I tell Ivy when she asks where you are?' Katy asked, keeping one eye on the door for Ivy's return.

'Tell her – I've gone for pies for lunch,' Ella said as she hurriedly snatched up her bag and left the shop.

Grabbing the attention of a cabbie, Ella climbed in, asking to be taken to the doctor's office. Once there, she was led into a room which smelled of disinfectant.

'Now, how can I help you, Miss…?'

'Ella Bancroft. It's not me, actually, it's my friend I need advice about.'

'I see. I'm not sure I can discuss another's problems; it goes against my ethics.'

'Please, doctor, I'm really in need of some help.'

The doctor chewed on his lower lip, then said, 'In a hypothetical situation, I may be able to help. Tell me what's worrying you, Miss Bancroft, and then I'll see what I can do.'

Ella did as she was bid and the man sitting behind his desk listened intently, his grey hair shining in the light and his spectacles in his hand. When Ella had finished speaking, he leaned back in his chair and placed his glasses on his desk.

'I've seen this before. We're not entirely sure what causes it, and so far we have no name for it. What I can tell you is – if it's the condition I suspect, it will likely get much worse over time.'

'Worse how? And over what length of time?'

'It depends on the person concerned. For some, it happens very quickly and for others, it can take years.'

'Is it contagious?'

'No, my dear. Let me explain what we in the medical profession *think* happens. It's all to do with the brain cells dying off, we assume, leaving the patient with broken memories or sometimes none at all. Usually, the patient can remember instances from many years ago, but recall from the day before is lost to them. This results in frustration, anger and later, aggression. In the end, they lose the power to speak, eat and even swallow. I'm afraid that's when...'

'I see!' Ella cut across, not wanting to hear the

doctor say any more. 'How can I help my friend? What can I do?'

'Try not to lose your patience with her, she doesn't realise what's happening to her.'

'She's going to die, isn't she?' Ella asked, surprised at the gathering tears which she blinked away.

'We don't know, and I wouldn't like to hazard a guess. Hiring a full-time nurse would be advantageous to you both.'

'Thank you for your time, doctor,' Ella said, getting to her feet.

'I'm sorry I couldn't give you better news.' He shook his head sadly as he watched Ella leave, tears beginning to roll down her face. In his experience, Ella Bancroft could well have her work cut out for her in the next months or even years.

On her way back to the shop, Ella stopped to buy the pies she had promised for their lunches.

'This is nice,' Ivy said as she took the pies to the kitchen.

In the sales area, Ella took the opportunity of Ivy's absence to have a word with Katy.

'After work, you, Thora and Freda come to my house – don't let Ivy know,' Ella whispered.

Katy nodded.

Ivy returned, holding out two plates with pies on them. 'Shall I take these upstairs?'

'I'll do it,' Katy said quickly and, giving Ella a wink, she took the plates from Ivy.

Ella knew the message would be passed along with the pies. For the rest of the day, her nerves were stretched taut. She needed the others to know what the doctor had told her and then they needed to plan out Ivy's future – however long that might be.

At six o'clock that evening, Ella welcomed Katy, Thora and Freda with hot tea before banging on the wall to alert Flossie that a brew was waiting.

Flossie came in, surprised to see everyone gathered. 'What's up?' she asked, taking the cup offered.

'I went to see the doctor today.'

'Why? You ain't poorly, are you?' Flossie asked, full of concern.

'No, but Ivy is.' Ella then went on to explain what she knew. At the end, she said, 'What we have to decide is how we manage this.'

'Bloody hell!' Flossie gasped.

'We did wonder, didn't we, Freda?' Thora said.

Freda nodded. 'She keeps asking the same thing over and over.'

'Has she got a funeral plan paid up?' Flossie asked.

'I don't know; how can I ask a question like that?' Ella felt the tears sting her eyes once more.

'Tell her you're thinking of starting one and ask her advice, then you'll know,' Flossie replied.

'That's good thinking,' Thora said.

With a nod, Ella went on, 'I'll do that tomorrow if I get a chance. What we all have to be prepared for is her anger and possible aggression.'

'We'll look out for it. We'll keep the scissors away from her,' Thora said as an afterthought.

'We don't have a timescale on this, ladies, so if you prefer not to remain at Ivella, I will understand.' Ella's voice was hardly more than a whisper.

'Forget that,' Freda said, 'I've waited a long time to work with you.'

'Me an' all,' Thora added.

'You'll need the money now you're courting our Josh,' Flossie said to Katy, who blushed beetroot red.

Spontaneous applause rang out and Katy was

given hugs. 'I'm not leaving either,' she said once the noise had died down.

'Then, ladies, we have a big job on our hands, one which could last a short or a long time. Thank you all, I couldn't manage without any of you.'

Flossie raised her cup. 'To Ivy. Long may she live.'

The others joined in the toast, but Ella suspected they were thinking the same as she was. She didn't want Ivy to suffer for years; if her condition worsened quickly, it would be a blessing for Ivy if she passed on sooner rather than later.

25

Ella was glad to see Ivy excited at having received an invitation for Ella and herself to attend a dinner and soiree at the Sampson household.

'It's been such a long time since I've been out socially!' Ivy gushed. 'You will come, won't you?'

Ella nodded. 'Of course, I'm looking forward to it. I'll send a reply accepting the invite.'

The dinner was planned for the following Saturday, which meant they only had a couple of days to sort out appropriate evening wear.

'I wonder what will be served for dinner. Should we choose hats from our new range? That would be a good advert.'

Ella watched Ivy bustle about, trying to decide which hat to wear. When Ivy was like this, no one would ever guess there was anything wrong with her. Ella sighed inwardly, knowing it wouldn't last, and she determined not to dwell on what was to come. She would make a concerted effort to enjoy what time she and Ivy had together.

'What will you wear?' Ivy broke into Ella's thoughts.

'I have an emerald-green silk dress, it's old but it might do. However, I'm worried it might be too showy,' Ella said, getting caught up in the excitement.

'Nonsense! One can never been too showy at an event such as this. Wear it proudly, it will be beautiful with your dark hair.'

'Then I will. How about you, Ivy, what are you wearing?'

'My royal blue organza! Like you, I've had it for years, but I intend to make a statement. After all, it might be the last time I get to go out in the evening.'

Ella looked at the woman fussing over a blue hat with large feathers. Did Ivy know what was happening to her? Was she aware of what the future held and preparing herself?

'That sounds perfect,' Ella mumbled.

'This will match nicely,' Ivy said, holding up the hat. 'Ella, come on! Choose a hat to go with your dress.'

Doing as she was bid, Ella plastered a smile on her face, her worries about Ivy having sucked the joy right out of their planning.

The following days seemed to pass quickly and, before they knew it, Ella and Ivy were boarding the cab which would take them to Birmingham.

'We should have taken the train,' Ivy said.

'I don't like travelling on the train at night, Ivy, you never know who's hanging around. A cab is much safer.'

'I wonder who will be at the supper,' Ivy said as the cab moved off.

'Men of standing and their wives, I would think,' Ella replied.

Arriving at the Sampson estate, the cab wound its way up the long gravel drive and halted outside a massive house. It was lit from the ground to the roof in electric light, and Ella gasped as a footman helped her to alight. Led indoors by a butler, their wraps were taken by a maid, then Ella and Ivy were shown to a huge sitting room. Here they were greeted by their host, Paul Sampson and his beautiful wife, Immelda. Welcomed with a glass of sherry, the two women were introduced to industrial barons, judges, lawyers and doctors, along with their spouses.

'Nicholas, meet Ella Bancroft and Ivy Gladwin – ladies, this is my partner, Nicholas Gerard.'

Ella thought her heart had stopped as she stared into the green eyes smiling at her. The stranger's hair was as dark as a raven's wing and framed a face as handsome as any Ella had ever seen. Lips parted to reveal white, even teeth, then closed again as they kissed the back of her hand.

A dig in the ribs from Ivy brought Ella back to the moment and her cheeks held a gentle blush.

'Yes, Mr Gerard, we are partners in Ivella,' Ivy said. Ella had not even heard the question.

'Paul has told me a lot about you, ladies, and I've been instructed to visit your salon,' Nicholas said.

'You won't be disappointed.' Ella's voice was timid, and she flushed again at his answer.

'I won't if you are there to assist me.'

The dinner gong sounded and with Ella on one arm and Ivy on the other, Nicholas escorted them to the dining room.

Once in their seats, Ella stared around her. The long table down the centre of the room sat twenty people and was set with fine china and silver cutlery, as well as cut glass wine and water glasses. Small fresh flower decorations ran the length of the table and overhead, glass chandeliers distributed light in beautiful patterns around the room.

Wine was served, as was water, then out came onion soup. A veritable army of staff had been taken on for the occasion and each person had their own waiter.

Ella's eyes were drawn back to Nicholas Gerard sitting opposite her, and she smiled shyly. Rewarded with a grin, Ella felt her stomach turn over. If she continued to look at him, she wouldn't be able to eat a thing. Glancing down the table, she saw Ivy indulging in an animated conversation with a doctor's wife.

'I've heard very good things about your establishment, and I intend to visit very soon,' the lady next to Nicholas called out to Ella.

'Thank you, I'm sure we'll be able to help you,' Ella replied.

Once the soup was finished, roast beef dinners with all the trimmings were served, along with a delicious red wine to match.

Ella's eyes roamed the room as low chatter sounded. Large paintings adorned the walls and beaded voile swags in grey and white hung at the windows and French doors.

'Beautiful, isn't it?' Nicholas Gerard asked, his voice loud to be heard over the noise in the room and pulling Ella's attention back to him.

'It is indeed!' Ella said on a breath. 'I'd love a house like this one day.'

'I'm sure you will have it. Where is it you hail from?'

'Walsall. My home and business are there,' Ella said between bites of her delicious dinner.

'Ah, the town of all things leather, I believe.'

'Yes, we provide the King with his saddles,' Ella said, swelling with pride.

A tiny lemon-flavoured ice was served to cleanse the palate once the plates were removed, then out came chocolate pastries with fresh cream.

Ella looked at the sweet in front of her and sub-consciously blew out her cheeks. When she looked up, Nicholas was laughing. Despite her embarrass-ment, Ella laughed too. She watched as he pushed his plate away untouched, giving her leave to do the same. Smiling her gratitude, Ella sipped her water and dabbed her mouth daintily with her napkin. She caught snippets of conversation going on around her but could still feel Nicholas's eyes on her. Her heart hammered in her chest and her blood felt on fire. Pulling a small fan from the drawstring bag hanging on her chair, Ella wafted it in front of her face.

At the head of the table, Paul Sampson noted the movement and raised his eyebrows to the butler, who instructed a servant to throw open the French doors. Ella inclined her head to her host in thanks before closing her fan and laying it on the table. She basked in the cool fragrant air coming in from the garden, as did the other women.

The butler announced coffee would be served in the sitting room, and the ladies' chairs were pulled back by servants before the guests trooped out.

The sitting room also had French doors standing

wide open, showing a gravel path surrounding the extensive lawns. Candles in jars lit the whole scene with an almost ethereal glow.

'Would you care for coffee, or would you prefer a stroll around the gardens?'

Ella turned at Nicholas's question, setting her heart racing once more.

'A stroll sounds perfect after such a wonderful meal,' she replied.

He offered his elbow, and Ella slipped her arm through it and stepped out into the cool of the evening.

'Are you cold?' Nicholas asked, seeing her shiver a little.

'No, it's just that it was so hot indoors,' Ella said, knowing it was nothing of the sort. She knew she was reacting to being in such close proximity to this most handsome and charming man.

She also knew she was going to enjoy every single moment of this walk.

26

Hearing the musicians warming up in the music room, Nicholas led Ella back inside to be seated for the entertainment.

When everyone was settled, a man stood in the bow of a baby grand piano. Nodding to the pianist, the keys began to tinkle and the man began to sing. Ella gasped at the sound he emitted. She had expected a bass or tenor but what she heard was soprano.

'He's a castrato,' Nicholas whispered quietly. Seeing her frown, he lowered his eyes to his lap then snipped his fingers like scissors. He grinned wickedly at her horrified look, but the singer's voice drew her back to its beauty and carried her to another world.

The man bowed and blew kisses at the standing ovation which greeted him at the end of his performance, and as he and the pianist left the room, Ella and other ladies dabbed their eyes on lacy handkerchiefs.

Next came a comedian who had no intention of apologising to the high-society audience for his bawdy jokes. Polite titters soon turned into booming belly laughs. Taking his leave to rapturous applause, the comedian waved and tipped his top hat.

'Unusual for a soiree, but rather entertaining,' Ella heard someone say.

The final performance was from a choir boy who sang his heart out unaccompanied, then the ladies retired to the sitting room once more. The gentlemen moved to the games room for brandy, cigars and a game of snooker.

All too soon, the evening came to an end, and carriages and cabs lined the driveway to take the guests home. After goodnights and thanks for a wonderful time were given, Ella and Ivy climbed into their cab and as they travelled, Ivy commented

on the singer who had opened the evening's entertainment. When Ella explained that the man was a
castrato, Ivy muttered, 'Poor man, he doesn't know
what he's missing.'

Ella laughed, saying, 'Apparently the procedure
happens when they are boys so he wouldn't know. It
prevents their voices from breaking.'

'It's barbaric, if you ask me, but I can't deny he
sang beautifully. I saw you take a turn around the
gardens with that handsome fellow.'

'Nicholas Gerard, he's Paul's partner in the business,' Ella said.

'He seemed very taken with you.'

'He was just being polite,' Ella said, thankful her
blush couldn't be seen in the darkness of the cab.

'I think it was more than that. I suspect we could
be seeing a lot more of Mr Gerard,' Ivy stated.

'Well, I must admit that would be nice, I did
rather like him,' Ella confessed.

'It would do you good to have a young man in
your life again, you've been mourning Harper too
long.'

'I would feel guilty, Ivy.'

'Why? Harper's gone, Ella, and no amount of

grieving will bring him back. It's time you found a new love.'

Ella was surprised by Ivy's words, for they almost never spoke about things so personal. In the hiatus that followed, Ella considered what Ivy had said and determined the older woman was right.

* * *

The following morning, over tea and before work for the day began, Ella and Ivy were telling Katy, Thora and Freda all about their evening.

'I've heard about them men who sing like women,' Freda said.

Freda began to explain with, 'Don't they have their do-dahs removed when they'm little kids?'

Thora put in, 'That's what I should have done to my old man – with two house bricks!'

Katy and Freda burst out laughing, then laughed harder at Ella and Ivy's shocked expressions.

'We'd best get the shop open, we can't sell anything with a locked door,' Ivy said. She and Katy went to the shop area and Thora and Freda went to the workroom, while Ella gathered the cups and washed them up in Ivy's kitchen. Then she returned to the back room to work on some new designs.

It was around mid-morning when Katy came rushing through. 'Someone wants to see you, Ella.'

Ella frowned as she got to her feet. 'Who is it?'

'A Mr Nicholas Gerard and – oh, Ella – he's really handsome!' Katy answered dreamily.

Ella drew in a breath, stepped to the mirror on the wall and patted her hair in place. She pinched her cheeks to give them a little colour, then smoothing down her long fawn skirt, she nodded.

'Mr Gerard, how very nice to see you again!' Ella gushed as she held out her hand in greeting.

'You also, Miss Bancroft,' Nicholas replied, giving her a beaming smile before shaking her out-stretched hand. 'I trust you enjoyed your evening at Paul and Imelda's.'

'Yes, indeed.'

'Paul recommended I visit for a new top hat, mine has seen better days, I'm afraid.'

'Of course. Katy will be happy to see to all your needs,' Ella said.

'I was hoping – that is – no matter,' Nicholas blustered.

Katy pulled out a range of toppers in different sizes for him to try. 'I have a small head, although some might disagree with that,' he said as the first he tried slipped down to cover his green eyes. Removing it, he saw Ella turn to leave the room. 'I wonder if you would help me choose, Miss Bancroft.'

Ella blushed prettily as she turned back to him. 'Of course.'

Katy watched the interaction between the two closely and sighed longingly. Nicholas Gerard only had eyes for Ella, it was so obvious even a blind man could see. They chatted long after the topper was bought and paid for, during which time Katy served two other customers.

Eventually, Nicholas said, 'I'm sorry, I seem to have taken up a lot of your time.'

'That's all right, please don't concern yourself,' Ella answered with a smile which made the gold flecks in her eyes twinkle.

'I'm only concerned that I must leave you now,' he said in a whisper.

Ella blushed to the roots of her hair, and holding

out her hand once more, she said, 'Thank you for your custom and we hope to see you again.'

Kissing the back of her hand rather than shaking it, Nicholas then held her gaze before turning to leave.

'Mr Gerard – don't forget your hat!' Ella called as he reached the door.

'Thank you.' Nicholas grinned then left the shop.

'Blimey! He's got it bad for you!' Katy said to her employer.

'Nonsense, he's just...' Ella began.

'Polite?' Ivy said as she sauntered through.

Ella shook her head then returned to her designs, but she did wonder how much work she would get done now. She had a feeling Mr Nicholas Gerard wouldn't be far from her thoughts for some time to come.

27

Darcie Newland was throwing yet another tantrum. She paced the luxurious parlour of Mason's house as she yelled her questions.

'Why were we not invited? You are the son of a judge, Mason!'

'Clearly it wath a thelect few only, my darling, even father wath not invited,' Mason Landor replied.

'It's really not good enough! We should be included in all high-society functions!' Darcie paced the length of the spacious parlour, the rustling of her skirts loud in the quiet of the room.

'We will be, my thweet, we have to be pathient.'

'Mason, you must know by now that patience is not one of my virtues!'

Ain't that the truth! Mason thought but said instead, 'You could alwayth organithe a thoiree of your own, my queen.'

Darcie stopped dead in her tracks. 'What a good idea! I'll get on to it straight away. I'll need a list of the most important people to invite. That I'll leave to you, which will leave me free to engage caterers and staff. Oh, but I can't afford it!' Darcie said sulkily.

'You go right ahead, my love, and I will foot the bill.'

'You're so good to me, Mason,' Darcie fawned.

'It'th becauthe I love you.'

Darcie's smile never reached her eyes, and she was careful not to reply in the same vein. She didn't love this lisping fop and had no intention of saying she did. Mason Landor was only good for two things: the fact that he adored her and his money. Whilst she had those, Mason would remain in her life and although they were betrothed, Darcie would rather walk on hot coals than marry him. She liked things the way they were, so she saw no reason to change anything.

'I'll need a new gown,' she muttered as she began pacing again.

'Yeth, dear.'

'The best food money can buy.'

'Yeth, dear.'

'The most expensive wine and champagne.'

With a sigh, Mason wished he'd kept his mouth shut.

'Come, Mason, we have a lot to do!'

As Mason followed her from the parlour, Darcie smiled as she heard again, 'Yeth, dear.'

The next few days were taken up with the organisation of her soiree and Darcie considered whether or not to invite Ella Bancroft. She doubted the woman would accept, but out of devilment, she added her name to the list and wrote out the card anyway. Should Ella attend, it would be a good opportunity to show her up in front of her other esteemed guests. Darcie knew Ella would not come alone so made out the invitation for Miss Ella Bancroft plus one.

Although Paul Sampson had missed Mason and herself off his guest list, Darcie would ensure that Messrs Sampson and Gerard would be at her party.

As they were held in high regard by the wealthy, Darcie thought it prudent to court their favour. After all, one never knew when one might need a top-class accountant.

Darcie's mind moved on to the entertainment for the evening. A quartet was always a good idea, but she also wanted something different. The answer came to her like switching on one of those new-fangled electric lights.

Grabbing her bag and parasol, Darcie left the house and hailed a passing cabbie. Calling out the address, she waited for the driver to jump down and open the cab door for her.

Once settled, she smiled to herself. Her party guests would be amazed at her choice of divertissement, in fact they would be talking about it for months.

Reaching her destination, Darcie asked the cabbie to wait, she didn't plan on being long. After a sharp rap on the door, it was opened and Darcie was greeted with, 'Come in, Miss Newland.'

* * *

Nicholas Gerard sat staring into space. Seeing nothing of his grand surroundings in his office at Sampson & Gerard, his mind showed him pictures of one thing only – Ella Bancroft. He smiled as he saw again the gold-flecked eyes twinkle when she laughed. The small wisp of dark hair which strayed from its pins and curled enticingly around her high cheekbone. Her laugh, which could turn from tinkling water to a sensual invitation in the blink of an eye. Her figure, which she did nothing to hide but was wrapped elegantly in quality apparel.

Ella might be small and dainty, but Nicholas had no doubt she could be a fierce foe if the occasion called for it. Her reputation as *the* milliner to visit for all one's needs had spread far and wide and was still growing. Nicholas wondered how long it would take for her business to rival the stores in London, although something told him she was already doing so. One thing was for sure – he wanted to know more about the dark-haired beauty. Maybe it was time to buy himself another new hat.

* * *

A few streets away, Darcie sat in Tilda's dark and dingy room once more.

'Oh, I'm not sure,' Tilda Hunter said after hearing Darcie's request for her to attend the soiree and give some readings to the guests.

'Why ever not? I'm sure the recompense for your time would make it worth your while.'

The thought of earning good money was a significant incentive for Tilda, of that there was no doubt, but how could she get away with it? She had no idea who would be in attendance and ergo no information to draw upon.

'Can you tell me who would be coming?' Tilda asked.

'The wealthy and most notable, of course!' Darcie stated.

Tilda needed to know exactly so she could make her discreet enquiries and Miss Newland was not being very forthcoming.

'If you could give me a better idea of my audience, it would help me enormously. You see, I would have to channel my energies towards their dearly departed in order to give accurate readings.'

'Ah, yes, I understand.' Taking a small notebook

and pen from her bag, Darcie wrote down the names of the guests to be invited.

'The Lord Mayor!' Tilda said as she took the list.

Darcie nodded importantly.

'Sampson and Gerard, Ella Bancroft...' Seeing that name brought Tilda up sharply. It was this lady and her friend who had caught Tilda out previously, so how could she now agree to the proposition? Ella could call her out as a charlatan and her reputation would be ruined. Maybe Ella wouldn't attend, but could Tilda risk it?

Seeing the woman debating, Darcie said, 'I will double my previous offer and pay you ten pounds.' She desperately wanted Tilda to be her surprise entertainment and thereby have her soiree talked about for months.

The temptation of ten pounds was too hard to resist and Tilda said, 'All right, I'll do it.'

Darcie could not know at that moment, however, that her party would indeed be the talk of the town – but for all the wrong reasons.

28

Tilda Hunter was kept busy over the next few days, finding out all she could about the people on the guest list given to her by Miss Newland. She realised she would have to have a memory like an elephant to be able to recall details about all these dignitaries.

Sitting in her semi-dark living room, she contemplated the upcoming soiree. What had she been thinking to agree to such a thing? How could she hope to get away with it? If it was revealed that she was a fraud, then her life as a medium would be shattered. Could she be hauled off to jail for misleading her clients? Would it be considered to be a crime? She didn't see how, for everything she'd found out was the truth, as far as she was aware. The only fly in the ointment was Ella Bancroft.

Tapping her fingers on the chenille tablecloth, Tilda debated whether to take a little trip to Walsall and have a quiet word with Ella. She could explain how desperate she was for the money Darcie was paying her. She could beg Ella to keep her secret just this once. How would Ella react to that? She might laugh in Tilda's face and threaten to disclose what she knew of the so-called medium.

With a hefty sigh, Tilda wished now she hadn't agreed to Darcie's proposal, but then again – ten pounds! This would tide her over for a while, by which time her failing business might pick up again. She'd had no clients for a couple of weeks, other than Darcie Newland, that was. For a reason unknown to her, even her regulars had deserted her. Maybe they could no longer afford the half-crown she charged. She could reduce her prices, but those clients were probably lost to her now. She had begun to fret that she might have to return to her previous profession of prostitution to put food on her table. Now this unexpected opportunity had fallen into her lap and would stave off that worry for a while longer, but she still had to pay her rent.

Tilda gave an involuntary shiver as she thought about her landlord throwing her out onto the streets. He would have no qualms about it, as he could then rent the house to a family and charge a lot more for the privilege. In fact, Tilda was surprised it hadn't happened already, despite her having to keep him happy in other ways when he came to collect the rent money. Tilda's mouth twisted into a look of disgust when she remembered he would be calling in the next few days. How had she come to this? Growing up in a family of ten children had been difficult, to say the least. Her father had been a drunk and a bully who repeatedly beat her mother when there was no money for drink. Taking in washing, Tilda's mother was old before her time, work-worn and constantly tired.

A tear escaped the corner of her eye as the memories flooded back to her. Tilda's mother, Josie, had fought tooth and nail when her husband, Fred, had decided Tilda was old enough to earn money working the streets. Fred had beaten Josie so badly she couldn't rise from her bed for many a day; the other children had had to do the washing until she'd recovered.

Terrified, Tilda had been dragged out onto a street corner by her father where he had sold her services and so plunged her into the dark underworld of prostitution. Naturally, Tilda never saw a penny of her earnings, which she had to hand over to her father.

Josie had never forgiven Fred for what he'd done to Tilda and was planning to do to their other daughters.

Tilda's silent tears ran down her cheeks as she watched the moving pictures in her mind. She saw again the day Fred took his heavy leather belt to her mother, but this time, the blow never landed. Fred had felt the knife enter his back and as he turned to face his eldest child, Tilda had stuck another knife into his heart.

Wincing, Tilda remembered the horror of what she'd done and the blood – oh, there was so much blood!

Josie had quickly taken charge of the situation and they had pulled and heaved Fred's lifeless body and sat him in the communal privy outside. Then the kitchen floor and the knives were scalded and scrubbed with soda crystals until not a trace of blood could be seen.

It hadn't taken long for a neighbour to discover the body and the police were called. After an investigation, it was discovered Fred Hunter owed a lot of money to a lot of people, any one of whom could have come calling to collect their debt. With no evidence to connect anyone in particular to the crime, the case was closed. Tilda Hunter had got away with murder.

Now, as she sat in her rented property, she didn't regret what she'd done, her father had deserved everything he got. Tilda moved away soon after, for fear her crime could come back on her family. She'd heard since that half of the family had been wiped out by pneumonia, and where her remaining siblings were now, she had no idea. It had been many years since she had last seen them, and she couldn't face searching, only to be disappointed at not finding them.

Unable to find work, Tilda had remained on the streets until she had enough put aside to rent this house. It was then she had been able to change her profession and become a medium.

Wiping away her tears, Tilda determined she would never return to streetwalking, no matter what life held in store for her. Bringing her thoughts back to the present, she considered again a visit to Ella Bancroft. Maybe the woman would take pity on her and not divulge her secret. Deciding she had nothing to lose by asking, Tilda grabbed her bag and left the house. On the way to the railway station, she prayed she wasn't making a huge mistake.

The sun was setting by the time Tilda arrived at Ivella, only to find it closed for the day. Recalling Ella's address from her enquiries about the young woman, Tilda walked the short distance to Silver Street. Knocking on the door of number twenty-four, she waited. In her peripheral vision, Tilda saw the curtain twitch then the door opened.

'Tilda?' Ella queried, a look of puzzlement on her face.

'May I have a word with you? It's important.'

'Of course. Please come in.' Ella led her visitor through to the cosy kitchen and, indicating a seat, she set the kettle to boil.

A moment later, Flossie bustled in through the back door and glared at Tilda. 'I thought it was you I saw coming down the street.'

'Flossie, sit and have a cuppa, then we can hear what has brought Tilda to my door.'

With a nod, Flossie did as she was bid, her eyes never leaving the heavily made-up face of Tilda Hunter.

With tea made and cake sliced, Ella asked, 'Will you tell us why you are here?'

Tilda poured out her life story, unable to stop until she had brought the women to the reason for her being in Ella's kitchen.

'Good God above!' Flossie exclaimed as Tilda dissolved into a paroxysm of tears.

Ella and Flossie glanced at each other before Tilda sobbed, 'Please don't call the coppers on me!'

'We won't. I promise, Tilda, so don't worry about that,' Ella assured her.

'I need the money, that's why I agreed to do the soiree!' Tilda sniffed.

Ella nodded. 'I've not received an invite and would be very surprised if one came now.'

'It will, your name was on the list – look.' Tilda passed the paper over for Ella to see.

Ella frowned. 'What is Darcie up to? Why would she want me there? I would have thought I'd be the last person she'd want to attend.'

'Maybe she thinks you won't go and then she can tell all and sundry you've snubbed her,' Flossie put in.

'What should I do, then?'

'You should go, of course!' Flossie answered. 'It would put that madam firmly in her place, and she'll be looking over her shoulder all night.'

'What about me?' Tilda asked, as she took back the list of attendees.

'You attend and do your best. Get your money up front, just in case Darcie reneges on the deal,' Ella suggested.

'You won't...?'

'No, I won't inform on you. Please, though, don't come to me when you perform,' Ella said with a little smile, trying to ease the tension in the room.

'Thank you, Ella. I'm glad I came to see you.'

'So am I, because at least now I have fair warning and won't choke on my drink when you walk in.'

'I'd love to see that Darcie's face when you accept her invitation,' Flossie added.

'So would I!' Ella and Tilda said in unison, causing all three to burst out laughing, all tension gone now.

'I'll be getting off, then. Thanks again, and I'll see you at the soiree,' Tilda said, getting to her feet.

Ella saw her visitor out and returning to the kitchen, she shook her head. 'Who would have thought it? Tilda Hunter coming here and pouring her heart out.'

'Poor bugger, she's had it hard,' Flossie replied, helping herself to more tea.

'I felt so sorry for her, Flossie.'

'Me an' all, but it's you I worry about.'

'Why?'

'I can't help wondering why Darcie wants you at that party. What's her game? Does she intend to show you up about Harper jilting her for you?'

'I hadn't thought of that, but it's been five years, Flossie. I can't believe she still bears a grudge!'

'Put yourself in her shoes. If Harper had jilted you for her, would you...?'

'Yes, I suppose I might,' Ella interrupted.

'You just watch your back is all I'm saying,' Flossie warned.

'I will.'

'You could do with a nice young man to go with,' Flossie said with a grin.

Ella smiled and shook her head but couldn't prevent an image of Nicholas Gerard forming in her mind.

29

'It's not difficult!' Ivy yelled at the top of her voice. 'I told you what was to be done and you obviously didn't listen!' She flung the hat on the work bench in front of Freda.

'I did what you asked, it ain't my fault if you've changed your mind,' Freda replied.

'I said to use a peacock feather!' Ivy kicked out at the table leg in her anger.

'What's going on? I could hear the shouting from downstairs,' Ella asked as she entered the workroom.

Freda tried to explain whilst being constantly interrupted by Ivy, arguing the point.

'All right, enough!' Ella called out and turning to Thora, she asked, 'Who's right here?'

'Freda. I'm sorry, Ivy, but originally a grouse feather was agreed upon.'

'Come on, Ivy, let's leave the girls to it, they know what they're doing.' Ella snaked an arm around Ivy's shoulder and led her from the room.

'Ta for that,' Freda said.

'I told the truth. I fear Ivy is getting worse, she's getting violent now.' Thora shook her head, feeling sorry for the woman. 'That kick could have been aimed at you.'

'I know and that's what worries me. Next time, she could pick up the scissors!' Freda said, her voice cracking with emotion.

'Right then, we'll just have to keep them in the drawer. It's too much of a risk to leave them lying around. I also think it's time to have another word with Ella, because we can't go on like this for much longer,' Thora instructed.

'I agree, and we need to include Katy so that she's aware of how we feel,' Freda concurred.

'Good idea. We'll tell her next time she comes up

here. Then, after closing time, we should visit Ella at home.'

'Fair enough, but quite what Ella can do, I don't know,' Freda said quietly as she threaded a needle.

'Nor me, but at least she'll know how we feel.'

The two milliners heaved a sigh in unison as they returned their attention to their work.

Downstairs, Ivy was still ranting about the hat. 'I distinctly remember...'

'Ivy, it doesn't matter, the girls will sort it out,' Ella said gently.

'Don't treat me like a child! I know what I said!' Ivy again kicked out, this time at the armchair, and yowled at the pain shooting through her toe.

Ella was shocked at Ivy's behaviour. She knew to expect it as the doctor had forewarned her, but she didn't think it would come so soon.

'All right, perhaps Freda mistook your instructions.' Ella was trying to calm Ivy's temper but her heart went out to the woman whose memory was failing faster than anyone thought possible. Whatever was wrong with Ivy was very cruel, the more so because Ivy seemed unaware of it happening.

'Let's have a cup of tea, I'm parched,' Ella said as she moved to the kitchen. In her mind, she thought, I don't know what to do! Maybe it was time to speak with the doctor again. Ella wondered if there was a hospital Ivy could be admitted to where they could take care of her.

Having made the tea, Ella returned to the back room but there was no sign of Ivy. Walking through to the shop, she glanced around.

'You lost something?' Katy asked.

'Yes, Ivy.'

'Oh, she just went out.'

'Did she say where she was going?'

Katy shook her head as a look of concern crossed her face.

Alarm bells rang in Ella's head, and she dashed out of the door. Glancing left and right, she spotted Ivy stamping up the street. Ella ran after her, calling out her name.

When Ivy stopped and turned around, Ella asked, 'Where are you off to?'

'I'm going home to Birmingham.'

'Ivy, you live here, you've never lived in Birmingham.'

Ivy looked around her then back at Ella.

Ella's heart cracked as she saw the pain in Ivy's eyes. The woman had no idea where she was and as her tears glistened, Ella held out her arms. Ivy stepped into the embrace and sobbed with despair. It was all Ella could do to hold back her own tears as she led Ivy back to the shop and settled her with a cup of tea.

* * *

Over in Birmingham, Darcie Newland was in full swing, organising her soiree. The invitations had gone out and the house was being cleaned from top to bottom by a troop of women sent by the Servants' Registry.

Now she was in a meeting with her cook. 'Seafood to start with, I think.'

'And for main course?' the cook asked.

'Beef and fowl of some sort.'

The cook nodded. 'Dessert?'

Darcie frowned – she had no idea, as she didn't usually eat a pudding.

'May I suggest something light, maybe a lemon

sorbet?'

'Yes, whatever you think,' Darcie replied. 'Now, I must get on, I have so much to do!' Darcie flicked her fingers, dismissing the cook.

As she left the parlour, the cook wondered what else was left in the way of preparations.

Glancing again at the list of invitees, Darcie clapped her hands like a little child. Her guests were in for the shock of their lives when Tilda Hunter began her readings. Afterwards, Darcie Newland would be the talk of the town, and Ella Bancroft's reputation would fade into the background like smoke on the wind.

* * *

That evening, Ella answered the knock to her front door and she wasn't surprised to see Katy, Thora and Freda standing there.

'Come in, ladies, I thought you might call round.' Ushering them into the kitchen, Ella made tea as Thora explained the reason for their visit.

'It's about Ivy. We're worried about her being aggressive, so much so we're now hiding the scissors.'

'I guessed as much. When she left the shop earlier today, she said she was going home to Birmingham. She had no memory of living here, so I think I should speak with the doctor again,' Ella replied as she provided scones, jam and cream.

'Ain't there anywhere they can put her?' Thora asked, eyeing up the food.

'Thora!' Freda gasped.

'What? A hospital or something was what I meant.'

'I wondered about that myself, so I'll ask,' Ella said.

'Summat has to be done, Ella, if she slips out again, God knows where she'll end up,' Katy put in.

'I know, but – oh, the look in her eyes when I caught up with her almost broke my heart! There are times she's fine, then all of a sudden, it's like her mind has gone somewhere else and she doesn't know,' Ella said on a dry sob.

'Don't upset yourself, just see what the doctor advises first off.' Thora's voice was soft, not wanting to see Ella burst into tears.

Ella nodded. 'I'm not having her put in the asylum.'

All the friends shook their heads as Ella looked from one to the next, but they were all thinking the same thing – it might come to that in the end.

30

Bright and early the following morning, Ella visited the doctor before he set out on his rounds. She explained her reason for being there and her heart sank as she saw his face fall.

'I was expecting this, but not nearly so soon. This disease has her firmly in its clutches and I'm sorry to say it will only get worse. I've not often seen a decline so rapid, I have to admit.' The man shook his head and Ella saw the sadness in his eyes.

'Is there anything that can be done?' Ella asked.

'I'm afraid not, we don't know enough about the condition as yet, so we don't have any treatments we can offer.'

'Can we get my friend into hospital?' Ella pushed but even as she said it, she didn't hold out much hope.

'No, they wouldn't take her. They're not equipped to deal with illnesses such as this; the beds are full of patients with pneumonia and the like.'

'There must be somewhere she could go to receive the care she needs!' Ella was becoming distressed.

'The best I can suggest is a full-time nurse,' the doctor said.

'She would never accept that. I don't think she realises she's ill.'

'It's often the case, my dear, but think on what I've said because the time will come when you need to employ someone to take care of your friend, or take care of her yourself.'

Thanking the doctor, Ella walked home in the summer sunshine, her mind turning over his advice. She was in agreement that Ivy would be in need of round-the-clock care, but when? If Ella tried to employ a nurse now, she felt sure Ivy would not accept it and would most probably throw one of her tantrums. What if Ella explained that she was worried that Ivy might hurt herself? That if Ivy put something in the range and forgot about it, she could burn the shop down? But Ella knew Ivy would argue that she was perfectly capable of looking after herself.

All the way back to Ivella, Ella worried about finding a solution to the problem, but by the time she arrived, she still had no answers.

Throughout the morning, Ella managed to sneakily speak with Katy, Thora and Freda and disclose what the doctor had told her, but unfortunately none of them could see a way around the problem either.

It was around mid-afternoon when Ella smelled burning and when she rushed into the kitchen, she found it full of smoke. This was exactly what she'd been afraid of. Grabbing the thick cloth, she opened the range door and pulled out a blackened pie. Opening the back door which led onto a small yard, Ella threw the pie out, its pastry, burnt to a crisp, still smoking. Propping the door open with a chair, she opened the window wide, and with a tea towel she began to waft the foul-smelling air out through the door.

'I can smell...' Katy yelled as she came rushing through. 'Oh, my God! What happened?'

'Ivy. She must have made a pie and forgot about it,' Ella explained.

'Oh, no. Ella, we have to do something and quickly, otherwise we could end up like that pie!'

'I know. Go back to the shop and keep this door closed. Prop the shop door open in case it smells in there. Leave this with me.'

Katy did as she was instructed, leaving Ella frantically waving the cloth to clear the air. Once the room began to smell fresher, Ella decided now was as good a time as any to be having a word with Ivy. Then a thought struck – where was Ivy? She hadn't gone through the shop, for Katy would have mentioned it, so she must be upstairs with Thora and Freda.

Ella climbed the stairs to be greeted with, 'What's that bloody awful smell?' It was Thora who had asked, with a wrinkle of her nose.

Ella looked around but of Ivy there was no sign. 'Where's Ivy?'

'We ain't seen her all day,' Freda answered.

'Oh, no, she must have gone out again. She

baked a pie which is now a cinder in the yard and the kitchen was full of smoke.'

'Bloody hell! We could have been burned alive!' Thora said, the fear evident in her voice.

'I'll have to go looking for her,' Ella said and dashed out of the room, leaving Thora and Freda sharing a look of horror.

'I'm going to find Ivy,' Ella said as she swept through the shop, out of the open door and onto the street. Looking both ways, Ella couldn't decide which direction to take. She had no idea how long ago Ivy had left and she could be anywhere by now. Deciding her search would be futile if she went one way and Ivy had gone the other, Ella stepped back into the shop.

Looking at Katy, who had concern written all over her face, Ella said, 'I don't know where to look.'

'Come on, I'll put the kettle to boil while you watch the shop a minute,' Katy responded.

Ella nodded as she wondered where Ivy could be. She thought about the illness that was taking over Ivy's mind and how swiftly it had developed. Then, with a frown, she began to recall incidents which she had dismissed as Ivy just being Ivy. Like, for instance, her temper, which had grown far worse over the last few years. Ella had thought it might be something to do with age. Then there were times when Ivy had difficulty bringing a word to mind as they talked.

It was as Katy brought the tea through that realisation hit Ella like a thunderbolt. Ivy's illness had begun some years ago and no one had known, not even Ivy herself!

'There you go, drink that and try not to worry. Ivy will come back, you'll see,' Katy said, proffering the cup and saucer.

'But what if she doesn't?' Ella's hands shook as she took the drink.

'She will. Besides, everybody knows Ivy, so if she's looking a bit lost, someone will bring her home.'

What Katy said was true, Ivy was very well known in the town. Sipping her hot tea, Ella relaxed a bit, there was little more she could do.

As the afternoon wore on, Ivy had still not returned and Ella was frantic. 'I can't lock up until she's home, otherwise she won't get in!'

Thora, Freda and Katy sat in Ivy's living room

with Ella. 'It's early yet, so she might be back before the shop closes up for the night,' Katy said.

'Besides, you can't sit up here all night waiting,' Thora said.

'I agree, you'll make yourself ill,' Freda added.

'I have to! If she's not home by morning, I'll go to the police,' Ella said.

'Do you want me to stay with you?' Katy asked.

'No, you get off home, you're seeing Josh later, aren't you?'

'Yes, but he'd understand.'

'No, Katy, there's no point in us both being here. I have nothing to go home to anyway.' Ella didn't see the look of sadness pass between Thora and Freda at her statement.

'If you're sure?'

'I am, Katy.'

It was then that the bell over the shop door tinkled, and Ella jumped to her feet. 'I hope that's Ivy!'

Katy and the others followed Ella through and stopped dead in their tracks.

'Ella Bancroft?' the policeman asked, tucking his helmet under his arm.

31

Try as he might, Nicholas Gerard couldn't get Ella out of his mind. His sleep was suffering, as was his work, he couldn't concentrate on anything. He was tired and irritable, and he nodded when Paul Sampson's voice, with its deep timbre, sounded quietly. 'Go and see Ella, Nicholas. Tell her how you feel.'

'I'm sorry, Paul, I'm fit for nothing today.'

'Take my advice, my friend, and declare your love, at least then she'll know.'

'I want to, God knows I do, but what if she laughs in my face?' Nicholas asked, dragging a hand through his thick dark hair.

'What if she doesn't?'

Nicholas brought his hand down to rub his chin as he considered his business partner's words.

'I want to marry her, Paul,' he said at last.

'I guessed as much, despite you barely knowing the girl, but if you don't visit her, how can you ask the question?'

'I don't mean right now! After a suitable courtship time...'

'I know, I'm teasing you. Look, take your courage in both hands and go and invite her to dinner and the theatre. If she says no, then you will have your answer. On the other hand, she may say yes and – you'll still be hell to work with!' Paul's booming laughter filled the office.

Reaching down Nicholas's hat from the coat stand, Paul dropped it on the desk. 'Go and buy yourself a new hat and, while you're there, ask Ella Bancroft out.' With that, Paul left the room.

Nicholas snatched up the hat and dashed from the office – he would have to hurry before Ivella closed for the evening. Hailing a cab, Nicholas yelled up to the driver. 'Ivella, Walsall, as fast as you can!'

Climbing aboard, Nicholas fell into the seat as the cab lurched forward. The train would have been faster, but he had no idea of the times it left the station. He heard the clip-clop of the horse's hooves and willed it to run. He knew they couldn't pick up speed until they left the city streets and he prayed they would be in time. If he missed this opportunity, he wasn't sure he'd be able to find the courage again.

Pulling on his gold Albert chain, he flipped open his fob watch. Four-thirty. Snapping the watch closed, he returned it to his waistcoat pocket. They wouldn't make it. He'd left it too late and missed his chance. Slumping back in the seat, Nicholas Gerard felt the adrenaline drain from his body. When he arrived, the shop would be shut and he'd have to go home. The poor horse pulling the cab would be exhausted. The thought brought a feeling of guilt with it, and he decided a big tip would most definitely be in order.

Suddenly the cab picked up speed and began thundering along. Should he forget the whole idea and ask the cabbie to slow the horse and take him home? Checking the time again, he decided at least to try. Maybe by some miracle Ella would still be at the shop.

Ella was indeed still at Ivella, now sitting in the

living room, listening with mounting horror to what the policeman was telling her.

'The train driver saw a woman walking in the middle of the train tracks. He slammed on the brakes, but he couldn't avoid hitting her, I'm afraid. Once he managed to stop the train, a female passenger identified the woman as Ivy Gladwin. I'm very sorry to say Miss Gladwin was confirmed dead at the scene. The train knocked her to the side of the track, but her injuries were too great for her to survive. Please accept my condolences.'

The policeman accepted the tea Katy had made and glanced at the women's shocked faces one by one.

'I need to ask – have you any idea why Miss Gladwin would be walking the train tracks?'

'She was – unwell. She was losing her memory and was very confused. The doctor suggested I employ a full-time nurse as Ivy would only get worse as time went on,' Ella managed quietly.

'Was Miss Gladwin aware of her illness?'

'I think so – at times. At other times, she had no understanding of what was happening to her. She thought she lived in Birmingham.'

'Ah, that would explain the direction she took,' the constable said as he made notes before sipping his tea.

'What I don't understand is how Ivy didn't hear the train coming,' Ella muttered.

'You say she was forgetful?' the constable asked.

'Yes. Oh, no, do you suppose she didn't know what a train was? Could it be she was living in one of her episodes in the past before the trains came into service?'

The constable nodded. 'It's possible, and I have to say, I was wondering the same thing.'

'The poor woman,' Katy said quietly.

'Where is she?' Ella asked, her voice cracking with emotion.

'At the coroner's office. You'll be notified when her body can be released for burial.' The policeman knew this was one part of his job he would never get used to, and his heart went out to the grieving women.

'Thank you,' Ella whispered before bursting into tears.

The constable gave an imperceptible sigh of relief at seeing the woman crying. He knew all too well what bottled-up grief could do to a person, and he was further relieved when the others began to weep too. He slurped his tea as he waited for the women to gain some control over their emotions.

Eventually the weeping eased, and their handkerchiefs stifled the sniffs.

'I have one more question, and I'm so sorry, but I must ask it – do you think Miss Gladwin intended to take her own life?'

'No! Most certainly not! Ivy would never do such a thing. It's my contention she was trying to get to Birmingham and had no idea she was on the train track,' Ella stated firmly.

'Thank you, that's all I need for now. As I said, the coroner will let you know when you can collect Miss Gladwin. Once again, I'm sorry for your loss.' The constable stood and with his helmet again under his arm, he was led out through the shop by Ella.

'Thank you, constable,' Ella said as she saw him don his helmet.

'I hate bringing bad news. Good afternoon to you, Miss Bancroft.'

Ella nodded and watched the policeman stride

away. She was about to step back inside when she saw a cab come hurtling down the street, grinding to a halt in front of her.

Nicholas Gerard jumped down and said breathlessly, 'Miss Bancroft, thank goodness you're still here!'

'Mr Gerard, forgive me, but I've just received some dreadful news and I have to close the shop now. Would you be kind enough to call again another day?'

'Why yes, of course.' He could see she'd been crying by her red puffy eyes. 'Is there anything I can do?'

'No, but thank you. Now, if you'll excuse me, I don't wish to be rude but...' Ella said, stepping inside and locking the door.

Nicholas stared at the door and his heart sank. After charging from one town to another, he had arrived in time to speak to her, but something terrible had happened and she was distraught. He wondered what had had her in tears. Whatever it was, it had left her devastated. He felt disappointed – having gathered his courage at last, he was unable to speak with her. Turning back to the cab, he said with a hitch in his voice, 'Home, please – there's no rush, save your horse.'

Once his passenger was safely inside, the cabbie clicked the reins and the horse walked on. Whatever the rush was, it seemed the man was too late; the cabbie shook his head sadly.

* * *

Tilda Hunter was doing her best to learn and remember what she'd found out about the people on the list she'd been given. Unfortunately, it wasn't much. People were reluctant to speak to her about the dignitaries she enquired about, and Tilda had a strong sense of foreboding. It was all going to go wrong, she could feel it. For once, she wished she really did have the sight, because if she messed this up, she could well find herself ridiculed. If that happened, she'd have no more clients and in order to live and pay her rent, she would have to return to the streets.

Staring at the list of names, she rubbed her forehead as her mind tried to find a way out of the problem she'd brought upon herself. It was her own fault, she knew that. The thought of ten pounds in her pocket had turned her head. It was greed that had landed her in this position and now she was neck-deep in trouble.

Tilda considered cancelling by letter but that would bring an irate Darcie Newland back to her doorstep. If that happened, she could simply refuse to attend, but Darcie would most likely bandy her name about town, branding her a fraud. She was a charlatan, she took people's money under false pretences, which also made her a thief, something she could go to jail for.

No, she *had* to attend the soiree and do her best. Maybe she'd be lucky enough to have some good tells, signs or words from her audience, to lead her on the right track. Some of the folk there could be believers, but she guessed the majority would not be, otherwise she would have made their acquaintance already.

The more Tilda thought of the upcoming function, the more she fretted. Getting to her feet, she looked at her reflection in the old cracked mirror on the wall.

You still have the look of a prostitute about you, it's

something you'll never get rid of, so why try to deny your fate?

A lone tear rolled down her cheek as Tilda imagined herself once more in the profession that was as old as time; one that she'd fought so hard to leave.

32

Thora made fresh tea for want of something to do and asked, 'What will you do now, Ella?'

'I don't know. I suppose I'll have to search for a Will and a funeral plan if Ivy had one. I never did get around to asking about that.'

'We'll help,' Freda said gently.

'Thank you,' Ella replied with a sniff.

'Who was the fella you were talking to after the copper left? I had a look, but I couldn't see very well,' Katy asked.

'Oh, it was Mr Gerard.'

'What did he want?' Katy pursued.

'I have no idea. I asked him to call by another day.'

'He was after a new hat, I expect,' Freda said.

'He's just had a new one,' Katy stated.

'Maybe he wanted another!' Thora snapped.

'Ladies, please, it's not important. Right now, I need to concentrate on sorting out Ivy's paperwork,' Ella reprimanded the women gently. 'Look, you've all had a busy day, so why don't you go home?'

'I ain't going and leaving you here,' Katy said hotly.

'Me neither,' Thora said.

'Nor me,' Freda added.

'Well, in that case, let's all go home. I'll close the shop tomorrow as a sign of respect and put a notice in the window,' Ella suggested.

'Fair enough, but I'll be back in the morning to help you go through Ivy's stuff,' Katy said adamantly.

'All right. That would be very helpful indeed. Come on, let's go.'

Saying their farewells, they parted company as Ella locked the shop and set off for Silver Street.

No doubt Flossie would have heard the news by

now, but if not, Ella would have to tell her. As she slowly walked home, Ella was still trying to come to terms with Ivy's death. The final question the constable had asked came into her mind and she deliberated the answer she'd given. She had resolutely stated that Ivy would not have taken her own life, but as she thought more on it, she wondered. Did Ivy know what was happening to her? Was she aware that her illness was progressing rapidly? Would she have decided that death was preferable to losing her mind completely and having to be shut up in the asylum?

Or was it as she said, that Ivy didn't know where she was and hence her death was just an accident? Ella would never know the answer to the questions rattling around in her brain, but one thing she did know, Ivy would have a good send-off. Even if Ivy had no funeral savings plan, Ella would make sure she went out in style. Black horses with feathered plumes, a nice casket, on the top of which she would have flowers in the form of a huge hat. Ivy would have liked that, she felt sure.

She wondered who would sort out her own funeral when the time came. Shaking off the morbid thoughts, she braced herself to share the sorrowful news with Flossie.

Ella set out two cups and saucers. As usual, Flossie bustled in through the back door and plonked herself down on a kitchen chair. 'I was sorry to hear about Ivy,' she said.

Ella nodded, she wasn't surprised the news had travelled fast. Such a dreadful accident would have been spread far and wide in no time by the train passengers.

'Has she left a Will, do you know?'

'We're going through her things tomorrow. Then I'll have to organise the funeral,' Ella answered sadly.

'Look, I know you and she didn't always see eye to eye, but I also know you came to be friends in the end.'

'We did, in a strange way.'

'Did she have any family? I mean, what will happen to the shop now?'

'I don't think she had family, and as for the shop – I haven't a clue. I wonder if Paul Sampson would know.'

'Why would he? Ain't he just an accountant?'

Flossie asked, helping herself to a biscuit from the plate on the table.

'Yes, but Ivy may have left some instructions with him about what to do with the shop and monies in the event of her death.'

'Oh, ar, I see what you mean. She might have had a solicitor an' all if she made a Will.' Flossie's voice was quiet as she spoke, for she could see Ella was on the verge of tears.

'It's all so dreadful, Flossie! Fancy being killed by a train!' Ella's tears began to fall and this time she let them come.

'Was it on a purpose, do you reckon?' Flossie asked as she poured more tea, knowing it was best to let Ella cry it all out, it did no good holding on to grief.

'I did wonder that myself earlier,' Ella said as she pulled herself together and blew her nose on her handkerchief.

'Either way, I think it's a blessing in disguise.' Seeing Ella look up sharply, Flossie went on, 'Ivy was angry and frustrated at what was happening to her and she couldn't understand why. She probably would have known the doctors couldn't help her.

She was aware that it would only get worse until she was lost completely to that awful disease. Maybe she couldn't face the inevitable.'

'I wish the doctors could find a cure for it, I wonder if they ever will.'

'One day, possibly, but for now we need to make sure Ivy goes out like a class act,' Flossie said with care. 'I'll help in any way I can.'

With a grateful nod, Ella explained about the funerary arrangements she intended to make.

'Oh, I nearly forgot! This came for you today, I took it in when I saw it being delivered.'

Ella took the envelope and opened it. 'An invitation to a soiree from – Darcie Newland!'

Flossie screwed her eyes up and said, 'It came, then. Why would she be inviting you to her party?'

Ella shook her head slowly as she scanned the writing again. 'Tilda was right that I would be asked to attend, but, of course, me going is out of the question now.'

'Why?'

'I couldn't possibly go with having to make all the preparations for Ivy.'

'Ella, Ivy ain't going nowhere just yet. You have to

wait until the coroner's finished with her, then she'll go to the undertaker's Chapel of Rest while they sort out a plot for her.'

'Oh, Flossie, it all sounds – so clinical!' Ella said on a breath.

'I'm being realistic, sweet 'eart, it's how it will be and that all takes time. So, take my advice and go to this swaree – if nowt else, you can keep an eye on Tilda.'

'I suppose you're right, although I don't much feel like socialising at the moment.'

'Remember what the old 'uns used to say; if you feel down in the dumps, buy yourself a new hat! Pick one out of your new range and wear it in honour of Ivy.'

Ella gave a small smile. 'That's a lovely idea, Flossie, I'll do just that.'

'Good, and try to remember everything, because I'll want all the details, especially about how Tilda Hunter gets away with being a lying, cheating charlatan!'

33

In the shop, Ella greeted Katy, Thora and Freda with a hot drink. A notice was in the window saying that due to bereavement, the shop would be closed for the day.

'I can't say I'm looking forward to this,' Ella said.

'I know, but it has to be done,' Thora stated.

With a nod, Ella led the others upstairs to Ivy's bedroom. Opening the door, she was surprised to see the flowery wallpaper and chintz curtains. The room was light and airy with a huge oak wardrobe along one wall. The single bed was neatly made and sported an eiderdown. There was a bedside cabinet and a jug and bowl set on a chest of drawers.

'I'll look in there,' Katy said, pointing to the wardrobe.

'I'll take the cabinet by the bed,' Ella said.

'We'll do the chest of drawers then,' Freda added.

Quietly the women went about their tasks for about half an hour before Ella said, 'I've found it – Ivy's Will and funeral plan.'

Downstairs again, and with some relief, Ella opened one of the documents. 'Her funeral is all paid up, we just have to arrange it.'

'What does the Will say?' Katy asked.

'I can't...' Ella began, very close to tears again.

Thora took up the envelope and then she gasped.

'What is it?' Ella asked, full of concern.

'Ivy's left everything to – you!' Thora said as she passed the Will over for Ella to see for herself.

'Oh, my goodness!' Ella whispered.

'That was nice of her,' Freda said.

'You just have to see her solicitor and get the arrangements all finalised,' Thora said.

'At least you can stop worrying about what's happening with the shop now,' Katy added.

Ella shook her head in disbelief. Although her relationship with Ivy had softened towards the end, it hadn't always been that way. Now Ivy had left all her worldly goods to Ella. The shock had left her lost for words. The others watched as Ella dropped into a chair, still trying to process what she'd learned.

Eventually finding her tongue, Ella said, 'There's no point staying here today as we've found what we were looking for, so I suggest you all go home, and we'll open up again tomorrow.'

'What about you?' Thora asked.

'I'll take the Will to the solicitor. Then I'll visit the undertaker and let them know what's occurring with the coroner. I can sort out a package at the same time,' Ella said.

Locking up, Ella bid her staff a good day and set off for the solicitor's office. The weather was hot and before long, Ella could feel beads of sweat forming on her brow. Slowing her pace, she heard children laughing as they played in the street. She felt the ground shake beneath her feet as the tram rattled past, and she squinted her eyes against the glare of the sun, feeling cross with herself at having forgotten her parasol. Birds twittered high in the canopies of trees standing tall in the well-to-do gardens, and the church bell chimed the hour of ten o'clock. A cat yowled, followed by a dog barking as they thundered across the street in front of her.

Eventually reaching her destination, she entered the offices of Daly & Son and was led through into a room to be met by Mr Daly, who she thought must have been as old as Methuselah.

Ella handed over the Will to the kindly-looking elderly gent and smiled. His eyes belied his age and twinkled with youthful mischief.

'I'm very sorry for your loss,' Daly said as he scanned the Will.

'Thank you. I thought it best to come and see you right away. My apologies – I am Ella Bancroft.'

'I know,' Daly said, his smile lighting up his whole face, 'as does everyone in these parts.'

Surprise registered on Ella's countenance as a delicate blush rose to her cheeks.

'Miss Bancroft, your reputation is known far and wide, as is your beauty,' Daly senior said cheekily.

Ella's blush deepened and her eyes swept round the room to cover her embarrassment.

'Forgive an old man enjoying reliving his youth in admiring a charming young lady,' Daly said before getting down to business. 'This Will is in order, as it was updated five years ago.' Mr Daly pulled a folder from a cabinet next to his desk. 'Ivy came to see me when you and she became partners. She requested that you become the sole beneficiary to her estate, which includes the shop premises and the monies in her private bank account amounting to five thousand pounds.'

Ella gasped. Five thousand pounds! 'That was so very kind of her.'

'Ivy knew then she was ill, Miss Bancroft, and she wanted everything in order in case she forgot to see to it.'

'I didn't know, I didn't see it coming,' Ella whispered, her tears threatening once more.

'She wouldn't have allowed that. She was a very proud woman, Miss Bancroft, as I'm sure you know. Clearly her health deteriorated rather quickly – such a shame.' Mr Daly's eyes lost their twinkle for only a moment before he went on, 'I have to ask you to sign this document stating the estate will pass to you when it has been approved by the London Probate Office. Once that is complete, you will be informed by letter and you will have access to the bank account and the deeds to the property.'

'Thank you, and payment?' Ella asked, fumbling with her bag.

'All taken care of, Miss Bancroft, Ivy had everything in hand.'

'I see. Well, thank you again, Mr Daly.'

Ella left the elderly man wishing he was thirty years younger as he watched her sashay her way out of his office.

Walking through the town, Ella was still trying to come to terms with being named Ivy's sole beneficiary. She'd had no idea, and Ivy had never breathed a word. Giving herself an internal shake, Ella braced herself as she reached the undertaker's parlour.

A kindly woman helped her organise the funeral. A casket was chosen, and the horses and carriage arranged. The lady smiled broadly when Ella told her about the flower arrangement she had in mind.

'Most appropriate. Would you like me to order these for you?'

'Yes please, but we are awaiting notification from the coroner,' Ella explained.

'That's all right. If you let us know when you have heard from the coroner's office, we can do the rest.'

Ella thanked the woman for making the whole process as easy as it could be, before she left the parlour. Ella was pleased everything had gone so smoothly. Making her way home, she decided she would design herself a hat especially for Ivy's interment, and it would have a large feather – Ivy's favourite adornment.

No sooner had she arrived home than Flossie came rushing in. 'A bloke's been here looking for you!' she huffed.

'Who was it?' Ella asked, intrigued.

Flossie passed over a business card and after glancing at it, Ella said, 'I wonder what Nicholas Gerard wants that he would call at my home.'

Flossie shook her head, a smile on her face and her tongue pushing out her cheek. She didn't know, but she could hazard a pretty good guess.

34

Ella heard the birds singing as she walked to the shop. There were children playing and laughing in the streets and women were gossiping on their doorsteps. She returned their greetings as she passed by, shielding her eyes with her hand from the brilliant sunlight.

Arriving at Ivella, she took down the bereavement notice so that people would know it was business as usual, propping open the door for good measure. Before long, Katy arrived and immediately set about making a much-needed cup of tea. Thora and Freda followed and over their hot beverages,

Ella explained about her visits to the solicitor and undertaker.

'What's happening about Ivy's stuff?' Thora asked.

'I hadn't thought that far ahead, but it will need to be cleared out, I suppose.'

'We could do it, there's more than enough stock to see us through for a while,' Freda volunteered.

'Thank you, that would be a great help. I'm not sure Ivy's clothes would fit any of us, but if you know of anyone in need, please do help yourselves. I'm sure Ivy wouldn't want them to go into the rubbish. Katy, you can give a hand and I'll mind the shop, if you wish.'

'I'm happy to help.'

The three women trooped upstairs, leaving Ella alone with her thoughts. In the blink of an eye, everything had changed. Ivy's passing had turned Ella's world on its head and although outwardly she appeared to be coping well, on the inside, Ella was grieving. Her one-time rival who had become her business partner and friend was dead, and Ella was mourning the loss.

The sound of a little cough shattered her thoughts and Ella was surprised to see Nicholas Gerard smiling at her.

'Good morning, Mr Gerard, how may I help you?'

'You can start by calling me Nicholas,' he answered with a broad grin.

With a flush, Ella nodded.

'How are you? The last time I called, you were somewhat distressed,' Nicholas said, not wanting to pry, but needing to know she was feeling a little better.

'I am fine, thank you for asking,' Ella responded. She felt this was not the place to discuss such matters.

'May I ask, have you by chance received an invitation to the Newland soiree?'

'As a matter of fact, I have, Nicholas.'

His name on her lips sounded divine, and Nicholas felt the heat rush through his body. 'Good, so have I. Would you do me the honour of accompanying me?'

The blush on Ella's cheeks deepened as she boldly gave her answer. 'I'd be pleased to.'

'Excellent! I shall call for you at your home on Saturday at seven o'clock.'

'Thank you, I look forward to it.'

With a wave, Nicholas left the shop, a wide grin splitting his face.

Ella's smile spread as she realised he had travelled all the way from Birmingham to see her and ask her out. He could, of course, have business in Walsall, but she rather liked the idea he had come especially for her.

'Ooh,' Katy said as she entered the shop area. 'I heard what he was saying, so I waited till he'd gone.'

'That's unlike you, normally you would have come straight in to earwig.' Ella's little laugh said there was no malice in her words.

'What will you be wearing?' Katy asked, not at all offended.

'I only have one decent dress, the same one I wore to Paul's soiree.' Ella made a mental note to buy herself some new clothes as and when her inheritance came through. 'How's it going upstairs?'

'Almost done, Ivy didn't have that much, to be honest. I came down to ask if I could have this, please.' Katy held up a cream-coloured fur cape.

'Of course you can. It will go well with your colouring. Like I said, if there's anything...'

'Well, Freda has asked for the boots 'cos they fit her and Thora knows a family who have a daughter about Ivy's size.'

'I'm sure Ivy would approve.'

'Ta, I'll just go and tell the others, then.'

When Katy disappeared back upstairs, Ella's mind returned to Nicholas Gerard and his suggestion they attend the party together. That must have been why he had called at her house. Ella's stomach fluttered as she contemplated spending the evening with Nicholas, albeit in the company of others as well. But before she had time to dwell, her thoughts were disturbed by the trilling of the telephone.

* * *

Nicholas was also excited that Ella had accepted his proposal, and in the cab back to his office, he grinned like a cat who'd got the cream. Nicholas was very taken with Ella and had known from their very first meeting that he would pursue her. She set his blood on fire and his dreams were full of her. As the cab rolled along, Nicholas whistled a little ditty, barely able to wait for Saturday to arrive.

Coming to his destination, Nicholas's whistling continued until he was interrupted by his partner, Paul Sampson.

'Someone sounds happy.'

'I am, Paul. I've just made arrangements to take Ella Bancroft to the Newland soiree.'

Paul grinned. 'You dog!'

'Oh, no, it's not like that, my friend. I intend to treat this lady with total respect,' Nicholas stated.

'I'm pleased for you, and I hope it all goes well. God knows, Ella deserves some happiness in her life. She's just suffered another bereavement.'

'Oh, who?'

'Her business partner, Ivy Gladwin. I heard it on the grapevine, and I've spoken with Ella on the telephone to pay our respects.'

'I didn't know, I've just come from Ivella and she never mentioned it,' Nicholas said with a frown.

'Why would she? I'm sure you two had other things to discuss, am I right?'

'Yes, of course.'

Paul turned to leave Nicholas's office, saying, 'Don't forget to buy her a corsage.'

'I won't,' Nicholas answered before he began whistling once more. He could hear Paul's deep laugh as he walked to his own office.

I'll take Ella a bouquet as well, Nicholas thought, as he rifled through the papers in front of him. Unable to concentrate, he pushed back his chair, propped his feet on the corner of his desk, clasped his hands behind his head and with closed eyes, he conjured up an image of Ella.

'Hmm,' he said on a sigh, 'beautiful.'

* * *

On Saturday night, at seven on the dot, Nicholas banged on Ella's door and presented her with a bouquet of flowers.

'How lovely, thank you. Please come in while I put them in water,' Ella said.

Nicholas watched as Ella bustled about, finding a large jug which she half-filled with water then arranged the flowers as best as she could.

'There's this also,' Nicholas said, passing over a gardenia attached to a green ribbon. He deftly tied it about her wrist and held out her stole, which had been draped over a kitchen chair. As he laid it over her shoulders, he breathed in the fragrance of her hair and closed his eyes in an effort to commit it to memory.

Locking the door, Ella dropped the key into her drawstring bag and smiled her thanks as Nicholas helped her into the waiting carriage.

The two fell into easy conversation as they progressed towards their destination. Ella told him of how she had come to be in partnership with Ivy Gladwin and how much she loved making hats. In turn, Nicholas regaled her with his own story of studying accountancy and joining forces with Paul Sampson. Ella was very excited to be out socialising again, especially with a handsome young man like Nicholas.

When they arrived, Ella was amused to see that Darcie had hired a Master of Ceremonies, usually only seen at grand balls, for her small affair. However, Ella said nothing as Nicholas relieved her of her stole and handed it to the maid.

They were greeted at the parlour door by Darcie, who wore a bright red evening gown. 'Mr Gerard, how very nice to see you!' Darcie gushed.

'Miss Newland,' Nicholas replied, shaking the outstretched hand.

'May I introduce my fiancé, Mason Landor.'

'We are acquainted already. How are you, Mason?'

'Good, very good, Nicholath.'

Ella smiled when Darcie turned to her and said, 'You came, then.'

It was a statement which didn't call for an answer, but Ella gave one anyway. 'It would have been rude not to.'

Nicholas and Ella moved further into the room and waved at people they knew. A waiter appeared with a tray of drinks and Nicholas took two glasses of punch, handing one to Ella.

'Darcie wasn't very welcoming to you,' Nicholas whispered.

'We have a history, she and I, but the tale is not for telling this evening,' Ella replied.

Nicholas nodded with understanding. As they

mingled and spoke with other guests, neither noticed Darcie glaring at them from the doorway, a scowl on her face.

35

Rows of chairs were set out facing the huge fireplace and to the right, the French doors were propped open, leading the eye out onto the well-manicured lawns. The fragrance of jasmine floated into the room on the warm breeze and Ella moved away from its cloying scent, the rustle of her emerald-green silk dress barely audible amid the mounting chatter. Glancing through the window, she saw the sun was low in the sky and she could hear the refrains of the quartet playing in the garden. Turning, she looked around the room at the many feathered fans fluttering near faces that were flushed in the remaining heat of the day.

Taking a seat towards the back, Ella wondered how the evening would progress and whether Tilda Hunter would pull off her readings. Part of her hoped she would, for it was plain the girl needed the money. She silently prayed Tilda would adhere to her promise to ignore Ella as she moved amongst the guests.

Ella was surprised to learn that the entertainment was to take place before the meal, when usually dining took precedence. Sipping her glass of punch, Ella's eyes scanned the thickening crowd, and she smiled widely at the woman approaching her.

'Good evening, Miss Bancroft.'

'And to you, Mrs Bowen. Nice hat you have there,' Ella said with a wry grin.

'Thank you. It's an Ivella special,' Mrs Bowen said with a laugh.

Stoles, wraps and capelets were handed over to waiting maids on arrival, but the ladies' hats remained firmly pinned to high-piled curls. It was an excellent way to show off newly acquired millinery.

'I wonder what Darcie has in store for us

tonight,' Mrs Bowen mused quietly from behind her fan.

'I'm sure it will be something we will remember for a long time,' Ella replied.

'Are you in the know? Oh, do tell!'

'I'm as wise as you, Mrs Bowen.' The little white lie slipped from Ella's lips as she hoped the woman would not pursue her line of enquiry.

'Ah, then we must wait until everyone has arrived, I suppose. Excuse me, dear, I really must tell Audrey Flowers she should shop at Ivella – I can't imagine where she got that dreadful hat from.'

Ella inclined her head as the woman swept across the room.

'Do you think she'll be tactful?' Nicholas whispered in Ella's ear, making her start.

'I doubt it somehow,' she laughed as he took the seat next to her.

'Oh dear, although if Mrs Flowers takes the advice, then it will do your sales good.'

'There is that, I suppose,' Ella grinned.

'Excuse me a moment while I have a word with a colleague,' Nicholas said, then added, 'will you be all right?'

'I'll be fine,' Ella replied with a nod.

As Nicholas rose and crossed the room, Ella stood and moved towards the doorway to speak to another of her customers.

It was then that Darcie saw her opportunity and intercepted Ella whilst she had the chance. 'Why did you come tonight? I really didn't think you would have the gall to attend!'

Taken aback, Ella quickly composed herself. 'Why did you invite me?'

'I know what you're up to, Ella Bancroft, and let me tell you right now – it won't work!'

'I'm not sure what you are referring to, Darcie, but I'm certain you are wrong.'

'You don't fool me! You stole Harper Fortescue from me...'

Ella sighed. Not this again!

'... but you won't get your grubby hands on Mason!'

Ella couldn't believe what she was hearing. 'I have no designs on your intended, so let's be clear on that. Now, you didn't invite me here just to warn me off your fiancé, so what's the real reason?'

'You made my life a misery and I want you to

know that I will have recompense!' Darcie ground out.

'Revenge, you mean. And how precisely do you intend to exact that revenge?'

'You'll see. Before the night is out, everyone will know you for what you are – a jumped-up hat maker who wrecks lives! I will ensure that all and sundry ostracise you. Your business will be in ruins!'

Darcie walked away before Ella could reply. Ella felt her blood run cold at the threat. What did Darcie have planned? Ella's frown remained as Nicholas joined her once more.

'Is something wrong?' he asked as he cast a glance at Darcie, who laughed loudly at something Mason said to her.

'No, all is well,' Ella assured him, but in her heart, she knew it to be a lie. How could she relax, wondering what Darcie had in store for her? Ella deliberated feigning illness in order to leave but then she'd never know Darcie's intentions, but really she just wanted to get it over with. All she could do for now was to grin and bear it and see what transpired.

Unbeknown to either of the women, Tilda Hunter

had heard every word. She had stood behind the slightly open door and listened intently to the threats Darcie issued. Knowing a good deal about both Ella and Darcie from her enquiries, Tilda knew that it had been Harper who had called off his engagement to the bad-tempered Miss Newland. Ella was innocent of the accusations thrown at her, and Tilda found her to be a kind and caring person. As far as she knew, Ella had not breathed a word of what Tilda had told her about her past, as she had promised.

Tilda nodded as she thought, one good deed deserves another. Her mind made up, she readied herself for the performance of her life.

'Ladies and gentlemen, please be seated.' The voice of the Master of Ceremonies boomed out and the music and conversations ceased. There was a scraping of chairs on the polished mahogany floor as ladies settled their ball gowns comfortably into place. Low mutterings began as people tried to guess what was to come.

Ella's heartbeat increased as Darcie took centre stage and called for attention. 'I have something very special for your delectation, which I know you will enjoy. Ladies and gentlemen, please welcome my guest, Tilda Hunter!'

There was polite applause as Darcie took her seat.

Ella swallowed and waved her fan beneath her chin. This was it!

Tilda entered the room, her heavily painted face causing a few gasps from the women in her audience. Her dress was cotton and had seen better days, but it was clean, and her boots had been given a polish.

'Hello, everyone, I'm Tilda and I'm a medium.'

More gasps greeted this pronouncement as she stood facing the guests. Surprised glances were exchanged as excited chatter began.

Ella noticed some of the men rolling their eyes, clearly disbelievers.

'I have a lady here who says her name is Maud. Is there a connection anywhere in the room, please?'

Ella winced, reminded of Flossie's words about how Tilda should be telling rather than asking. Her head swung round as a woman called out, 'Yes, here!'

Tilda moved a couple of steps towards the

woman who had spoken. 'Thank you, this is your mother?'

'Yes, she passed some years ago!' the woman said, already seemingly taken in by Tilda.

'I see a walking stick...' Tilda went on.

'Yes! She had a limp!'

'She's thrown the stick away. She's telling me she no longer has need of it.'

'Thank the good Lord!' the woman said, dabbing her eyes with a small lacy handkerchief.

Tilda smiled when the mutterings began again. It was working, they were being drawn in. All she had to do was hold her nerve and everything would be all right. 'Maud is saying your husband will prosper further with his business of saddlery.'

Hearing the sharp intake of breath, Tilda pushed on. 'There will be a christening and you will be asked to be godmother.'

'How wonderful!' the woman sobbed openly now.

'Who is Albert?'

The woman shook her head. 'I don't know.'

'Anyone else? Who knows an Albert?'

Ella felt her stomach clench as no one admitted

to knowing an Albert who had passed over, despite the popularity of the name.

'No matter. I have a tall man in a dark suit – he's asking for Miss Newland.'

Darcie's face lit up at the news, enjoying all eyes on her.

'He's saying there are times when your temper gets the better of you and you must beware of this.'

The grin slipped from Darcie's face to be replaced by a scowl, but Tilda added quickly, 'I see a wedding. It will be a grand affair and there will be children in the not too distant future.'

Polite applause filled the room and Darcie nodded in response.

'Yes, the lady in question, I'm being told, is not a friend as such, but she will be happy for the rest of her life.'

Darcie clamped her teeth together in order not to call out her dismay.

'You were betrothed once before, but it was not meant to be, the gentleman is saying...'

Ella gave a little cough as she sipped her punch and it caught in the back of her throat. Harper! Could it be true? Smiling at Nicholas, who tapped her back gently, Ella nodded, affirming she was fine. She knew Tilda was a fake, but she still so wanted to believe.

The quiet buzz of voices faded as Tilda went on, oblivious to the glare aimed at her by Darcie. 'The wedding was called off and you were left...'

'Thank you, Tilda! Maybe the other guests might like a message.' Darcie was furious. How dare the stupid girl bandy about such private information! How did she know that Darcie had been jilted by Harper Fortescue?

Mason placed a hand on Darcie's arm, but she shrugged it off angrily.

Taking the hint, Tilda moved on around the room and as she went from person to person, she felt her confidence increasing. But it wasn't long before she began to drop in little things that would have been better kept secret, as far as Ella was concerned. Tilda informed a chain-making giant that his rival – who unbeknown to her was sitting a few seats away – would cause ructions over pricing anomalies. To another man, she said he would soon be marrying the girl who he had been courting, much to his wife's disgust. The pair had not been sitting close together and Tilda had no idea they were married. The more Tilda went on, the more everything began spiralling out of control.

Voices were raised in anger as couples argued. Women screeched as they accused their husbands of being unfaithful, their men trying in vain to deny any such thing ever having taken place.

Darcie attempted to regain some sense of decorum, but to no avail, and she shrank back when her guests turned on her, shouting with displeasure at her choice of entertainment.

People started to file out of the room, calling for their capes and stoles. They marched out of the house, yelling for their carriages to be brought round, letting Darcie know in no uncertain terms that they would not be attending any more of her soirees in the future.

Darcie was aghast at how the evening had disintegrated before it had even begun. She was running around, trying desperately to coax her guests back into the house so they could enjoy their dinner. She was apologising left, right and centre in the hope that folk would forgive her faux pas and stay, but it was a forlorn wish. There was a mass exodus as people fled, pushing her aside in their hurry to leave.

Tilda Hunter, seeing how her performance had gone, had slipped out of the French doors and took to her heels across the lawns, down the drive and out onto the streets, glad she had taken Ella's advice and got payment first.

Ella and Nicholas stared around them, their mouths open in disbelief at the chaos surrounding them. Then Nicholas helped Ella to her feet. 'Time for us to go, I think,' he said quietly.

'I agree,' Ella replied.

Nicholas retrieved her stole and they too left via the open doors into the garden.

Seeing her safely into his carriage, Nicholas asked, 'Are you hungry?'

'I'm famished! I was rather looking forward to dinner,' Ella replied.

'Then that is what you shall have.' Nicholas called out to his jarvey and the carriage slowly manoeuvred its way through the throng of very disgruntled people to roll down the gravel driveway.

36

It was over dinner in a swanky hotel that Ella quietly told Nicholas about Darcie being jilted by Harper, so that he could become engaged to Ella. With sadness, she explained about Harper's death, then went on to relate how Darcie had been whisked off to Scotland by her embarrassed parents.

'A sorry tale – for you both,' Nicholas said with feeling as she finished speaking.

Ella nodded. 'I met Tilda a little while ago and my friend and neighbour exposed her as a fraud.'

'I did wonder,' Nicholas said with a little smile.

'I'm afraid Darcie's soiree was not the success she had hoped it would be.'

'Indeed not. The gossip will abound, and Judge Landor will not be at all amused,' Nicholas concurred.

'Poor Darcie. I can't help but feel sorry for her,' Ella added.

'I know it sounds harsh, but she brought it on herself.'

Ella sighed heavily, knowing Nicholas was right in what he said.

'Now, tell me more about you,' Nicholas said and was pleased to see Ella smile once more.

The evening passed pleasantly, and eventually Nicholas delivered Ella safely to her door. 'May I call on you again?'

'I'd like that.' Ella's cheeks burned as he kissed her hand, and she was glad it was too dark for him to see her longing that the kiss might have been on her lips.

'Until the next time,' Nicholas said as she let herself into the house.

'Thank you for a lovely evening.' Ella closed and re-locked the door after watching Nicholas climb into his carriage. Going straight to bed, Ella guessed that sleep would evade her, thoughts of her delightful time spent with Nicholas Gerard crowding her mind.

* * *

Darcie Newland was screaming with disgust at how her soiree had been ruined by Tilda Hunter.

'Calm down, my cherub,' Mason tried to placate his irate fiancée.

'How can I? That stupid woman has made me a laughing-stock! By the morning, it will be all over town how disastrous the whole thing was! I won't be able to hold my head up in polite society!'

'Don't take on, my darling, it wathn't that bad,' Mason lisped.

'But it was! It was a complete and utter shambles! All that money spent and food wasted!'

'It'th of no importanth, my thweet.'

'Mason, it's of the utmost importance! Whatever will your father say when he hears about it?' Seeing his pallor change, Darcie spat, 'Precisely!'

* * *

Ella was still feeling sleepy when she answered the knock on her door and was astounded to see Tilda Hunter standing there, looking sheepish.

'Come in and have some tea.'

Tilda followed Ella into the kitchen and took a seat. She almost jumped out of her skin when Flossie came bursting in. 'Well, how did it go?'

Ella and Tilda exchanged a worried glance, then Tilda said, 'Exactly to plan.'

Ella frowned. 'What do you mean? It was a complete disaster!'

'Exactly!'

Over tea, Tilda explained how she'd overheard the conversation between Ella and Darcie. 'So I thought to myself, I'm not having that! Darcie Newland was out to ruin your good name, Ella, but before she could, I decided to throw a spanner in her works.'

'Ooh! How?' Flossie asked. 'Tell me everything!' She leaned forward in her chair and rested her arms on the table.

Tilda did, and when she'd finished, Flossie and Ella were grinning.

'We shouldn't laugh, there are some very unhappy people in Birmingham today,' Ella said.

'Not for long,' Tilda put in. 'I've written to everyone who attended last night. I told them what Darcie was up to, but I didn't divulge what was said between you two, just that she was out to besmirch your reputation out of pure spite. I also apologised for telling them lies, which was what my readings were, because I'm not a medium at all. I ended with hoping to be forgiven and that I would be changing my profession.'

'Well, damn my eyes!' Flossie gasped.

'Oh, Tilda, thank you for saving me but at the cost of your work! What will you do now?' Ella asked.

'I don't know, but I have to get out of Birmingham. I can't pay my rent, so I'll be kicked out by the landlord, and I don't fancy having Darcie bloody Newland bringing the coppers down on me.'

'She couldn't do that, could she?' Ella asked worriedly.

'I ain't sure, but I agree with Tilda, she needs to get gone and as soon as possible,' Flossie answered.

As Tilda got to her feet to leave, a thought struck

Ella like a thunderbolt. 'How would you like to live in Walsall?' she asked.

* * *

Judge Joseph Landor stared down at his son as they sat in the study of the Judge's massive house, whisky glasses in hand.

The judge was rotund with a red nose and cheeks acquired from years of imbibing alcohol. His silver hair, beard and moustache were neatly trimmed, and his dark eyes appeared to hold no mercy.

'I warned you, Mason. I told you not to get involved with that woman.'

Mason stared at his drink, unable to meet his father's cruel eyes.

'But no, you wouldn't listen. Now you find yourself at the centre of a scandal. Do you realise how badly this reflects on my name and my being a judge? I'll be a laughing-stock in my own court room!'

'I'm thorry, father, but I love Darthie,' Mason protested.

'Don't be ridiculous, Mason!' Joseph snapped. 'You are infatuated, nothing more! The woman is a divorcée, for God's sake! I also heard she stabbed her husband but no charges were brought against her. It's a good job she didn't find herself in my court, otherwise she'd have been in jail by now!'

'Father...' Mason tried again.

Joseph held up his hand to forestall his son whining in defence of Darcie. 'I don't want to hear it, Mason! Now, if you wish to remain living under my roof, you will distance yourself from the Newland girl. Though why you are still residing here at your age defeats logic as far as I'm concerned.'

'Mother thaid...' Mason began.

'Of course. Your mother has you tied to her apron strings. You have your own house, Mason, the one I paid for, may I remind you, but you moved *her* into it! I don't understand you, boy!'

Joseph swallowed the last of his drink and poured himself another before speaking again. 'You have a life of luxury in my house, you eat food I pay for, and you don't work, but let me tell you right now – that is about to change! Firstly, you will break off your engagement to

Newland, then you must oust her from your property.'

'Where will thee go?' Mason asked.

'I don't know and what's more, I don't care! As of today, the woman is no longer your problem.'

'But Father...'

'I'll hear no more, Mason. You get rid of her today or I'll cut you off without a penny!'

Mason knew he was beaten. He couldn't envisage having to work for a living. He relied upon his father for everything and couldn't contemplate any other way of life. Mason nodded compliantly.

'Good. Ensure you see to it today!' Joseph didn't wait for a reply but strode from the study, leaving his son feeling wretched.

Throughout the day, the notes Tilda had penned were delivered and read. The upset of the previous night between husbands and wives, as well as business rivals, was smoothed over by her words. However, the matter would not rest there, for gossip would keep it alive for a while to come.

Good news travelled fast, but bad news was transferred even more rapidly, and before the day's end, Darcie Newland was considered an outcast by people of import. Her telephone calls went unanswered and her visits would be shunned from now on. Darcie found herself ostracised, unable to do a damned thing about it.

Staring at Mason, standing now in what she considered *her* parlour, Darcie tapped her foot.

'I have been inthructed to break off our engagement by Father,' Mason said.

'You're not serious?' Darcie asked incredulously.

'I'm afraid I am.'

'Mason, you're a man now! You don't have to obey your father like a little boy!' Darcie spat.

'I'm thorry, my dear.' Mason turned to leave, then added, 'I will need you to leave the houthe, too. You have until the end of the day to vacate the property.' He walked out without a backward glance. He loved Darcie, but he loved money more.

Darcie dropped onto a chair and looked around her. How had it all gone so wrong? Her soiree had been a shambles and now her name was mud. Mason had left her and she had to give up the house he had set her up in. Where would she go? How would she live? Despair gripped her in its icy fist as an image of the workhouse crept into her mind.

Then the picture changed to first Tilda Hunter then to Ella Bancroft; despair turned to anger as she considered these two women to be the cause of her downfall.

Picking up an ornament, a porcelain shepherd boy, she threw it with all her might into the fireplace, where it shattered into a thousand pieces. 'You won't get away with this, either of you!' she muttered. 'I'll see you ruined yet, Ella Bancroft!'

37

By the time Ella and Tilda reached Ivella, the news of the disastrous soiree was abroad.

After asking Tilda to wait outside for a moment while she spoke to everyone, Ella called a meeting of the staff and outlined her plan before asking for their opinions.

'It's fine by me,' Katy said.

'Me an' all,' Thora added.

'Freda?' Ella asked.

'After what you've just told us, I believe Tilda should be given a chance. I agree.'

Ella nodded and, going to the door, she beckoned Tilda to join them. 'Everyone is in agreement;

welcome to Ivella, Tilda. I just have one request – leave off the make-up, please. You really don't need it, you're pretty enough without it.'

'Fair dos. Thank you, everyone.'

'Bring your things today. We need to get you moved in as soon as possible.'

'I'll go now then.' With that, Tilda left to gather her few belongings.

'Now we have a cook and cleaner,' Ella said. 'I hope it all works out.'

'That Miss Newland sounds a right sort, and it's my guess she ain't finished with you yet,' Thora added.

'I suspect you could be right,' Ella replied as a shiver took her. 'We'll have to wait and see what she has planned, but for now, we should get back to work.'

Tilda arrived back in the afternoon by cab but with very little in the way of possessions. Ella had said she could live in Ivy's private quarters and, before long, she was settled. Once in the kitchen, Tilda made tea, saying, 'That bloody landlord tried to make me pay rent to the end of the month!'

'That's outrageous!' Ella exclaimed.

'I told him where to go. Then he said as I should show him a good time before I left.'

'Good grief, has the man no scruples?'

'No, Ella.' Then, on a sob, Tilda explained how she'd had to pay in kind when she'd had no money.

'Oh, Tilda!' Ella wrapped her arm about the young woman's shoulder. 'It's over now, you don't have to do that ever again.'

'Thanks to you,' Tilda sniffed. 'I won't let you down, Ella, I promise. You've been good to me and I won't forget it.'

'Good, now how about we both do some work?'

Tilda smiled and, after rooting around in the kitchen, she set herself to making some bread.

Ella left her to it and went to the back room to continue adjusting her sketches. She was designing a new range of hats for the autumn, which she realised would be upon them in no time. Looking at her drawings, Ella wondered how long the large hats would be fashionable. With a sigh, Ella thought there was no telling, but she certainly hoped it would last until the year's end. This was one time she wished Tilda was a true medium and could foretell the future; with a shake of her head, she picked up her pencil and began work.

At closing time, Ella presented Tilda with Ivy's set of keys. 'I'll see you in the morning. Will you be all right here alone?'

'I'll be fine. Thanks, Ella.'

Once everyone had gone, Tilda wandered around the place, familiarising herself with her new surroundings. She'd landed on her feet and knew she was very lucky. She would adhere to her promise not to let Ella down and felt fortunate to be able to call Ella her friend.

Back in the kitchen, Tilda cut the fresh bread and, with some cheese and chutney and a cup of tea, she sat by the open door of the range. After a while, the heat from the oven made her drowsy so, after washing the plate and cup, Tilda made her way to bed. Leaving the curtains open, she watched the clouds pass over the moon and sighed with contentment.

'Thanks again, Ella,' she whispered as she snuggled down on the soft mattress. Closing her eyes, Tilda instinctively knew she would have the best night's sleep of her life.

* * *

The pattering of rain on the windows woke Ella the next morning and she rose with a sigh. Umbrella weather, she thought, as she washed and dressed. Gazing out of the window drinking her tea, Ella wondered how Tilda had fared overnight. The girl was used to living alone, but in new accommodation, would loneliness have made its presence known? It did for Ella, often. Shaking off the depressing thought, she readied herself for what the oncoming day had to offer.

Trudging through the streets, her umbrella low over her head, she heard the delighted shouts of children as they splashed in the dirty puddles. Mothers yelled for their offspring to 'get out of the bloody 'ossroad!' Picking up her skirt, Ella dodged a pile of faeces left behind by a stray dog. She saw the filthy water running down the road and jumped over the stream so as not to soak her boots.

Arriving at the shop as the church clock struck eight, Ella was surprised to be greeted by a clean-faced Tilda holding out a steaming cup of coffee. Shaking her umbrella outdoors, she smiled and took the cup. 'Thank you. What a day! You look lovely, Tilda.'

The lack of heavy make-up had not gone unnoticed, and Tilda beamed. 'Ta. I've swept and polished and I thought to make fish pie for lunch.'

'Sounds wonderful,' Ella remarked as she followed Tilda into the kitchen, where she placed her umbrella over the sink to dry out.

'You'll need to go to the market then, I take it?'

'Yes, if we're to have pie, I will.'

Ella passed over some money for Tilda to get what was needed for the larder.

'How did you sleep?'

'Like the dead.' Tilda grinned. 'I'll need something to keep me busy, though, once the pie is made.'

Ella blew out her cheeks as she considered Tilda's words. She should have realised that making meals and dusting around would not be enough to keep the young woman busy for long. 'Can you sew?'

'Yes, why?'

'Come with me.' Ella led Tilda to the workroom and showed her what Thora and Freda did for a living.

'I could do that,' Tilda said as she examined the work.

'When you've finished downstairs, come to Thora and Freda. They'll give you some instruction. That would be a massive help.'

'What would?' Thora asked as she and Freda came in and took off their wet coats.

Ella explained and requested that the women induct Tilda into the world of millinery.

'Certainly we will. Come up when you're ready,' Freda said, taking her place at the work bench.

'Thank you, ladies. I'll have some new ideas for you soon.' Ella smiled and left them to chat, while Tilda set off for the market.

It was around mid-morning when Katy rushed through to where Ella was working. 'There's a bloke here for you!'

'Who is it?' Ella asked with a frown.

'Ella, I'm up to my eyeballs in women and hats! That gossip about the soiree is bringing them in here in droves. They're coming out of the woodwork!'

'Sorry, I'll come at once.'

Waiting patiently in the shop was Nicholas Gerard. He smiled as he watched the gaggle of women try on the hats, all talking at once.

'Hello, would you mind? I'll only be a moment,' Ella said as she waved an arm in the direction of the gossiping women.

Nicholas grinned and nodded towards the customers.

Ella dived in, asking who she could help first. With Ella and Katy working flat out, the customers were soon served, and Ella invited Nicholas into the back room.

'You're very busy today,' he said, taking a seat.

'The soiree, it seems everyone is looking for gossip as well as a hat,' Ella said by way of explanation.

'Ah, of course.'

Over tea, he showed her the letter he'd received from Tilda and she told him about Tilda's new home and employment. She then went on to relate the conversation between Darcie and herself and how Tilda had thwarted the woman's attempt to sully her reputation.

'So we thought it best for her to come here in case of any repercussions from Darcie.'

'Sensible, there's no knowing what might happen,' Nicholas concurred.

Ella was pleased he agreed with her decision to provide Tilda with a home and job.

Nicholas picked up one of her sketches. 'You are very talented,' he said as he glanced through the others laid out on the small table.

'Thank you.' Ella blushed prettily.

'I came to invite you to dine with me,' Nicholas said, looking her directly in the eye.

'Oh, well... yes, I'd be delighted.'

'I'll collect you at seven, then.'

Ella nodded, her heart racing. Seeing him out, she returned to the back room, but her excitement would give her no peace.

She had loved Harper Fortescue with every fibre of her being, but she knew it was time now to leave him in the past. Chewing the end of her pencil, Ella hoped she was doing the right thing in allowing herself to become involved with Nicholas. As she thought about their forthcoming evening together, she knew it was already too late to worry – she was head over heels in love with Nicholas Gerard.

38

Darcie Newland had sat for a long time, trying to fathom out how she had become reduced to being alone once more. Mason had left her. That in itself was no great loss, she decided, for she had never intended to marry the lisping fool anyway. However, with him had gone her abode and the money he provided, to say nothing of the prestige.

There would be no more shopping in the best stores or visiting the theatre, and invites to parties and balls would cease. She had nowhere to go and nothing to go with, having depleted her coffers.

What she needed was another rich man to pander to her needs. The question was, how would she find one now she would no longer be amongst the elite?

Clenching her fists, she banged them on her skirts. *Damn you, Ella Bancroft, this is your doing!* The thought sliced through her mind like a dagger.

Unable to decide how to proceed, she had stamped off to bed in a foul temper. Now, in the cold light of day, Darcie made up her mind – she would stay put. She defied Mason to throw her out onto the streets, for if he tried, she would kick up a stink. The name of Mason Landor would be on everyone's lips as a cad for heartlessly dumping his fiancée. She would ensure that he would be seen as the villain of the piece; that he had callously jilted her because of the unfortunate incident at her soiree.

Her plan had been to guide Tilda to centre her attention on Ella and bring forth all the details of the girl's background. Had that idea not come to fruition, it was of no consequence, for Darcie fully intended to whisper into ears as she circulated amongst her guests. She wanted it known that Ella Bancroft was the cause of her misery. That Darcie's parents had had to flee to Scotland to avoid the scandal surrounding their daughter's failed marriage to a man she had wed but never loved, after Ella had stolen Harper away from her.

Darcie felt the catch in her throat as she was reminded of the heartache of being jilted previously, and now Mason had done the same thing. Was she destined never to be happily married? Would she go through life bouncing from one man to the next without ever being able to settle? All she wanted was a rich husband who would treat her like a queen, which she didn't think was too much to ask for.

Until that time, Darcie would continue to live in the house Mason provided for her. She would have a box at the theatre and go alone, and she would still do her shopping at the most expensive places, with the bills being sent to Mason as usual. And just in case, Darcie would set out to purchase some high-quality jewellery as insurance. It would be a good investment and one never knew when desperation might call for it to be sold on and the proceeds pocketed. Now would be the best time to buy – before Mason refused to pay any more towards her upkeep.

Darcie snatched up her drawstring bag and marched out into the street where she waved to a cabbie, feeling a whole lot better about the situation she found herself in. She was going on the mother of all shopping sprees while she still had the chance.

* * *

Ella had received the letter from the coroner's office. She opened it and read that Ivy's body was being released for burial. It had been concluded that Ivy's death was accidental, at which Ella let out a sigh of relief. The thought that Ivy might have taken her own life had worried Ella, and would have made it impossible for the interment to have taken place on consecrated ground. Now that worry could be laid to rest with her friend.

Going up to the workroom to inform the others of the outcome of the coroner's report, Ella was pleased to see Tilda was getting along splendidly with Thora and Freda.

'I'll take this letter to the undertaker and then finally Ivy can be buried,' Ella said sadly.

Once Ella had left, talk in the workroom turned to Ella's past.

'I learned a lot about her from the market wenches,' Tilda said.

'Ella's had it hard over the years,' Freda added, 'but it hasn't changed her. She's still a lovely young woman. All she needs is a husband.'

'That Mr Gerard would fit that role, if you ask me,' Thora said, her eyes on the needle stitching a crown band to a straw boater.

'I think she's scared,' Freda replied.

'Of what?' Tilda asked.

'Of getting too attached.'

'Why?' Thora laid down her work.

'In case anything should happen to him.'

'Like Harper Fortescue dying before they could be wed, you mean?'

Freda nodded.

Turning to Tilda, Thora said, 'It's a pity you ain't really got the sight.'

Tilda merely shrugged her shoulders. How many times had she wished the same thing? Instead, she said, 'I'll go and make us all a drink.'

Ella had arranged for Ivy to be buried two days hence. The funeral parlour, having all the details now, had given Ella the next available time slot in their busy schedule. After a short service in the small church in White Street, Ivy would be conveyed to the town cemetery, which lay next to the gas works. Thinking about her friend as she walked along, Ella hoped Ivy would approve of the funeral package Ella had chosen for her. A small smile played on Ella's lips as she thought Ivy would complain at the extra monies paid for the black-plumed horses and the flowers in the shape of a hat. Ella hadn't minded stumping up the extra few pounds in order to give Ivy the good send-off she'd promised.

The sun beat down on Ella's shoulders as she meandered the streets towards Ivella. She watched a gang of children dashing along, following their leader, who rolled a hoop with a stick. Their shrieks of laughter echoed between the buildings as the hoop fell and another child took a turn. A cat with its back arched hissed from a garden wall at the little dog who yapped and jumped in an effort to reach the feline. The coal man whistled a happy tune from the seat of his cart as it trundled past, his hands and face covered in black dust.

Arriving back at the shop, Ella was greeted by Tilda and Katy and a glass of cool lemonade. She then informed everyone that the shop would be closed on the day of the funeral as a mark of respect.

'Oh, by the way, Ella, a note came for you while you were out,' Katy said as she handed over the envelope.

Ella read the note in the back room and the colour drained from her face.

I warned you! Keep looking over your shoulder, Ella Bancroft!

39

In Birmingham, Darcie had also received a letter – from Mason Landor's solicitor. It was to instruct her she must vacate Mr Landor's property forthwith. Should she not comply with this request by the end of the week, police would be despatched to remove her and her belongings.

Darcie slammed the letter onto the table in disgust. She had only a few days to find alternative accommodation before the bobbies landed on the doorstep to physically turf her out. Initially she had planned to stay in the property, but on second thoughts, she realised it would only harm her reputation even more.

Leaving the note where it was, Darcie ran upstairs to pack her clothes. The house and furniture belonged to Mason, so she had no worries about having to rent storage space.

As she folded her clothes and placed them in a trunk, Darcie ground out, 'You're a pig, Mason Landor! I will ensure your name is dragged through the mud for this!'

Once the packing was finished, Darcie returned to the lower floor and rang for the maid.

'Fetch a cabbie!' she instructed.

The maid bobbed a knee and left, returning moments later. 'Cabbie's here, miss.'

Flicking her fingers to dismiss the maid, Darcie told the cabbie to bring her luggage downstairs and load it into his cab.

The cabbie was about to protest that he drove the cab and was not a porter, but seeing the scowl on Darcie's face, he thought better of it. The man muttered under his breath as he ascended the staircase. 'Bloody woman, there'd better be a big tip for all this.'

Darcie ignored his mumblings as she returned to the parlour and began selecting items and placing them in a Gladstone bag. She was after useful things to sell on when her money ran low – not that she had much to begin with. A silver snuff box followed a small clock, along with porcelain figurines. Closing the bag, she carried it into the hall. She watched the cabbie struggling with the trunk, but eventually he managed to load it onto the cab. Taking the bag outside, she snapped, 'Be careful with that!'

Returning to the parlour, she grabbed her drawstring bag and parasol. With a last look around, she turned on her heel and left the house for the final time.

The maid and cook had been peeking around the kitchen door, and once the mistress had left, they scuttled into the parlour to look out of the window.

'The clock's gone – and some other stuff,' the maid said as she glanced around.

'I ain't surprised, look at this.' The cook passed the letter over which she'd picked up off the table.

'You know I can't read!' the maid said as she held out the letter.

'Give it here!' The cook snatched the paper back and read it aloud to the maid.

'Bloody hell!' the maid gasped. 'What happens to us now?'

The cook shook her head, replying, 'Buggered if I know.'

* * *

Darcie glowered as the cabbie took her to a hotel as instructed. Helping her to alight, he turned to unload her luggage.

'Be careful...'

'I know, I heard you the first time,' the cabbie said.

Darcie snorted, watching him place the Gladstone bag on the ground beside her. He then heaved the heavy trunk down and set it next to the bag, before holding out his hand for payment.

'You'll have to carry it inside,' Darcie said sternly.

'I'm a cabbie, missus, not a porter,' he replied, having had enough of being told what to do by this woman.

'How am I to manage?'

'Look, lady, that's not my problem. Now pay up before I fetch a bobby.'

Darcie rummaged in her bag and found the exact coinage.

Tipping his hat, the cabbie dropped the money into his pocket and climbed aboard. 'Miser,' he mumbled. He'd guessed from the outset that a tip, if any at all, would be small. Therefore, when he received nothing, he was not surprised, but he was most disgruntled.

Darcie watched the cab roll away then glanced down at her baggage. Picking up the bag, she walked into the hotel and immediately spying a porter, she sent him to collect her trunk.

With what remained of her allowance from Mason, she booked a room and meals for a week. She considered that to be quite long enough to conduct her business. Once that was completed, Darcie intended to board a train to London. If one wished to bag a rich gentleman, then the capital was the place to be.

* * *

Ella had pushed the poisonous note into her bag and tried to forget about it, but it would give her no peace. Although there had been no signature, Ella was certain she knew who it was from. It had to be Darcie Newland.

Ella guessed that one day there would be a face-to-face confrontation, and it would not be pretty. She was also aware that she would have to keep an eye out, for there was no telling what Darcie might do.

Glancing at her bag, she wondered if it might be sensible to tell someone about the note. She thought it unwise to mention it to her staff, she didn't want them to worry about her. She also didn't want them to be uncomfortable or afraid to come to work. Ella considered telling Nicholas but quickly dismissed the idea. She didn't know him nearly well enough as yet to lay something like this on him. She was embarrassed about her connection with Darcie, as it linked back to Harper.

Ella sighed, trying her best to concentrate on her designs. In the end, she threw down her pencil and wandered into the shop, just in time to hear the tail end of a conversation between two customers.

'Mason Landor has thrown her out, I tell you! I have it on the best authority!' one said.

'It's hardly surprising after that farce of a party. Whatever was she thinking?' replied the other.

'I don't know, but the stuck-up Miss Newland is no longer betrothed to the judge's son.'

Ella slipped quietly to the back room, where she tried to process what she'd heard. Had Landor called off the engagement, or had Darcie? If she no longer lived in that house, then where was she? Was she still in Birmingham? Or had she come to Walsall? Ella wondered if she was in danger. The words on the note came to mind again and Ella felt a shiver run down her spine.

40

That evening, when Ella locked the shop, she looked warily around her before she rushed home, all the time aware that she could be being watched. She wondered if she was being paranoid, but felt she should be cautious nevertheless.

Once home and safely indoors, a sigh of relief escaped her lips. She set the kettle to boil and fed the range. Then she sat at the table, feeling tears prick her eyes. It was ridiculous, but her fear was almost tangible. She had only received the note that day and already she was scared witless.

The back door opened, and Ella jumped up.

'Blimey, cocka, you're jumpy,' Flossie said as she walked in.

'Sorry, I didn't hear you,' Ella replied.

Making tea for them both, Ella's hands shook, and it didn't go unnoticed by her neighbour. 'What's up?'

'Nothing,' Ella said quietly.

'Well, that *nothing* has you shaking like a leaf, so much so that I fear that cup and saucer will meet the floor sometime soon.'

All day, Ella had fretted, now she was overcome and she burst into tears.

Flossie rushed to wrap her arms around her young friend. 'That's it, lass, let it come, then we can have a sup and you can tell me all about it.'

Dragging her emotions under control, Ella pulled out the note and passed it to Flossie.

'What the...? Is this from that bloody Newland girl, do you think?'

'I'm not sure, but I suspect so,' Ella said with a sniff.

'You should take this to the coppers, see what they have to say about it,' Flossie advised.

'The police won't do anything, Flossie, we can't prove Darcie sent it.'

'True, but you can't let it get to you like this. Look at the state of you!'

'I can't deny I'm worried, but there's nothing to be done until whoever sent that makes a move.' Ella nodded at the note on the table as she spoke.

'I see your point, but I ain't happy about it. What about we visit Newland and have it out with her once and for all?'

Ella then explained about the conversation she'd overheard in the shop. 'So you see, she could be anywhere.'

Flossie sighed loudly before muttering, 'Bloody woman! She's a menace!' Then, as an afterthought, she asked, 'Ain't you off out with Nicholas tonight?'

Ella nodded.

'Right then, you best get yourself ready. When he gets here, you show him this.' Flossie waved the note in the air before replacing it on the table.

'Flossie, I don't think that's such a good idea.'

'Yes, it is. He might have a solution, but you won't know that if you keep it a secret. Besides, you'll be poorly and terrible company if you worry about it all the time.'

'I'll consider it,' Ella relented, knowing her friend was right.

That evening, over dinner in a swanky hotel, Ella was quiet. She was consumed with the note and whether it was, in fact, from Darcie. Who else could it be?

'Are you quite well, Ella?' Nicholas asked, concerned that Ella's mind was elsewhere.

'Yes, I'm sorry. I'm just tired.'

'You should have cancelled.'

'Oh, no! I wouldn't dream of it. I...'

Nicholas waited for her to continue. There was definitely something she needed to get off her chest.

Reaching into her bag, Ella pulled out the note and passed it over. She watched his eyebrows rise before his eyes moved back to hers.

'Have you any idea who sent it?'

Ella voiced her suspicions. 'I can't prove it, of course.'

'You must take it to the police,' Nicholas insisted.

'What can they do? There's no signature, no proof.'

Nicholas nodded at the truth of her words. 'I'm worried for you, Ella! Let me inform the constabulary, they may be able to keep an eye on you.'

Ella smiled at his small admission of his feelings for her. Her heart skipped a beat and her stomach flipped as she returned the note to her bag.

'Thank you, but no. Let's speak no more about it. Instead, let us make the most of our time together,' she said boldly.

The rest of the evening passed with a visit to the music hall and, very slowly, Ella began to relax. By the time Nicholas took her home, Ella had all but forgotten the note.

* * *

Ella felt sad as she dressed. It was the morning of Ivy's funeral. Ella, Thora, Katy, Freda and Flossie met at the shop. Attired in black, they walked to the undertaker's.

The large wooden gates were open and the two black horses sporting feather plumes waited patiently. The carriage behind them held Ivy's coffin, and the floral hat tribute was carefully fastened to the top in case of a sudden gust of wind. The driver and conductor came forward and tipped their top hats in respect before taking up their positions. Ella was almost undone at the beautiful gesture.

The conductor led the procession forward and the five mourners walked behind the carriage towards the cemetery.

Ella appreciated the respect shown by people as they passed. Men removed their flat caps and rested them on their chests. Women gathered their unruly children close to them, making the sign of the cross as the cortege passed by.

At the graveside, the five women said a silent goodbye to Ivy as the vicar droned on about the deceased, a woman he had never met. Ella struggled to hold back her tears as the vicar spoke, but when it came to dropping a handful of earth on the coffin, Ella's emotions erupted. She sobbed as the others completed the ritual and she felt Flossie's arm around her waist.

The short service over, Ella thanked the clergyman, who then walked away, leaving the women to their grief. Gathered around the grave, the women came together in a huddle, their arms around each other as they sobbed over the passing of their friend. After a while, Ella, Thora, Katy, Freda and Flossie walked solemnly back to the shop.

Not having known Ivy, Tilda had opted to stay behind and prepare a small wake. With immaculate timing, she was just making a pot of tea when the others walked in. Removing their hats and coats, they sat to have a sandwich and a much-needed brew.

'How did it go?' Tilda asked.

'It was a nice service,' Flossie replied.

They continued to discuss the interment for a while. 'Funerals are such sad affairs,' Katy said.

'That's the nature of the beast, though, ain't it?' Thora put in.

'How do you mean?'

'Well, everybody who's left behind cries because their loved one has gone to ground, as it were.'

'I wonder where your spirit goes after you die,' Katy mused.

Ella and Tilda shared a wry smile. 'I'm glad Ivy's laid to rest and, wherever her spirit is, I hope it flies high,' Ella said as she stood to put on her coat.

They then parted company to return home. Tomorrow would be a working day but for now they would honour Ivy with a day of rest.

Ella realised as she walked back to Silver Street with Flossie that there was a chill in the air, and she pulled her coat tighter about her body.

Ella's eyes darted this way and that as the note again came to mind. As a shudder crept down her spine once more, she increased her pace.

'Weather's turning,' Flossie mumbled, thinking Ella was hurrying to get out of the cold.

'It is,' Ella replied, trying to hide her feelings of fear. She sighed with relief only when indoors and the key turned in the lock.

Again, she deliberated going to the police. One thing was certain, she couldn't afford to be constantly scared.

41

Darcie Newland had booked the hotel room for another week, which would give her time to decide what she would do next. She had no idea how she was going to settle her bill, but she would meet that challenge when it arrived. Sitting in the dining room over afternoon tea, Darcie thought again about the note she had sent to Ella. It had never been her intention to physically harm Ella, the underlying threat would be enough to frighten her.

Nibbling on the small salmon sandwiches, Darcie considered her future. She would have to sell the jewellery, clock and figurines in order to have ready cash at her disposal. Then the next step would be to find herself another man to take care of her. This would be impossible in Birmingham due to her disastrous soiree, so she would need to move to somewhere else. Maybe it was time now, or at least very soon, to go to London, where she would have a better chance of meeting someone new. However, before she did, Darcie fully intended to ruin Ella's reputation.

Reaching for a cream cake from the tiered cake stand, Darcie decided the following day was soon enough to begin her trail of destruction. With a short train ride to Walsall and a visit to as many shops as she could manage, Darcie would blacken Ella's name with lies and deceit.

Having made her plans, Darcie finished her tea before returning to her room for a nap.

The following day, Darcie took the jewellery, clock and figurines to the nearest pawn shop. Given far less than what they were worth, she had to accept the situation for what it was. She was selling stolen goods, so the pawn shop was her best bet to avoid being caught by the police.

Returning to the hotel, Darcie thought about how she could make more money. With her clothes hung in the single wardrobe, she smiled. She would sell her trunk. Once she had sufficient cash, she could leave Birmingham, taking only clothing that would fit in the Gladstone bag. Confident she would soon find a rich man in London who would buy her more garments, Darcie was undaunted at leaving behind her fine dresses. After all, she could only carry so much, and the swelling of her coffers was more important.

As she entered the hotel, she was greeted by the owner's wife, Mrs Freeman.

'I wonder, can you tell me where I might sell my trunk?' Darcie asked.

'I'll buy it off yer if it ain't too dear,' Mrs Freeman answered. 'Our daughter is going overseas with her husband, so I could give it to her as a gift. Can I see it?'

'Yes, of course.'

Mrs Freeman followed Darcie upstairs to her room. 'Oh, this is perfect! How much are you looking for?'

'What can you pay?'

'Not much, I'm afraid, I could manage ten pounds. Business has been poor of late.'

Darcie thought at ten pounds it was a steal for the woman, but then again, she needed the money. 'It's worth an awful lot more than that, it's of the highest quality leather.'

'I realise that it's beautifully made, but it's all I can afford,' Mrs Freeman replied, hoping Darcie would accept her offer. 'Never mind, I'll have to look elsewhere for a cheaper one.'

Darcie could see the opportunity slipping away from her and said quickly, 'Very well. I'd be obliged if you would have it removed as soon as possible.'

'I'll fetch you the cash right away,' Mrs Freeman said, mentally rubbing her hands together as she bustled out of the room.

A few moments later, the tap on the door told Darcie that Mrs Freeman was back. 'Your money, and Alfie is here to shift the trunk.' Mrs Freeman moved aside to reveal her son.

Alfie lifted the trunk easily with well-muscled arms, then carried it away.

'Thank you,' Mrs Freeman said as she again left Darcie alone.

Putting the money in her bag, Darcie walked out, locking the door behind her. It was time to catch a train to Walsall. She had some mischief to cause.

* * *

Everyone was back at Ivella, working on Ella's new autumn range. The shop felt strange without Ivy, but Ella kept herself busy with her sketches.

Around mid-morning, Katy came through to the back room. 'A letter's come for you,' she said, handing over the envelope.

Ella blanched. Was this another note from Darcie? 'Thank you.' Once Katy had returned to the shop area, Ella opened the letter and breathed a sigh of relief. It was from the London Probate Office. She had been granted probate, which meant she could now access Ivy's bank account.

Deciding to visit the bank immediately in order to transfer the money into her own account, Ella donned her hat and coat.

Explaining to Katy where she was going, Ella set off. As she walked, she noticed how the leaves had changed colour. Some had already begun to fall and lay on the ground like a multi-coloured carpet. Crows cawed as she passed gardens which held tall trees. She saw spirals of smoke from household chimneys which left behind the smell of burnt coal.

At the bank, Ella produced the letter and the transaction went smoothly. The deeds to the shop she pushed into her bag to be stored in the safe.

Once her business was completed, Ella returned to the shop, all the time keeping a wary eye out for Darcie Newland. Arriving back safely, Ella settled again to her work.

The new range of hats was coming along nicely. Ella had chosen to base her collection on the out-door pursuits of the elite – hunting, shooting and fishing. The hats were smaller, some in a trilby style and sporting a couple of grouse or pheasant feath-ers. Others retained a more feminine fashion, adorned with silk roses and ribbons which were ruched and curled.

Taking her latest designs up to the workroom where Freda and Thora were chatting as they worked, Ella asked, 'How are we doing, ladies?'

Thora nodded to the completed millinery laid out on the longer counter.

'Oh, my goodness! These are beautiful, do we have enough for a window change, do you think?'

'Yes, there's plenty if they're placed strategically,' Thora answered.

'Excellent. I'll let Katy know, then I'll make us all a hot drink. Tilda is busy with lunch. Thank you, ladies, you are marvellous.' With that, Ella left to complete her tasks.

'She's always so nice,' Freda commented.

'Yeah, grateful an' all,' Thora replied. 'We are lucky to work for her.'

'It don't feel like we'm working *for* her, though. It's like we're all on the same level.'

'It is; she doesn't come the big *I am* around any of us. She really appreciates what we produce and is always ready with thanks and praise,' Freda said.

'We dropped on our feet when she took us on and that's a fact.'

The women continued to sing Ella's praises until she returned with the promised tray of tea and home-made biscuits.

'I've been to the bank, ladies, and I think the business can stretch to giving you all a raise in wages.'

Thora and Freda clapped with pleasure as they voiced their thanks.

Ella grinned and went downstairs to tell Katy and Tilda, who were in the sales area, the same good news.

Answering the ringing telephone, Ella was delighted to hear Nicholas on the other end. 'Will you have dinner with me tonight?'

'I'd love to,' Ella answered, glad he couldn't see the blush rising to her cheeks.

'Good. I'll collect you at seven.'

After saying goodbye, Ella was excited to be spending her evening with Nicholas and began to think about what she should wear.

42

Darcie had also been otherwise engaged. She had already begun to spread her nastiness in various shops, blackening Ella's good name. She stood in a textile store, listening to women gossiping, coincidently about Ella.

'I wouldn't buy a hat from anywhere else now,' one said.

'Nor me, Ella Bancroft's are the best,' her friend agreed.

Having waited patiently, Darcie knew this was her chance to join the conversation. 'The same person who would steal another woman's fiancé?' Darcie asked.

The gossipers turned to her with a look that could crisp bacon. 'What?'

'Ella stole my fiancé,' Darcie stated.

'That ain't how I heard it,' the first said.

'Well, it's true. She enticed my betrothed away, I should know, as it was me who was left broken-hearted.' Darcie forced a tear to accompany a dramatic sniff.

The women exchanged a glance.

'And that's not all. She accused her own sister of thieving.'

Frowns appeared on the shoppers' faces and Darcie guessed they were taking it all in.

'She bullied Ivy Gladwin into becoming partners in that shabby little shop, too.'

The first woman who had spoken had clearly had enough, as she rounded on Darcie. 'You'd best leave and take your filthy lies with you!'

'I'm not lying!' Darcie snapped.

'Well, I think you are, and I don't want to hear it. I, for one, will have nothing said against that girl!' The woman took a step towards Darcie menacingly.

Darcie quickly saw she would get no further here, so she turned to leave and her parting shot was, 'I'd watch your husbands, Ella could lure them away!' Then she was gone, a grin splitting her face. *On to the next*, she thought as she strode away.

* * *

Nicholas had listened to what Paul Sampson told him before he rang Ella.

'I received a telephone call from Imelda and what she imparted to me, I thought you should know. She overheard some talk in a shop about Ella.'

It appeared that Darcie Newland, well known in Walsall and Birmingham, was causing ructions in the shops. She was spreading lies about Ella Bancroft which could turn out to be libellous. If nothing else, it wasn't doing Ella's reputation any good.

'Oh, Lord! That woman is an absolute menace!' Nicholas said, feeling exasperated.

'Get Ella to a solicitor,' Paul advised.

'I will, thanks, Paul.'

Nicholas had then telephoned Ella to invite her to dinner, so that he could let her know what was going on.

Paul's idea to visit a solicitor was a good one –

maybe a letter could be sent to Darcie threatening court action if she continued with her slander. It might help, but firstly they had to discover where she was now living. It had quickly become common knowledge that Mason Landor had called off his engagement and had forced Darcie out of his property. So where was she now? Was she living in Birmingham still or had she moved back to Walsall?

* * *

Having garnered no support at the previous shop, Darcie moved on. In the greengrocers, she again determined to pursue her campaign of spite. Her opportunity came when the grocer was overheard to compliment his customer's hat. This was her opportunity, and Darcie wasted no time in taking it.

The customer replied it was an Ivella creation and Darcie moved in for the kill. 'How you can support that woman, after what she's done, defies me!'

The woman frowned. 'What?'

'Ella Bancroft. I'm sure you are aware of her background. She accused her sister of stealing, you know.' Darcie deliberately left out the fact that Ella's sister, Sally, had admitted to the theft of Ella's designs.

'Ella's private life is of no consequence to me. I buy her hats because I like them and I can afford them,' the woman replied.

'It's all tat! What about the fact that she was the cause of a betrothal break-up?' Darcie pushed on, hoping to get the woman on side.

'How would you know?'

'Because it was my fiancé that she stole!' Darcie retorted angrily.

'That has nothing to do with her millinery,' the woman countered.

'You mean that cheap rubbish?'

The woman bristled as her hand went to her hat. 'It's not rubbish! It's affordable to the likes of us who don't live in big houses and have lots of servants!'

The grocer had taken a few steps back, wishing he'd kept his mouth shut.

'Of course it's up to you if you want to parade around the town in that...' Darcie stabbed a gloved hand in the direction of the woman's headgear, 'but I wouldn't be seen dead in one of those!'

Seeing a physical altercation brewing, the grocer

intervened. 'Ladies, please!' Turning to Darcie, he asked, 'Is there anything I can get for you?'

Darcie shook her head. 'No.'

'Then may I suggest—'

'I'm going!' Turning on her heel, she walked out of the shop. Striding to the next place, she began to wonder why it was proving so difficult to besmirch Ella's name. The woman's followers were spread far and wide and, try as she might, Darcie's efforts were being thwarted at every turn.

Tired and fed up, Darcie entered a tea shop. She would have a drink and think about a new strategy, for this one wasn't working.

* * *

As she walked home, despite the chill, Ella noticed the children in the street playing, but there seemed no joy in it. Having no shoes or boots, their toes were red with cold. They shivered as they huddled together in the ginnel, their thin rags providing no warmth. These were the poorest families in the town and the children knew nothing different. All they were sure of was that they would probably go to bed on an empty stomach yet again.

Ella's heart went out to them but there was little she could do to help. If she held out a coin to them, in a second, she would be surrounded by raga-muffins and she couldn't give to them all.

As she moved on, the wind picked up, plucking dying leaves from boughs and swirling them high into the air, before gently laying them on the ground where they would either dry and crisp or become soggy with the rain.

Ella noticed people passing by. Only a few weeks ago, they had walked tall and straight, now they bowed their heads into the inclement weather.

The sun fought valiantly to warm the people and streets alike, but it struggled to break through the roiling dark cloudbank. It was threatening rain and as Ella glanced up, an icy raindrop plopped into her eye. The rain then began to fall in earnest and Ella was drenched by the time she got home. This au-tumn, it seemed, was set to be wet.

Hanging her coat over the back of a kitchen chair to dry off, Ella shivered with cold as she fed the range and put the kettle to boil. Watching the rain patter against the window, she wished she didn't have to go out in it again later. However, the thought of spending another evening with Nicholas had her heart hammering in her chest. It would be worth braving the weather just to see him.

A blast of cold air preceded Flossie as she hurried through the back door. 'Bloody hell! It's raining cats and dogs out there,' Flossie blustered as she took off her shawl and draped it over another chair.

'Tea's on,' Ella said.

'Ta, sweet 'eart. You off out again with that nice young fella?'

'Yes, he's taking me to dinner,' Ella replied with a little blush.

'I'm glad, he does you good. Our Josh is taking Katy to the music hall later. I think it's serious between them, and I do like her,' Flossie said with a smile.

'So do I. Maybe there'll be a wedding?'

'I'm hoping so, gel, but where they would live beats me. I ain't got the room to take in another body or the means to feed another mouth.'

Ella nodded, knowing how crowded her friend's house was with Flossie and her husband, Josh,

Phoebe and Margaret. With only two bedrooms, Josh had to sleep in the living room on an old sofa.

As she poured the tea, a thought occurred to Ella. If Josh and Katy did eventually wed, maybe Ella could move into the spare room at Ivella and rent her house to the newlyweds.

For now, however, she would keep the thought to herself and see how things went.

After they had had tea and Flossie had gone home, Ella began to prepare herself for her evening out with Nicholas, and she felt her excitement rising once more.

43

Darcie Newland had returned to her hotel room exhausted from tramping the streets. She had travelled third class on the train to conserve her money, but the carriage had been full of what she saw as lower social class passengers. Children screaming and running around causing havoc, frustrated mothers yelling for their offspring to behave, to no avail. Darcie couldn't wait to get back to have a rest.

After a wash and change of clothes, she went down to the dining room for dinner. It was packed and so she had been placed on a table with three other people. Darcie did not join in the conversation, choosing instead to eat in silence. She ignored the strange looks from the other diners and kept her eyes on her food. Having finished her lamb, potatoes and vegetables along with a fine red wine, she was about to go back upstairs when the hotel owner called to her.

'Ah, Miss Newland, I wonder if I may request your payment, please.'

Darcie nodded. 'Of course.'

Following the man to the reception desk, Darcie dug in her bag and paid the man.

'Many thanks,' he said with a smile.

Darcie returned to her room where she emptied her bag onto the bed. Counting out the remainder of her money as she sat on the bed, she blanched. She had been living far too extravagantly since being evicted from Mason's house. She had sold her trunk, the jewellery, clock and figurines and now she had nothing left but her clothes and a few pounds.

If she stayed here, she would have another hotel bill to pay and not enough money to cover it. If she moved out, where could she go? How would she transport her clothing? Berating herself for being so stupid, Darcie banged a fist on her knee in frustration.

Instead of trawling the streets endeavouring to blacken Ella's name, she should have been seeking out a new man to take care of her. She should have had afternoon tea in the best places in the better part of town where she could have possibly met someone she could sucker in. As it was, she had wasted her time and money, and for what? Nothing. The women hereabouts were sworn followers of Ella Bancroft, very few seeing Ella as the villain of the piece.

Somehow Darcie had to get her hands on some more cash, but how? She could try for a job, but the thought sickened her. She felt herself too high-born to lower herself to working for a living. She could go back to her parents in Scotland, cap in hand, but she held the belief her father would refuse to take her in again.

No, Darcie knew she was on her own, and as she undressed for bed, she fretted as to how she would manage.

* * *

Over in Walsall, Ella and Nicholas were enjoying a candle-lit dinner of roast beef. 'Ella, I need to speak with you about something important,' Nicholas began.

Ella felt her heart plummet into her stomach. What was he about to say? Was he going to apologise and tell her he was married? Or would he say he didn't want to see her again? Had he met someone new, someone he wanted to wed?

'I spoke with Paul earlier today, and it seems Darcie Newland has been spreading gossip about you. Paul suggested I take you to a solicitor who could write to the woman and warn her if she did not cease and desist from her slander, then court action would be taken. The problem with that is we don't know where Miss Newland is living at present.'

Ella breathed with relief. It was none of the things she had fretted about, it was merely something to do with the elusive Darcie. 'I wouldn't worry about it, Nicholas.'

'Ella, she's out to ruin your good name! She could very easily adversely affect your business.'

This last sentence brought Ella up sharply. 'Do you think she could?'

'I do, and if she did, how would you pay your staff and your bills?'

'I see your point, but what can I do about it?'

'We need to discover her whereabouts then have a solicitor's letter delivered. Then you need to think about consolidating and re-affirming your client base. In other words, make sure your regular clients remain loyal, as well as bringing in more custom,' Nicholas advised.

'How?'

'Well, you could have a sale in your shop.'

'That's a good idea. I'll put it to the girls tomorrow.'

Nicholas held out his hand across the table, and when she placed hers in it, he squeezed her fingers gently. 'Be positive, we'll sort it out one way or another, my love.'

My love! Ella's heart leapt at the words and suddenly all she could see was Nicholas. Everything else faded into the background as they shared a loving smile.

Early the next morning, before the shop opened, Ella repeated what Nicholas had said and his suggestion about a sale day.

'As long as I don't have to shift any furniture like I had to for Ivy,' Katy said, with a twinkle in her eye.

'No, we'll leave everything in place. We'll let it be known that our millinery will be greatly reduced on Thursday for one day only,' Ella said.

'We have a lot of old stock in the workroom cupboards,' Freda put in.

'We could fetch it out and you can cast a beady eye over it,' Thora added.

'Thank you, ladies, that would be a great help.'

An hour later, Ella shook her head as she looked at the hats pulled from their resting places. All Ivy's creations, they were big and gaudy. Feathers and flowers smothered the felt and satin.

'We could soon strip 'em down if you don't think they'll sell as is,' Thora said gently as she saw Ella's face fall.

'Yes, then you can tell us what's needed and we can update them,' Freda said helpfully.

'It will be a lot of work,' Ella said on a sigh.

'They'm doing nothing in the cupboards, so let's at least see if we can make them saleable,' Katy added forcefully. 'I can unpick while there's nobody in the shop, and Tilda could help with that as well.'

Tilda nodded. 'I tell you what, let's have a cuppa with some pikelets and we'll thrash out some suggestions.'

They all agreed and whilst Tilda made herself busy in the kitchen, Ella jotted down some notes about what to do with Ivy's abominations. 'Sorry, Ivy,' Ella said quietly, hoping her friend would understand if she could hear her. Thora and Freda set about removing all the adornments so they would be left with the simple shapes. Katy found some old boxes for the milliners to use as storage, one for feathers, one for jewellery and one for flowers. Slowly the hats were being stripped of their décor and Ella had a better idea of how to make them sale ready.

After tea, Katy opened the shop and placed a sign Ella had drawn up in the window, advertising that a Grand Sale was to take place on Thursday – two days hence.

Ella remained in the workshop to help out.

'You should put a bit in the paper about it,' Tilda said, 'I can pop it to the news office for you if you want. I need to go out and get some food in anyway.'

'That would help enormously, Tilda, thank you.'

Ella drafted an advert and gave it to Tilda with some money.

'I won't be long, oh, and I've a stew on the go for lunch,' Tilda said before she left.

'You did a good thing there,' Thora said, without taking her eyes from her work.

'Sorry, what?'

'Taking that wench in, it was a good deed on your part. Look at how happy Tilda is now, and the same goes for us lot an' all.'

Ella smiled.

'I agree, we're like family,' Freda added.

They were right, the little coterie had come together and gelled straight away, and it did indeed feel like Ella had a family around her once more.

44

The following two days were spent working hard in the workroom and although she was tired, Ella readily accepted Nicholas's invitations to take her to dinner and the music hall.

The weather had, as Ella had guessed it would, turned cold and wet. The incessant rain had everyone grumbling and foretelling an early and harsh winter. The streets were strewn with soggy leaves as well as the usual detritus of bits of paper, cigarette butts and dog and horse manure. Chimneys smoked, sending out particles of coal, which were caught in the raindrops to fall into an inky black stream on the roads. Skirt hems were held up so as to avoid being soaked, and large puddles were stepped around.

Ella began to fret that no one would brave the foul weather in order to take advantage of the sale.

'Folk will come, you mark my words,' Thora had told her, but as Ella stared out onto the street and the pelting rain, she had her doubts. All she could do was wait and see – and pray for a successful day.

In Birmingham, Darcie had been approached to once again pay her hotel bill for the previous few days. The hotel was extremely busy, and she was told in no uncertain terms to pay up or leave. Darcie deferred, saying she needed to visit the bank. She had used the last of her money taking tea in the most up-market establishments, in the hope of meeting a rich stranger. However, her efforts had been thwarted and she had left – alone and miserable.

A rap on her door forced Darcie to answer and be faced with the hotel owner and his wife. 'I am, for the last time, demanding you pay what you owe,' the man said as he and his wife pushed their way into Darcie's room.

'I have yet to visit the bank…' Darcie began.

'You said that yesterday,' the man said sharply.

'And the day before,' his wife added.

'I assure you…'

'No, Miss Newland, it is my opinion you are not in a position to pay your arrears, therefore I must ask you to vacate these premises forthwith.'

Darcie stared at the owner. How dare he treat her in this manner! 'Sir, I don't like your tone!' she snapped.

'Madam, I don't give a bugger!' the owner raged. 'You owe me money and if you cannot pay then you can get out – now!'

'You can leave those clothes as recompense an' all,' the wife added.

'I most certainly will not!'

'You will, or I'll send for a constable!'

Seeing she was beaten, Darcie snatched up her bag and stamped from the room, the owner and his wife's laughter filling her ears as she went.

Outside in the rain, Darcie felt wretched. All she had to her name was the clothes she stood up in. She had nowhere to go and no money to go with. How would she survive out on the streets, cold and alone? Why was life treating her so badly? All she had ever wanted was to be married to a rich man who doted on her, lots of money of her own and a big mansion to live in. Was that too much to ask for?

The hotel door opened, and the wife tossed out Darcie's coat, which thankfully she caught.

'Thank you, you're all heart,' Darcie said sarcastically.

The woman slammed the door and Darcie donned her coat and wandered away, her head down against the lashing rain.

Darcie walked the streets all day. She was wet, cold, tired and hungry and she had no idea where she was. All the shops had closed up for the night and, finding a doorway on the lea side of a building, she sat down and wept. She wondered if all of her spiteful ways were coming back on her. It was too late to worry about it now, for the past was the past and she couldn't rectify it. Was she sorry for the things she had done and the way she had treated people? Drying her eyes, Darcie deliberated, but at thought of Ella and Tilda, she shook her head fiercely. Those two women were responsible for the predicament she found herself in so, no, she was not sorry.

Slowly darkness descended and Darcie shivered, both with cold and fear. For the first time in her life, Darcie Newland was scared. She knew this doorway would shelter her from further rainfall, but there were bad people about and she could be murdered in her sleep. As full night fell, she began to relax a little. She had not seen or heard a soul since coming here, and with heavy eyelids closing, she drifted off to sleep.

Birdsong snapped Darcie awake with a jolt. She looked around her and realisation dawned. It had not been a nightmare, she really was in a shop doorway with nothing to her name. Getting to her feet, she groaned as she stretched out her aching muscles. She needed to find food and water, her throat felt dry and tight.

Stepping out onto the street, she glanced around. It was still not properly light, but she could see enough to know she was lost. Then again, she had nowhere to call home, she had no roots. Wandering away, she wondered what would become of her.

Would she die of starvation with no one to mourn her passing? The thought of presenting herself at the workhouse gates through sheer desperation made her shiver. She had no way of knowing that life had chosen a completely different path for her.

* * *

Ivella was bustling with life as Ella and her staff prepared to open the doors. It was sale day and already, to Ella's delight, a queue was forming outside.

'I can't thank you ladies enough for all your hard work,' Ella said. 'Well done, everyone. I shall ensure you have a bonus in your wages.'

A round of applause rippled around the workroom.

'Now, let's open those doors.'

It had been agreed that Thora and Freda would help serving in the shop, as well as Katy and Ella. Tilda said she preferred to remain in the background and keep the others fed and watered.

Unlocking and opening the door, Ella stood aside as women of all ages, sizes and shapes poured into the shop. The noise of customers talking and laughing was loud, but there was no pushing and shoving.

Ella overheard compliments and she smiled. Her hats were yet again proving successful. The till rattled and clanged as the money went in and as fast as one customer left, another took her place.

Katy ran up to the workroom to bring down more millinery, which was quickly snapped up by eager buyers. All morning, the shop heaved with bodies and by the lunchtime lull, the workers were exhausted but happy.

Ella closed up for an hour so they could rest and eat their meal of faggots with grey peas and bacon, prepared by Tilda. Over a cup of tea, they spoke animatedly about the morning's sales.

'I had one lady buy two hats,' Freda said proudly.

'There was a woman trying every hat she could get her hands on, she was loving it. I had to turn away to laugh when she made up her mind, though, because she chose that big fawn feathered one. Well, she looked so funny, it reminded me of the arse end of an ostrich!' Katy said.

Everyone burst out laughing.

'Before we open up again, we should replenish our stock. What's left upstairs?' Ella asked.

'There's still lots, we'll fetch them down now,' Thora said as she dug Freda in the ribs.

'I'll help,' Katy added.

The afternoon was just as busy and by five o'clock, when Ella locked up, all of the refurbished hats and some of the shop stock had been sold.

Tilda had made an evening meal, realising they would all be too tired to bother once they got home. A rich cottage pie, cabbage and fresh crusty bread was consumed hungrily.

With thanks all round, they wound their way home, tired but happy.

Ella was secretly pleased not to be going out with Nicholas, as she was weary to the bone. She would have liked to see him, but in truth all she wanted was her bed. When she eventually climbed in, she nestled down with a satisfied sigh. It had been a really good day and on that thought, but with a picture of Nicholas in her mind, Ella fell asleep immediately.

45

Darcie had paced the streets looking for food. She had taken a drink of water from a standpipe in someone's garden and had been chased off by a belligerent woman wielding a broom. Feeling her stomach rumble, she swallowed. It growled again in its insistence at needing to be fed and Darcie tried her best to ignore it. She knew, however, that if she was to survive, she would have to eat. She also had to find somewhere to spend the night. She couldn't remember how to get back to the doorway she had slept safely in, so she scoured the district for another hiding place.

Her coat was still damp and was now dirty from

lying on the ground. Her hair was a mess and her boots were muddy. She realised she must look frightful, but that was the least of her problems. Staying alive was her first priority and the only way she could see to do it was to beg.

Sitting on the cold ground on a street corner, she held out her hand to passers-by. For the most part, people pretended they hadn't seen her, then an old man dropped a threepenny bit in her palm before he walked on. Staring at the coin, Darcie thought again how low she had sunk. Tears formed at the kindness of the man who had surely saved her from starvation.

Clutching her money, Darcie stood and followed a tantalising aroma. Further down, a street vendor was selling hot potatoes.

'Just threppance – sixpence for two if you'm hungry,' the seller called out.

Darcie held out her money and was given the hot fare wrapped in paper. She eyed the slab of butter before looking up at the man hopefully.

'Butter is a penny,' he said, seeing the query in her eyes.

Darcie turned and walked away. Even without a

knob of butter to moisten it, the potato would make good eating. After devouring her food, Darcie began to look for a place to sleep.

Following the street, she turned the corner into yet another thoroughfare. Birmingham was like a rabbit warren and this area was totally unfamiliar to her.

She heard men calling to each other and the rattle of a travelling crane overhead, so she must be near a goods depot of some sort. She passed a synagogue which stood next to a school. She was almost knocked over by two men laughing loudly as they bowled out of the door of a public house.

'Hey up, hello, darlin',' one said.

Darcie ignored him and tried to move on.

'She ain't interested in you, mate,' his friend said with a grin, as he stood in front of Darcie.

Shrugging his shoulders, the first spoke again. 'I ain't bothered, she ain't much to look at anyway.'

His friend sneered, 'You don't look at the mantel shelf when you'm poking the fire!'

Howling at the statement, the two drunken friends ambled away, an arm around each other's shoulder, leaving Darcie feeling wretched.

Walking on, she commenced her search for a safe hideaway in which to spend the night.

As darkness fell, Darcie settled herself in a shop doorway, hoping the night would pass peacefully. She could not have been more wrong.

The electric streetlights flicked on and slowly the place came alive. Darcie watched as one woman after another appeared and stood in little groups in the glow of the lamps. Then she saw a man approach one group and, after a short conversation, he wandered away with one of the women on his arm.

It was then that Darcie realised that she had stumbled into the streetwalkers' territory. Staying silent in the shadow of the doorway, Darcie watched as men came and went, on foot and in carriages. She was shocked at how busy the women were, no sooner arriving back than they took off with yet another customer.

Darcie's stomach turned at thought of what was taking place in nearby alleys. How could women do such things? What had happened in their lives that would drive them to earn a coin in this dreadful manner? Unable to sleep due to the laughing, shouting and carriage wheels grinding on cobblestones, Darcie continued to watch the scene playing out in front of her. Only as a sliver of light cracked open the dark sky did Darcie finally close her eyes for some much-needed rest.

* * *

Outside Ivella, around nine o'clock the following day, a black carriage pulled by two chestnut roans stopped. The jarvey jumped down, opened the door and pulled down the steps for his passenger to alight. The man nodded his thanks, smoothed his dark woollen coat, set his bowler on his head, and with an umbrella doubling as a walking cane, he stepped into the shop.

'Good morning, may I help you?' Katy asked jovially.

'Good morning. I'm here to see Miss Ella Bancroft.'

'Oh, may I take your name?'

'Shotton.'

'One moment, Mr Shotton, and I'll fetch her.' Katy hurried into the back room and whispered, 'There's a Mr Shotton to see you. He looks posh!'

Ella frowned, she didn't know anyone of that name.

Following Katy through, Ella greeted her visitor with an outstretched hand, which was shaken by his gloved one.

'Mr Shotton, how may I be of service?'

'Miss Bancroft. I wonder, is there somewhere we can speak alone?'

It was a strange request, but Ella felt she was safe enough as Katy would be in the next room. 'Of course, please come through.' Ella led the man to the back room and gestured for him to take a seat.

Inclining his head, Mr Shotton sat on the sofa and placed his bowler beside him. The umbrella he propped up next to it, then carefully peeled off his kid gloves, almost as daintily as a woman would do.

'May I offer you some tea?' Ella asked.

'Thank you, no.' Mr Shotton waved a hand in dismissal then laid both hands on his knees, which were placed tight together.

'What can I help you with, Mr Shotton?'

Mr Shotton reached into his inside pocket and pulled out a small leather case. Taking a business card out, he passed it to Ella before replacing the case in his jacket.

Ella looked at the card. Over the top of his name sat the royal coat of arms. Her eyes shot to Mr Shotton's and her mouth fell open in shock. As she made to return the card, Mr Shotton shook his head. 'Keep it.'

'Thank you, I...'

'Miss Bancroft...'

'Ella.'

Another nod and Mr Shotton went on. 'Ella, I realise this has come as a surprise to you,' he smiled as her head wobbled up and down. 'I have something important to discuss with you. May I be so bold as to ask you close your shop for an hour and assemble your staff?'

'Yes, I... I'll see to it straight away and – I need tea!'

'Splendid!'

Ella locked up and led Katy, Thora and Freda to the back room. Tilda was asked if she'd mind making tea – in Ivy's best china tea service.

Once they were all gathered and the beverages provided, Ella passed round the card for all to see.

'God love us!' Freda breathed.

'I'll second that!' Thora added.

Mr Shotton smiled warmly before he set down his cup and saucer, having drained his drink. He had completed this type of mission before many times and he was aware of the startling effect it had on people.

'What I have to say must be kept in the strictest secrecy. May I have your word on this?' He acknowledged each nod. 'Very well. Now, as I'm sure you are aware, King Edward only ever purchases his saddles from Walsall.'

More nods. 'Naturally he only wants the very best, which are made here. The King is due to be making a visit to the saddlers on Monday morning, which must, at all costs, be kept under wraps. On this visit, Queen Alexandra will accompany him but whilst he is busy, the Queen has expressed a wish to be a guest at Ivella.'

Mr Shotton paused as sharp intakes of breath sounded. He waited while his words sank in before going on. 'The Queen has heard very good reports of your work, Ella, and it is her intention to purchase some of your millinery.'

Excited looks passed from one woman to the next, then Ella said, 'We would be honoured to host the Queen, of course, but however are we to keep it a secret?'

'Ah, well, we would request you black out your window, giving the impression to the public that you are changing your display, which I would suggest you do.'

'Of course,' was all that Ella could manage.

'Her Majesty will arrive at ten o'clock on the dot and will expect the door to be open so she can slip inside undetected.'

'Won't people see her carriage?' Katy asked.

'The Royal crest will be covered, so it will look like any other wealthy patron's mode of transport.'

'Will we provide refreshments?' Tilda asked.

'You can certainly be prepared just in case,' Mr Shotton replied.

'I'd best bake some little fancies then,' Tilda said with a grin.

'Wonderful idea. Now, may I ask – do you have plenty of stock for the Queen to peruse?'

'Yes, although we can make more, just to be on the safe side,' Ella answered.

'Good. Do you have any questions?'

'Pardon my saying so, but I know our lovely Queen is a little small, so we will need her hat size.'

Mr Shotton again produced a slip of paper from his pocket and handed it over. 'Thank you, I almost forgot that!' he said with a horrified look. 'Now, is there anything more you wish to know?'

All heads shook except Ella's. 'May I ask how we address the Queen?'

'Your Majesty in the first instance, then Ma'am as in jam, after that,' Mr Shotton replied. 'Anything else?'

'No, thank you,' Ella said. Her nerves were stretched taut, and her stomach was roiling with excitement.

'Then I will be on my way, but please remember – not a word to anyone or heads will roll – namely mine!'

Ella led Mr Shotton back through the shop. 'Thank you, sir.'

'I'm not a sir, but I live in hope.' The man gave a little giggle and Ella smiled.

She watched as he climbed aboard and the carriage rolled away. Rushing to the back room, Ella began to pace. 'Oh, my! Oh, my goodness! A royal visit to our little shop, would you believe it? Good grief, do we in fact have enough items for display?'

'We have some, maybe we should check,' Freda answered. 'Because we sold such a lot on our open day sale.'

'I think we need to get working on more,' Thora answered.

'And I think we need to find a decent chair in case Her Maj wants to park her arse!' Katy said.

Howls of laughter sounded as everyone dashed upstairs to check just how much stock they actually had.

46

Ella and Tilda were in the workroom with Thora and Freda, doing their best to create new designs for the impending royal visit.

Katy yelled up the stairs that Nicholas was on the telephone and Ella raced down to speak with him. She explained that they had just had the possibility of a big order so they would probably be working late into the night and over the weekend. She agreed to see him on Tuesday evening, saying she was looking forward to it, and was pleased Nicholas accepted her reason for putting him off.

Ella had tasked Katy to come up with a new design for the window, which would be revealed on

Monday afternoon. On Sunday night, they would hang up some dark material Ella had found in a trunk in the spare room upstairs.

Katy had sent a message to Josh, via a street urchin runner, telling him the same thing Ella had said to Nicholas. Tilda volunteered to cook as well as help out where she could with the new creations.

Sunday afternoon was to be spent cleaning the shop, everything had to be spick and span. The little coterie agreed that no one would be going home until Queen Alexandra had been and gone.

The excitement was building as one hat after another was finished and the day wore on. Ella suggested they took turns in getting some rest – they could grab some sleep on the back room sofa. Tilda also offered the use of her bed for those who wished to use it.

Once the shop was locked up for the evening, the friends sat to enjoy a meal of broth and fresh bread, followed by suet pudding and custard. After a period of digestion time, the women all went to the workroom to begin work again.

Ella knew it would be a back-breaking few days but her staff – no, her friends – had not baulked at the prospect. All were eager to ensure the Queen enjoyed her time spent at Ivella.

* * *

Darcie Newland had once more sat on the street corner. She looked exactly what she was – a beggar. The once fierce light in her eyes had dimmed and died at finding herself one of the downtrodden. She had come to realise that she was not now in a position to get even with Ella or Tilda, and the thought saddened her immeasurably. All she could do was try to stay alive and dream that one day a Prince Charming would rescue her from this dreadful state of affairs. It was this thought that gave her the strength to fight for one more day of life.

The rumbling of her stomach made Darcie grimace and she doubled over as hunger pains struck again. She had to find a way of getting enough money together to feed herself. Her thoughts strayed to the women she had seen on the street the night before. Clearly they were earning and their services appeared to be in high demand, but could she do the same? Shaking her head, she very much doubted it. The idea of selling her body for coin sickened her, but if things didn't improve soon, it might very well come to that.

Holding out her hand to a man passing by, Darcie was shocked when he kicked out at her. 'Get a job!' he snapped before spitting on the roadway and moving on. Tears welled in her eyes and the groaning in her stomach grew louder.

Eventually a lady gave Darcie a penny, which would buy her some bread. On her feet, she rushed off to find a baker's, and with a small loaf in her hands, she chomped hungrily whilst walking back to her place. The bread was dry but most welcome. When she saw a couple approaching, Darcie hid the loaf under her coat and held out her hand.

She watched as the young pair disagreed about whether to give the unfortunate beggar some money. The woman was for it, but the man shook his head. Darcie wondered what the outcome would be and was delighted when the lady dug in her bag and produced a shilling.

'Thank you!' Darcie managed, her throat still dry from the bread.

The woman smiled and walked on.

Darcie watched as the argument between the pair raged on as they walked. Then she stood and went in search of a tea shop. She could afford a cup of tea now. Her mood lightened a little at the kindness shown her, and suddenly life didn't seem so bad. Then again, the thought of returning to the corner plunged her back down into the depths of despair.

Finding a shabby café, Darcie rushed in and ordered a pot of tea. The room smelled of burnt food and the tables were dirty and greasy. The curtain at the window was grey with grime and the floor was sticky. Darcie wasn't put off, she was desperate for a hot drink.

'You want anything to eat?' a miserable-looking waitress enquired.

'What can I get for this after I've paid for my tea?' Darcie asked, producing her coin.

'A bacon sandwich.'

'Yes, please.'

'Do yer want yer bread dipped in the liquor?'

'Erm... yes.' The bread soaked in the fat from the frying bacon would help put a lining on her stomach and encourage the whole thing to slip down a little easier.

The waitress nodded and wandered away.

Darcie sighed and silently thanked her bene-factor yet again.

Feeling so much better for having eaten, Darcie walked back and sat on the ground. Would this be her life from now on? Was there any way she could claw her way back to the higher echelons of society? In her heart she knew there was not, and in truth, she didn't think she would ever find the strength to try. These last days of living out on the streets had sucked the life out of her; she was never meant to live hand to mouth. Sitting in the cold, she prayed it would not rain but as she glanced at the sky, the dark clouds told a different story.

* * *

Ella and her team worked throughout the night, only taking rest breaks when tired watery eyes pre-vented them from seeing the tiny stitches on the millinery.

At nine o'clock in the morning, the shop was

opened and the first person through the door was Flossie Woolley.

'What's going on?' she demanded to know.

'You'd best speak to Ella, she's in the back room,' Katy said, pointing the way with a yawn.

Finding Ella snoozing on an armchair, Flossie asked her question again then added, 'I called round last night and you were nowhere to be seen.'

'We have a large order to fill so we're all working flat out,' Ella said sheepishly.

'Ar, that's what our Josh told me, but I don't believe a word of it.'

Ella sighed. She'd been sworn to secrecy and desperately wanted to adhere to her word. On the other hand, Flossie had been so good to her over the years, could she really keep her friend in the dark?

'Come with me,' she said. Calling Katy to join them, they went to the workroom. Tilda was lending a hand and Thora and Freda were surrounded by cloth, feathers and ribbons.

'How do, Floss, how are you?' Thora asked.

'I'd be a bloody sight better if'n I knew what was afoot!' Flossie stood with her arms crossed beneath her bosom.

Glances were exchanged, as if each woman was trying to read the mind of another. Over time, they had all become firm friends with the plain-speaking Flossie, and Ella could see they felt as she did. Flossie had been a godsend during their special days at the shop, organising for her offspring to model the hats at their shows. She was like one of them, a member of the family, for all she didn't work at Ivella.

'Ladies?' Ella asked.

'We promised...' Freda began but faltered at Flossie's scowl.

'A nod or shake will give the answer I seek,' Ella went on. Looking at each in turn, Ella saw a nod from each. 'Right.'

Turning to Flossie, she said, 'Be here at nine o'clock on Monday morning – with your best frock on.'

Flossie frowned. 'What the...?'

'I can't tell you, Flossie, but I can show you. For your part, you must swear not to say a word to a soul.'

'I swear,' Flossie said, although the secrecy was already tormenting her.

'It's imperative, Flossie, you can't mention any-thing – even to your family,' Ella urged.

'I bloody swore, d'aint I?'

'Thank you. I promise by Monday lunchtime you'll know everything and will be the envy of all your friends.'

'Well, as I'm here, give me something to do. My lot have all gone to work so I can leave the chores for another day.'

Breathing a sigh of relief that Flossie did not pursue the matter any further, Ella set her neigh-bour and friend to work on stitching a frill on a parasol.

And so the day progressed. By mid-afternoon, Flossie left to attend to an evening meal for her hus-band and children. The others talked over their de-cision to bring Flossie into the conspiracy.

'I feel bad about breaking my word to Mr Shot-ton,' Freda said.

'Yer soft wench, he'll never know,' Thora replied sharply. 'He's just a lackey.'

'Even so, what if Flossie should...' Katy began.

'She won't. I've known her for years and if she's sworn an oath, she will stick to it. Besides, we haven't broken our word. We haven't told Flossie anything. All we said was to be here on Monday morning for her to discover our secret.' Ella was confident she was right. 'I suggest we close the shop early and have a couple of hours off.'

'Good idea, I'm about done in,' Thora agreed.

Ella went to lock up and turn off the lights, and the others followed to the comfortable back room.

Tilda conjured up a meat and potato pie, vegetables and gravy seemingly from nowhere and everyone tucked in hungrily.

When they had finished eating, they slept where they sat. A full belly and a little sleep ensured they would wake refreshed and ready to start again.

47

On Sunday evening, the dark material hung at the window and behind it sat a new display of some of Ella's finest creations. The shop was festooned with hats of all sizes, shapes and colours. In discreet places, small coloured paper crowns were situated, courtesy of Katy's clever thinking.

'Ladies, thank you. There's nothing more we can do, so I suggest we head home for a good night's sleep. Remember, be back at nine o'clock so we can be prepared.'

There were grateful groans of 'Thank God!' and Ella smiled.

Saying goodnight, they parted company and after locking up, Ella glanced at the window. Nothing could be seen other than the dark curtain, and she wandered home, tired to the bone but happy with the way everything had gone. Still, in the back of her mind, she had a niggling worry about Darcie, but she pushed it away. She had more pressing matters to think about now.

The following morning dawned with a fog so thick it could have been cut with a knife. As Ella hurried to the shop, she wondered if her special visitor would cancel her visit due to the foul weather. It would be a dreadful disappointment if the event was called off, especially after all the work they had put in.

Tilda had unlocked the door and welcomed everyone, including Flossie, with a hot cup of tea. They all watched the hands on the clock move exasperatingly slowly and their nerves tingled.

'At least the fog will keep folk indoors,' Thora said.

'Fingers crossed,' Katy added.

'Can't you tell me what's going on now?' Flossie asked.

'You'll see very soon, I hope.' Ella would have crossed her toes and eyes if she thought it would help.

At five minutes to ten, Ella had everyone line up in the shop before throwing open the door wide. An eerie stillness lay over the street, which was unusually quiet. Ella looked at the clock again, two minutes to go. She walked to the open door and stepped out, looking both ways. She could see nothing but a thick grey blanket, and she shuffled from foot to foot.

Then she heard it. The clip-clop of a horse's hooves. Her excitement was ready to burst out of her chest. Could this be it? Or was it just a carter going to market?

Slowly a shape formed out of the fog and a carriage appeared. It halted outside the shop and the jarvey leapt down to open the door and pull down the steps. A hand was extended, then a lady descended and hurried into the shop. Ella watched the maid look around her and nod, then she went to the door and nodded once more. Two large men climbed out of the carriage, dressed in identical livery, then out stepped a dark-haired lady. With one man either side of her, the lady walked smartly into the shop. Ella quickly followed, closing and locking the door behind her.

'Miss Bancroft.'

'Your Majesty,' Ella said with a deep curtsy. 'Welcome to Ivella.'

Flossie's mouth fell open as she at last understood the well-kept secret.

The Queen greeted each of the ladies by name as they were introduced, and they bent into a curtsy before her. 'I have to praise you for your discretion, ladies.'

'Mr Shotton said you might like to see our new range of millinery, Ma'am,' Ella said, waving an arm and remembering to pronounce the title to rhyme with jam.

'Indeed.'

'Can we offer you refreshments, Ma'am?'

'That would be most welcome. May I ask, do you have coffee, perchance? I have taken rather a liking to it.'

'Yes, Ma'am, and fancies an' all – erm – as well,' Tilda corrected herself.

'Splendid. Now, Miss Bancroft, show me what you have.'

Ella and the others brought forth the hats from their perches for the Queen to look at.

'This one. That one, and oh, yes, that one too.' A white teardrop in silk with a small net veil to cover the eyes was put aside, as was a black riding hat with a wide silk tie around the crown. The third was a red satin creation with black feathers neatly attached to the side, a silk rose holding them in place. The chosen articles were quickly boxed, strung and placed on the end of the long counter.

'Your coffee, Ma'am,' Tilda said tentatively.

The Queen was shown into the back room, which had been polished to within an inch of its life, and took a seat in the well-padded armchair. As she sipped her drink, she chatted openly with them all, asking about their lives and trade and complimenting them on their hard work. She requested a tour of the building and Ella showed the royal visitor everything from the workroom to the storage rooms. The Queen declined to see the private quarters, much to Tilda's relief, for she was not the tidiest of people.

Back in the shop, Queen Alexandra chose more hats before asking if her maid would be kind enough to inform her driver that she was ready to leave. The two bodyguards loaded the hat boxes into the carriage as the Queen gave each woman her thanks. Then she was gone.

Locking up once more, the women returned in silence to the comfortable chairs, still hardly able to comprehend what had just taken place.

'Bloody hellfire and damnation!' Flossie exclaimed, breaking the spell. 'I can't believe I've just met the Queen!'

'Now you see why it was hush-hush and why we've worked our fingers to the bone,' Ella replied with a grin.

'Wasn't she lovely? Did you see she had two of my fancies?' Tilda said proudly.

'Ladies, I could not have done this without you, and I thank you from the bottom of my heart,' Ella said tearfully.

'If not for you, we wouldn't have met the Queen. Oh, Ella, your dad would be so proud!' Flossie said, brushing away her own tears.

'Ivy would have loved it too,' Freda said a little sadly.

Ella nodded. She hoped her father, Ivy and Harper were aware of how far she'd come and they would indeed be proud of her.

After tea, Ella suggested they all went home for some much-needed rest, and they could unveil the new window display tomorrow.

Walking home with Flossie, Ella chatted animatedly about their visitor.

'It's unusual for the Queen to do a visit without the King, ain't it?' Flossie asked.

'I'm not sure, but I guess so,' Ella replied as they meandered their way through the fog. 'I'm still trying to take it all in.'

'Here, does that mean we can talk about it now?' Flossie asked.

'Oh, I don't know. Maybe I should have spoken to Mr Shotton about that. It might be prudent not to, though, don't you think?'

'I suppose.' Flossie was disappointed at not being allowed to boast to her friends that she had taken tea with the Queen.

'Perhaps Mr Shotton will be in touch again, then we can ask him,' Ella replied hopefully.

Ella had never been so glad to see her bed as she was that night and she slept like the dead.

The following day, an envoy delivered a letter to Ivella, and as Ella opened it, she gasped with amazement and delight.

48

The night before Ella and her staff were to entertain the Queen of England in their little shop, Darcie sat on the street corner. She knew she was slowly starving to death and if she didn't do something soon, she would pass over right there on the roadway.

She deliberated whether she could in fact do what the other women were doing for money, and although it turned her stomach, she knew she had to try.

Getting to her feet, she stood in the yellow pool of light from the street lamp. She was scared and didn't know exactly how to go about this, but she needed to eat – and soon.

The streetwalkers beneath another lamp watched her intently. Was that woman trying to invade their patch, intending to steal the custom they felt was theirs? They muttered quietly to each other as they waited for their customers to arrive.

'If she scores, I'll punch her bloody lights out!' Jinny said. She was the leader of the little band and was built like an outhouse.

'Don't bother, she won't,' another answered.

However, just then, a man approached Darcie and spoke to her. She nodded and walked away with him.

'Right, that's it! I'll have her when she comes back!' Jinny snapped, her hair swishing around her face as she spoke.

Darcie followed the man into a dark alley. She was scared witless. This man could be a murderer! He could kill her and no one would be any the wiser until she was found the following morning.

'C'mon then, get them drawers off,' the man said.

There was little light in the alley and Darcie looked back the way they had come. Could she make a run for it? Would he catch her before she could get away?

'What you waitin' for?'

'Money,' Darcie croaked.

'Oh, no, you bloody don't! Service first, then money.'

Darcie felt her blood run cold. Tears formed and ran down her cheeks. She didn't want to do this, she couldn't.

'I've changed my mind,' she said, turning on her heel. She was startled as the man caught her arm, swinging her around to face him.

'That ain't how this works,' he said. 'I'm guessing you're new to it, am I right?'

'Let go of me! Get your filthy hands off me!' Darcie said.

'You made an agreement and I'm gonna make sure you honour it!' The man grabbed her skirts and threw them up as he snatched at her underwear.

'Get off me!' Darcie yelled.

Try as she might, she couldn't release herself from his grip. She was weak from hunger and what strength she had soon left her as he abused her body. Sobbing like a baby, Darcie was swung around and forced to fold forward as he pushed and heaved at her from behind. She could smell the sweat, tobacco and beer on him and she gagged. The pain was excruciating, and she cried out her despair.

When he had finished with her, he pulled out a coin and dropped it at her feet before walking away.

Darcie stared at the money, glinting in the sliver of light from the streetlight. What had she done? She had been despoiled by a stranger and could never now hope to be wed to a gentleman. Sliding down the wall of the alley, she cried like she had never done before.

Eventually her tears ebbed and she got to her feet. She was tender where he had hurt her. She picked up the money, she'd earned it, so she might as well have it.

Wandering back down the alley, she emerged to see the women waiting for her.

'What the bloody hell do you think you're doing?' Jinny shouted.

Darcie shook her head. She felt wretched enough without this.

'This is our patch. You bugger off and find your

own!' With that, Jinny raised a hand and slapped Darcie's face.

Bringing her palm to her stinging cheek, Darcie felt she could sink no lower. She took the beating Jinny gave her without so much as a sound. Then, when the streetwalker had vented her anger, Darcie stumbled away, the pain in her body screaming in protest.

'And don't come back here!' Jinny shouted after her as she accepted the congratulations from her friends as they ambled back to their spot beneath the light.

49

Ella read out the letter to the staff.

As a mark of recognition to those who have supplied goods to Queen Alexandra, Ivella has been awarded a Royal Warrant of Appointment.

'What exactly does that mean?' Tilda asked.

'It means,' Ella waved the letter in the air, 'that this lends prestige to our business. We can now have a new sign with this incorporated onto it. Everyone will know that the Queen has purchased our goods!'

Spontaneous applause rang out, then Thora suggested, 'You'd best get that letter to the sign-writer right away then.'

With a jaunty laugh, Ella grabbed her coat and skipped out of the door. A moment later, she was back. 'Katy – the window!'

'Blimey, I forgot about that!' Katy gushed as she moved to unveil the new display.

The fog was not so thick today, more of a milky mist as Ella hurried along, though it was still cold. However, excitement kept her warm at thought of the new sign. She couldn't wait to see it over the shop. Clearly this was the permission they needed to be able to share their news, but Ella thought the better part of discretion would be to wait until the new sign was in place.

The day passed quickly, the display drawing in passing trade, and it was that evening that Tilda decided to visit her friends again who continued to walk the streets. She hadn't seen them for quite some time and was curious to see how many remained in the age-old profession.

Taking the train to Birmingham, Tilda left New Street station and headed towards her old haunts. As she walked, she thought how lucky she was at no longer having to sell her body to sleazy men who frequented that particular area. It was all thanks to Ella, and every day, Tilda prayed her luck would hold out and she wouldn't find herself back seeking work on the cold and lonely streets once more.

'Well, well, look who's here, girls!' a voice called out.

'Tilda, sorry, wench, your pitch has gone,' said another with a laugh.

Tilda greeted the women with hugs. 'I didn't know if you'd be here,' she said.

'Where else would we be?' Jinny asked.

'I was a bit nervous about coming here at night,' Tilda said.

'Why? You used to work nights here, remember?' Jinny replied.

Tilda nodded.

The laughter grew loud as the women went on to regale Tilda with their exploits.

'I had one fella who just wanted me to throw cream cakes at him!'

'Bloody hell, Jinny, what a waste of cakes,' Tilda said with a grin.

'That's what I told him, so we made a deal. I'd

throw six and keep the other six. He paid me an' all,' Jinny said, then her high-pitched cackle echoed along the empty street.

It was then that Jinny caught sight of the stranger standing beneath a streetlamp further along. It was the same woman she had given a beating to. 'Oi! I've told you once, this is our patch, so bugger off unless you want another pasting!'

'Who's that?' Tilda asked.

'Dunno, but she's been hanging around for a day or two. We've chased her away, but she keeps coming back. I gave her a hiding but clearly it wasn't enough to stop her.'

'Do you think she's one of us?' Tilda asked.

'One of *us*, you mean, you ain't any more, remember? No, I think she's new, she ain't got a clue.'

'Will you let her stay?'

'Not bloody likely! Can't have anyone nicking our punters,' Jinny said, rather loudly.

Tilda squinted at the lone woman. There was something familiar about her, but Tilda couldn't quite put her finger on what that was. The woman reminded her of someone. Shaking her head, she thought, no, it couldn't be – could it?

Tilda tentatively walked towards the woman, who was watching her. As she neared, Tilda drew in a breath. Was it who she thought? Was it Darcie Newland?

Dressed in clothes which had seen far better days, the once well-to-do woman looked thin. Her dirty hair had lost its lustre and hung limp and lank. She had shed a lot of weight and she looked entirely different.

'Miss Newland?' Tilda asked quietly.

'Do you know me?'

'Yes, we've met before.'

Suddenly a light blazed in Darcie's eyes as recognition dawned. 'Tilda Hunter!'

In an instant, Tilda regretted her action, wishing she hadn't approached the woman in the first place. A fear took hold of her as she saw Darcie's face covered in anger.

The streetwalkers moved as one to stand behind their friend.

'You ruined my life!' Darcie spat as she pushed her head forward in a threatening gesture.

'No, you did that yourself,' Tilda answered, feeling grateful for the support of the others.

'You wrecked my soiree!'

'That I can't deny, but you have to admit you asked for it.'

The prostitutes exchanged glances, trying to glean what was going on between the two women.

'Tilda the clairvoyant, what a joke!' Darcie spat.

'It's better than setting out to blacken another's name, someone who never did anything to warrant your spite.'

'Ella Bancroft stole my fiancé!'

'No, it was he who dumped you, but you've never allowed yourself to come to terms with it,' Tilda answered.

'Nonsense! You weren't there; what would you know about it?'

'I heard you threaten Ella at your soiree, that's why I did what I did.'

'Threaten Ella? I've no idea what you mean,' Darcie lied, some of her old swagger returning.

'Drop the pretence, Darcie, it's not going to help you now. Look at yourself, for goodness' sake, see where you've ended up.'

Darcie looked down at her torn coat, the muddy

hem of her dress, then looked at each of the women in turn.

'You're no better than any of us now,' Jinny said.

'I will never be as low as you!'

'Cheeky bugger!' another said.

'You've been trying to muscle in on our patch for a while now,' Jinny took up, 'so in my book, that puts you exactly on our level. We saw you go into that alley with that bloke, and it don't take much thinking about to know what went on.'

Tilda sucked in a breath as she realised what had been said. Darcie Newland had turned into a prostitute!

'This has nothing to do with you, so keep your mouth shut!' Darcie snapped spitefully.

Jinny's hand shot out and delivered a sharp slap to Darcie's cheek, knocking her back a step. 'I belted you once, do you want some more?'

Raising her own hand to cover her stinging cheek, Darcie rasped, 'I'll have the law on you!'

'Go ahead and try, but I warn you, it won't do you any good,' Jinny answered.

'The police will drag you all off to jail for assault!'

'I doubt it and I'll tell you why, shall I? Us girls *know* quite a lot of the bobbies who patrol this area.'

The others laughed loudly at Jinny's remark.

'So you see, the boys in blue would have no fun if we were carted off to jail.'

Seeing red, Darcie darted forward in a vicious attack and as Jinny was nearest, she was the one to feel the blows. Darcie's fists attempted to pummel the other woman, who now had Darcie's hair in her hand, pulling hard. Darcie fell to her knees and pain shot through her legs as Jinny continued to slap with her other hand.

The others stood back. Having seen Jinny fight before, they knew she could hold her own admirably.

'Stop it!' Tilda yelled and took a step forward.

She was held back. 'Let 'em finish it, Tilda, it's been coming so it's best over and done with.'

Just then, Darcie let out a howl and crouched into a ball, trying to protect herself from the on-slaught.

Out of breath, Jinny moved away from the woman lying on the ground, her arms covering her head.

After a minute, Darcie looked up. She saw at last that she was beaten and with a snarl, she got to her feet and turned to walk away. Over her shoulder, she yelled, 'This is not the end, Tilda Hunter!'

The group of women watched Darcie walk away and Tilda breathed a sigh of relief.

'You know she could have had a knife?' Tilda asked.

Jinny just nodded, realising how foolish she had been.

'I'd best get on home. Thanks, girls, I'm sure I'll see you soon.'

'Be careful, that woman could be waiting for you,' Jinny advised.

'I will.'

'Don't forget to come back and see us again,' one of the others called out.

Tilda waved as she set off for the railway station. Maybe it had been a mistake coming here again. She had felt the old familiar fear of standing in the street, albeit this time the threat came from a woman. Yes, from now on she would stay close to home where she was safe, with her new friends.

50

The following evening, Nicholas collected Ella from home. 'I'm glad you telephoned,' Ella said as they dined in a nice family-run eating house.

'I'm happy you could come, I know how busy you've been of late,' he replied, the glow from the candle lighting up his eyes.

'I'm sorry, but now we have lots of time to be together – if that's what you want.' Ella blushed at her own forthright manner.

'I most certainly do. I've missed seeing you, these last days.'

'Me, too.' Ella felt the heat flow through her veins and her heart beat a tattoo in her chest. It had been so long since she had felt this way; in fact, she had resigned herself to never having those feelings again.

'So, are you able to tell me about the big order which has kept you from me?' Nicholas asked with a mischievous grin.

'I... erm... Nicholas, it's difficult to explain. Please don't ask me about it, just trust me when I say all will be revealed very soon.'

Nicholas frowned but inclined his head in acceptance. Whatever it was, Ella would tell him in her own good time.

'Ella, I have something I wish to discuss with you.'

It was Ella's turn to nod and, glad for the subject to be changed, she gave him her full attention.

'We have not known each other for very long in the great scheme of things...'

Ella felt the heat rise to her cheeks. Could it be Nicholas was going to propose marriage and, if so, would becoming betrothed to this man turn out as badly as it had with Harper? Ella didn't know if she could go through that again, the heartbreak of losing yet another man she had come to love.

'However, you must know by now how much I love you.'

There, he had said it. Nicholas had declared his feelings for her. Should she do the same? Was it wise to pin her heart on her sleeve?

'Therefore – oh, Ella, would you consider becoming my wife?' Nicholas's words came out in a rush before he lost his courage.

Ella's hand moved to her chest as he produced a small box and flipped open the lid. There, on a black velvet cushion, sat a gold ring with a small diamond at its centre. She drew in a breath as she looked at the beauty of the precious jewel, which glittered in the candlelight. Then her eyes slid to his, where she saw the myriad of emotions, the longing, the desperation for her to say yes, the uncertainty of whether he was rushing her. Ella's heart swelled with her love for him, and she knew what her answer would be.

'Yes,' she said on a breath.

With a smile which lit up his whole face, Nicholas slipped the ring onto her finger and watched as she held out her hand to admire it.

Catching a waiter's eye, Nicholas beckoned him over. 'May we have a bottle of champagne, please?'

'My apologies, sir, but we don't carry it. There's no call for it as a rule,' the waiter replied awkwardly.

'A bottle of your finest wine will do nicely,' Nicholas said, seeing the relief cross the waiter's face.

'At once, sir.'

The couple drank a toast to a long and happy life together.

As she delved into her bag for a handkerchief, Ella was suddenly reminded of the note that she had kept there. 'Nicholas, what about that note?' She had not forgotten that in all probability Darcie Newland was still out to ruin her.

'Have you heard any more?'

'No, but...'

'Then try to forget it, my love.'

Ella gave a small smile. This was a celebration of their engagement and she knew she shouldn't spoil it with worries regarding the spiteful Miss Newland.

That prickle of fear was always with her when she thought about the note, but for now, she took Nicholas's advice and pushed it aside in order to enjoy the happiness of her betrothal.

* * *

Ella was greeted by squeals of delight from Katy and the others as she announced she was to be married. Her friends crowded around to see the ring and they all gave their congratulations.

'Does Flossie know?' Katy asked.

'Yes, I told her this morning. She was delighted for us,' Ella replied.

'When's the wedding?' Freda asked.

'Bloody hell, give the girl a chance, they've only just got engaged!' Thora said.

Ella laughed. 'We thought in the summer.'

'New hats all round, then,' Katy added.

Colours and styles were being discussed then Ella noticed Tilda was a little quiet. 'Are you all right?' she asked.

Tilda gave a curt nod. 'I went to Birmingham last night to see some old friends – streetwalkers.' She waited for the shock to register on their faces, but when it didn't show, she went on more confidently. No one was standing in judgement of her. 'You will never guess who I saw there.'

Ella and the others exchanged glances of puzzlement.

'Darcie Newland.'

'What?' Ella exclaimed. 'Are you sure it was her?'

Tilda nodded. Then she related what had occurred the previous night, finishing with how Darcie had disappeared into the darkness.

So that was why Ella had heard nothing more after receiving the note. She breathed a sigh of relief, then said, 'I wonder what will become of her.'

'Don't you feel sorry for her, Ella, she brought it on herself. Bear in mind what she had planned for you at her soiree, how she was going to try and blacken your name in front of all those high-fallutin' folk,' Tilda said firmly.

'I know, but even so...'

'Tilda's right, Ella, it's time to forget that woman and look forward to a happy life with Nicholas,' Thora put in quickly.

'You're correct, of course, and we have our new sign to enjoy too.'

The excited chatter began again around how Queen Alexandra had chosen their little shop to visit.

Ella received another surprise visit from Mr Shotton that afternoon. After he had been shown into the back room, he was given tea, again in Ivy's best chinaware.

'I have brought payment for Her Majesty's purchases, along with her thanks,' he said, handing over an envelope containing a banker's draft.

'Thank you so much, Mr Shotton. I'm still reeling over the whole thing. Oh, and look...' Ella drew out the letter which had informed her of the Royal Warrant.

Mr Shotton scanned the paper and smiled. 'I am aware of it, Ella, and in my opinion, it is richly deserved.'

Ella smiled shyly. 'Are we allowed to discuss the royal visit now?'

'It might be wiser to keep that to yourselves. A new sign over your shop will tell people all they need to know.'

'Very well,' Ella nodded, her disappointment evident.

'It wouldn't do for the general populace to know of the Queen's secretive visit, they may feel their chance of seeing royalty had been thwarted.'

'Yes, I can understand that,' Ella replied.

'Now I shall return to London, my task completed, but before I go, I extend my congratulations on your engagement. I hope you will both be very happy.'

Ella glanced at the diamond sparkling on her finger, amazed that he had noticed. 'Thank you, I'm certain we will be.'

Seeing her visitor out, a sudden thought sparked in her mind, and she asked, 'Mr Shotton, did the Queen travel by coach all the way from London?'

'No, my dear. She travelled on the royal train, the coach is held at the saddler's for just such occasions. Why do you ask?'

'I was just thinking she didn't look tired or harassed when she arrived. I would have thought coach travel over such a distance would have shaken her badly.'

'It would indeed. Now, I really must be on my way. Good day, Miss Bancroft.'

Tipping his hat, Mr Shotton climbed into the waiting carriage and wiggled his fingers in a little wave.

Ella returned the wave and watched as the carriage disappeared. Back indoors, she opened the envelope and took out the contents. The banker's draft more than covered her sales and along with it was a headed paper. 'With thanks,' it was signed by the Queen.

Ella clutched it to her chest before putting it with the letter of appointment into the safe.

Now all she had to do was await the new sign. Oh, and tell the girls they must take their secret to their graves.

51

That evening, Josh sat quietly, knowing he needed to speak with his mother. His father and his two sisters had gone to their beds already, and Josh had patiently awaited his chance.

'Mum, can I talk to you?'

'Yes, lovey, what's up?'

'How would you feel if I asked Katy to marry me?'

'Oh, darlin', I'd be as happy as a pig in muck!'

Josh grinned at Flossie's turn of phrase. 'My problem is where we'll live once we're wed.'

Flossie blew out her cheeks. 'I know, I've thought about that myself.'

'Oh, yes?' Josh's grin was back.

'Well, you two are so close, it was inevitable that you'd marry one day. As for afterwards...'

'I know we couldn't stay here, Mum, there just ain't the room.'

'Look, you get the question asked and leave the accommodation problem to me. We'll sort something out for you somehow.'

Josh hugged his mother, kissing her cheek. 'Well, it's funny you should say that. The truth is I've already asked, and she said yes.'

'You bugger!' Flossie said before tears welled in her eyes. Her boy would be leaving home. Flossie corrected her thoughts, he was a man now, soon to be a husband and hopefully, in time, a father. *I'll be a grandma!* Flossie laughed, already falling in love with the idea. 'I've got to go and tell Ella!'

Josh shook his head, a broad smile on his face. 'Best check to see if she's still up. I'll make a cuppa to celebrate when you get back.'

'If she ain't, she soon will be!' Flossie said on a laugh.

Ella was preparing to retire for the night when, a moment later, Flossie ran in through the back door.

'You'll never guess – our Josh and Katy are engaged!' she blurted out.

'That's wonderful news, Flossie!' Ella said.

'I'll need a new hat, and so will you and the girls!'

'A new outfit too!' Flossie's excitement was contagious and Ella found herself caught up in it, all thoughts of bed having been forgotten.

On they talked about who would be invited, what colours to wear, what style of hat to choose, and whether they would both cry at the wedding ceremony.

'We'm getting ahead of ourselves now,' Flossie said at last.

Eventually, as calm befell the two women, Flossie mentioned about trying to find somewhere for the couple to live.

'Flossie, I had wondered about that too, should a wedding take place. Now, hear me out and tell me what you think.' Ella went on to explain about her idea of moving to Ivella and renting out her house. 'I'd love for Josh and Katy to have it,' she finished.

'Oh, Ella! Oh, my...' Flossie burst into tears, sobbing into her shawl.

Ella hugged her friend. 'Go and tell Josh what

I've said and see if he agrees. If so, he'll have to help me shift my things.'

'Thanks, chick, he'll be over the moon.' Flossie disappeared, leaving Ella to enjoy the warm feeling which wrapped itself around her. She wondered how Tilda would feel about having to share with her, if Ella did move in. As she was engaged herself, she would be able to tell Tilda that hopefully it would not be for too long. It was Ella's shop now, so she could do whatever she wanted, but she would prefer Tilda to be all right with it, otherwise it could cause untold problems.

As Ella settled in the warmth the range threw out, Flossie was telling Josh the news next door.

'Mum... that's so good of her,' he said, his tears glistening in the lamplight.

'I expect she'll square it with Tilda tomorrow. Katy will be pleased an' all, I think,' Flossie muttered, her chest tightening at seeing her son so close to crying.

'She will be, Mum. You know what – we are very fortunate to have Ella as our neighbour.'

Flossie nodded in agreement, feeling her own

tears sting her eyes. 'Right, I'm away to my bed. Goodnight, lad.'

Josh folded his mother in his arms and whispered, 'Night, Mum. I love you.'

Flossie's chest now released of the tension, it swelled with pride. 'I love you an' all,' she said, as she hugged her son.

* * *

Ella requested five minutes of Tilda's time when she explained the events of the previous evening.

'Ooh, it'll be nice to have some company,' Tilda said.

Ella visibly relaxed on hearing that Tilda was comfortable about the upcoming new arrangements.

'I'll start to bring my things over bit by bit once I've cleaned out the spare room.'

'I'll give you a hand,' Tilda offered.

'Thank you. It'll be done in no time with both of us.'

Katy came through, flashing a pretty ring bought by Josh. 'Look, I'm engaged!'

'Blimey, everyone's at it!' Tilda said with a grin.

Hugs and congratulations were given before Katy shot upstairs to show Thora and Freda.

'When's the wedding, then?' Freda asked.

'And are we invited?' Thora added.

'Of course you are! We thought as soon as possible,' Katy answered excitedly. Seeing the looks on the faces watching her, she added, 'No, I'm not pregnant. I don't believe in any of that before marriage.'

'Good girl.' Thora was full of praise.

'Will you move in with Flossie's family, then?' Freda's question wiped the smile from Katy's face.

'No, there's no room. We'll have to find somewhere else – and quickly.'

Ella and Tilda walked in at that moment and Ella said, 'I've told Flossie to tell Josh that you can rent my house because I'm moving in here with Tilda.'

'Oh, my goodness! Ella, that's wonderful! Thank you so much!' Katy flung herself at Ella and hugged her tightly.

'Stop – I can't breathe!' Ella croaked.

Thora and Freda dashed a tear away as they watched the little scene before them.

'Tilda is going to help me clean the spare room so I can bring my belongings over,' Ella explained.

'You'll have to tell Nicholas as well,' Katy said. 'Otherwise he'll be knocking on the door of an empty house – for now, at least.'

'I'll do that tonight when I see him,' Ella nodded.

Katy was on cloud nine as she returned to the shop and all day, the ladies and their customers were serenaded by her lovely voice. Ella thought it was a beautiful addition to Ivella.

That evening, Ella decided to cook a meal for Nicholas and herself. Beef collected from the butcher on her way home was roasting in the range, the delicious aroma filling the house. Potatoes and vegetables were simmering nicely, and the gravy browning was on standby.

Nicholas knocked and walked in through the back door. 'Something smells good,' he said.

'I thought we'd eat here tonight,' Ella said as she checked the pans on the hot plates.

'Wonderful!' Nicholas removed his coat and Ella took it to the hall stand.

'Have a seat and open the wine. I bought it, although I have no idea whether it's any good.'

Nicholas looked at the label. 'Good vintage.' Pouring two glasses, they sat at the table and Ella excitedly shared the news of Katy and Josh becoming engaged. 'So I'll be living at Ivella, which I have to admit will be rather strange.' Then, with a cheeky grin, she added, 'But with luck, it won't be for long.'

'You have a heart of gold, Ella Bancroft.'

Ella smiled and, raising her glass, she said, 'To Josh and Katy, may they have a long and happy life together.'

Nicholas clinked his glass against hers. 'And may we have the same.'

52

Ella was reading the newspaper by a roaring fire when she caught her breath. She read the article again and then laid the paper in her lap. Staring into the dancing flames, her heart was heavy. A woman had been found in a shop doorway in Birmingham, where she had frozen to death. The woman had been named as Darcie Newland.

Part of Ella was relieved that she no longer had to worry about looking over her shoulder in fear of attack. The other part of her felt sorry for Darcie, having reached such a dreadful end.

Going through to the shop, Ella stood looking out of the window. Fat lazy snowflakes fell from the heavens, coating everything in a thick white cloak. There was no denying Mother Nature was beautiful, but she could also be cruel. How many others would succumb to the freezing temperature? And how many more would die from the influenza which always came with the winter months?

Ella shivered and drew her woollen shawl tighter about her shoulders. Business was slow because of the weather, so she turned and said, 'Katy, you and the others get off home. I don't think we'll see many more customers today.'

'Oooh, ta! I'll go and tell them,' Katy said.

Ella nodded and donned her outdoor clothes. To Tilda, she said, 'I think we'll wait for a change in the weather before we open the shop again.'

'Good idea, folk will stay by their firesides, I would think. Did you see that piece in the paper?'

'Yes, such a shame.'

'It happens, more than you'd imagine,' Tilda said. During her time as a prostitute, she had witnessed a few deaths of people who lived and begged on the streets. 'Anyway, you lot had best get off before you get snowed in here with me.'

Tilda locked up after everyone had left. She too

felt a little sorry for the unfortunate Darcie New-land, but she also had the sense to realise none of them would have been safe whilst that woman lived. With a shrug, she thought, *at least it saved me from putting her out of her misery in order to keep Ella alive!*

The snow continued to fall heavily for days, and Ella had insisted Nicholas didn't travel from Birm-ingham to see her. She explained she had closed the shop until the thaw came.

In truth, Ella was terrified something might happen to Nicholas – an accident on the icy roads, or a cold which turned to pneumonia. She knew it was ridiculous to worry so, but she could not stop her-self. She couldn't bear the thought that Nicholas might be taken from her. She so desperately wanted to be his wife and have his children, and she knew this irrational fear of losing him was not conducive to her own good health.

Sitting in her small kitchen, she glanced to where her father's wheelchair had sat. 'Oh, Dad, I wish you were here to advise me,' she muttered. 'What should I do? Should I bring the wedding forward?'

It was then she noticed the snow had stopped

falling and a weak ray of sunshine came through the window to land on a white hat she had been working on. Was it a sign? Had her father sent her a message to say he agreed with her thinking? Ella's heartbeat sped up as she thought it might be possible.

Putting on her coat, hat and gloves, she rushed out to brave the cold. She needed to telephone Nicholas, so she headed for Ivella.

As she neared the shop, she stopped dead in her tracks. The new sign had been hung. She silently blessed the sign-writer for his promise to deliver it as soon as possible. He had gone above and beyond to hang it in such awful weather.

Unlocking the door, she called out to Tilda. 'It's only me, I need to use the telephone.'

Tilda came through. 'Fancy a cuppa while you're here?'

'Wonderful.'

Wandering away to put the kettle to boil, Tilda gave Ella the privacy she needed.

'Nicholas, it's Ella,' she said as the call connected.

'Hello, darling. Are you all right?' he asked, concern etched in his voice.

'Yes, yes, I'm fine. Nicholas, how would you feel about bringing the wedding forward?'

'Oh, sweetheart, I'd love it!' Ella beamed as he went on, 'I'll see the vicar right away.'

'I'm so glad you agree,' Ella gushed.

'It should take no more than three weeks to have the banns read in church, then we can be man and wife.'

'I'm so excited,' Ella said on a laugh.

'Me too. You'd best get your hat made, you're going to a wedding!'

'I love you, Nicholas Gerard.'

'I love you too, Ella soon-to-be Mrs Gerard.'

Replacing the handset, Ella danced a little jig right there in the shop. Then she pulled out a box and took out the hat from within. The hat was covered in white velvet and held two silk roses on the small brim. A feather nestled between the flowers and a net veil hung down to cover the eyes.

Ella smiled. This was her wedding hat. Just then, the sun shone through the window again and Ella knew for certain she had her father's blessing.

Ella had thought long and hard about when to move to Ivella and she decided now would be a good time to hand over the house to Josh and Katy in order that they could make it their own.

Despite the snow, Ella and Tilda moved Ella's clothes and trinkets over to Ivella. The furniture she left for Josh and Katy to make use of. Josh borrowed a cart to tote Ella's bed and bedclothes and once it was installed, all that was left to move was Ella herself.

She had told Josh and Katy to do what they wanted with their new home, and the young couple eagerly began decorating. Walls and woodwork were badly in need of a coat of paint, and Josh and Katy worked happily together.

Ella felt a little strange on her first night at Ivella, but she had to admit it was nice having company and she and Tilda chatted easily before retiring to bed.

53

Josh and Katy's wedding was the following day, and everyone was looking forward to it, despite the snowy weather.

Flossie and Ella sat at Ivella with Tilda, having tea, when Flossie said, 'Katy thinks she'll have to walk down the aisle on her own.'

'What! Why?' Ella asked, shocked to her core.

'She says her father will be too drunk to stand up, never mind be able to give her away.'

'Poor wench,' Tilda commented.

'Is there no one else who could do it?' Ella asked.

Flossie shook her head. 'I don't think so, and I don't like to push it. Katy seems set on this way.'

'That's awful. It's a shame one of us couldn't step up,' Ella said sadly.

'It would never be allowed,' Flossie said with a shake of her head.

'At least we'll all be there to support her.' Ella's heart went out to her young friend.

'I'm off home before it starts to snow again,' Flossie said. 'See you tomorrow.'

Ella and Tilda chatted about Katy's predicament before they had lunch, Ella thinking maybe Nicholas could help out. Then again, she didn't want to upset Katy by poking her nose in, so she dismissed the idea.

'I'll be glad to open the shop again,' Ella said. 'We're losing money every day it's closed.'

'It won't be long, then folk will be eager to know all about the new sign,' Tilda replied.

Sitting by the fire in the afternoon, the two dozed, comfortable in each other's company.

The following morning was cold but bright. The weak sun shone down in an effort to thaw out the town, but it was having very little effect.

Ella had ordered a cab to collect them and transport them to the church. Wrapped warmly, Ella and

Tilda climbed aboard and settled in for the short journey. They winced as the carriage slid on the ice but were reassured hearing the cabbie's gentle encouragement to his horse.

Arriving safely, Ella and Tilda alighted and entered the church after paying the cabbie. They sat near the front behind Flossie and her family.

Ella returned Josh's smile. He stood smartly dressed, awaiting his beloved. One of his friends from the sawmills where he worked was next to him, acting as his best man.

Nicholas arrived in a fine brown suit and polished boots, his hat in his hand, and sat with Ella, and next to come were Paul and Imelda. Katy had come to know Paul from his visits to the shop to look over the books, and she was pleased he had accepted the invite.

The organist, a little old man, pumped the bellows and quickly sat to play the wedding march, and as the music sounded, all eyes turned to see Katy standing just inside the door, looking alone and forlorn.

It was Paul who tapped Ella on the shoulder. 'Where's her father?' he whispered.

'He's too drunk to come, as is her mother,' Ella whispered back. It was only then they realised that none of Katy's family were in attendance.

Paul looked at his wife, who nodded her approval, she knew exactly what he was thinking. He stood and walked to where Katy stood, all eyes now on him. He crooked an elbow with a beaming smile.

'May I?' he asked with a grin.

'Thank you,' Katy said, her tears welling at his kind act.

Slowly they walked down the aisle towards Josh, who was beaming with happiness. Placing Katy's hand into Josh's, Paul took a step back and the service began.

Flossie bawled her eyes out as she watched her son tie his life to that of the girl she had come to love like a daughter. Phoebe and Margaret sobbed too, as did Ella and the others.

At the close of the ceremony, applause broke out, Josh kissing his new bride passionately.

Everyone retired to the local public house for food and drinks, which had been organised by Flossie's husband. Beer flowed freely and the men guzzled it like they might never see another drop.

The women sipped their gins between eating plates of ham and cheese sandwiches, pork pies, pickles and sausages, as well as good wholesome bowls of hot broth with chunks of fresh, crusty bread. Just the job to warm a body on a cold winter's day.

A wonderful time was had by all, and Paul's hand was shaken so many times in congratulations at his kind act, there were times he thought it might fall off.

As the day wore on and the alcohol took effect, someone began to play a jaunty melody on the piano in the corner and Thora and Freda sang along and danced, happily kicking up their heels, holding their hemlines up by their knees.

Eventually people drifted away home, tired and happy; glad to be by their firesides once more.

* * *

True to his word, Nicholas booked the first available date for his wedding to Ella, so the following weeks were a flurry of activity.

Josh and Katy settled into married life beautifully, and Flossie was thrilled to have them living next door to her.

Ella and Flossie travelled to Birmingham on the steam train to find Ella a gown to go with the hat she had chosen. A simple white satin shift covered in the finest Nottingham lace fit the bill perfectly.

Paul Sampson was to be Nicholas's best man, and Ella was thrilled when Josh agreed to walk her down the aisle.

Although the weeks were busy, working and preparing for the wedding, for Ella, it was as if time stood still. She found herself hardly daring to believe it might actually happen at last. Many times, she realised she was thinking about how she and Harper had made plans, only for them to be snatched away by his untimely death and every moment leading up to *the* day, Ella felt afraid. She could barely eat, she couldn't sleep and when she managed a few hours, they were filled with terrible dreams of tears and loss.

Flossie and the others had tried talking to her, but Ella's fear of losing Nicholas remained. Even on the morning of her wedding day, Ella could only just hold back her emotions.

Helping her dress, Flossie stood back and said, 'You look beautiful, gel.'

'Thanks, Flossie. Do you think Nicholas is at the church yet?'

Flossie sighed. 'Ella, you *have* to stop your worrying. Everything will be fine.'

'I know you're right, but—'

'Stop it this minute!' Flossie growled. 'I'll have no more of this! You've fretted quite long enough, so let's see a smile now.' Flossie knew she had to snap Ella out of her morose mood. It was her wedding day, after all, and the girl should be giddy with happiness.

A knock to the door heralded Josh's arrival. He was spruced up in a new suit, and his boots shone like a mirror. 'Mum, your cab is here, and so is ours, Ella.'

With a last hug, Flossie disappeared.

'Right, Ella, if you're ready,' Josh said, crooking an elbow.

Ella grabbed her posy of roses and adjusted her white fur cape. With a nod, she took Josh's arm.

Arriving at the church after a short journey, Josh

led Ella down the aisle to the sound of the organ. She beamed when she saw Nicholas waiting for her.

The service passed in a blur for Ella, and only when the vicar said, 'I now pronounce you man and wife,' did Ella feel like she could finally breathe again. As she left the church on the arm of her new husband, Ella was contemplating what the future held for her.

MORE FROM LINDSEY HUTCHINSON

We hope you enjoyed reading *The Hat Girl's Heartbreak*. If you did, please leave a review.

If you'd like to gift a copy, this book is also available as an ebook, digital audio download and audiobook CD.

Sign up to Lindsey Hutchinson's mailing list for news, competitions and updates on future books.

http://bit.ly/LindseyHutchinsonMailingList

The Children From Gin Barrel Lane, a gritty Black Country saga from Lindsey Hutchinson, is available now.

The Children
From
Gin Barrel Lane

Finding a family,
against all the odds...

Lindsey
HUTCHINSON

ABOUT THE AUTHOR

Lindsey Hutchinson is a bestselling saga author whose novels include *The Workhouse Children*. She was born and raised in Wednesbury, and was always destined to follow in the footsteps of her mother, the multi-million selling Meg Hutchinson.

Follow Lindsey on social media:

- facebook.com/Lindsey-Hutchinson-1781901985422852
- twitter.com/LHutchAuthor
- bookbub.com/authors/lindsey-hutchinson

Sixpence Stories

Introducing Sixpence Stories!

Discover page-turning historical novels from your favourite authors, meet new friends and be transported back in time.

Join our book club Facebook group

https://bit.ly/SixpenceGroup

Sign up to our newsletter

https://bit.ly/SixpenceNews

Boldwood

Boldwood Books is an award-winning fiction publishing company seeking out the best stories from around the world.

Find out more at www.boldwoodbooks.com

Join our reader community for brilliant books, competitions and offers!

Follow us
@BoldwoodBooks
@BookandTonic

Sign up to our weekly deals newsletter

https://bit.ly/BoldwoodBNewsletter

www.ingramcontent.com/pod-product-compliance
Lightning Source LLC
Chambersburg PA
CBHW010657100726
47900CB00010B/2690